HIGHBALL: DEATH BY THE LOCH

The Lizzie's War series

Kevin O'Regan

Core Books

Published by Core Books

Paperback edition ISBN: 978-1-7392206-5-5
A CIP catalogue for this book is held by the British Library.

This is a work of fiction. Names, characters, businesses, organisations, places, events and incidents are the product of the author's imagination or are used fictitiously. Any resemblance to actual persons, living or dead, events or locales is entirely coincidental.

AI has not been used directly in the writing of this book though AI tools may have been part of search engines used when researching.

CONTENTS

Prologue

It is said that blood is thicker than water, the loyalties of family enduring despite the frustrations of the relationships within them. Perhaps that is the case but it is certain that relationships beyond family can become stronger, revealing the inadequacies of family ties which are, after all, an accident of birth. Loyalties grow in the troubled soil of war, roots creeping outwards with every shared trial whilst the treachery of siblings is recorded in the earliest of stories. Children turn on parents and parents mistreat, even abandon children. No one owes a duty to members of a family who act without kindness. Loyalty is no longer required when the hurt caused is too great for forgiveness but, where love takes charge, it will endure forever.

I wish either my father or my mother, or indeed both of them, as they were in duty equally bound to it, had minded what they were about when they begot me.

Laurence Sterne,
Tristram Shandy

Friday 7th May 1943, 6.00 pm

CHAPTER 1

Lady Blairbuie's glass clattered on the coffee table. "Do ring for Langford. I need a re-fill."

"Don't you think you've had enough Virginia?"

Lady Blairbuie stared at her husband with clear hostility. "I think I'm capable of deciding when I've had enough, James. I want another drink and I shall have another one." She stood and walked to the right hand side of the magnificent fire place where she pulled a knob to summon the butler. Returning to her seat, she lifted her nose in the air and glared defiantly at her husband.

He looked away to the windows which gave a wonderful view of the Loch, the evening sky spread like a watercolour over the hills of Bute beyond the finger of sea. He sighed. Thank God for the beauty of his home, for the joys it afforded him out in the woodlands and fields. The tensions of home life melted away out there, fresh, clean air washing his face like balm, the sounds of birds, perhaps an occasional barking deer the only disturbance. Sometimes, he did not even wish to shoot, for the explosion of the shotgun seemed a desecration of such peace.

Langford, the Butler, tapped on the door and entered. Before he had time to approach his employers, Lady Blairbuie lifted her glass with her elegant right hand adorned with rings. "Another Highball if you please Langford."

There was the swiftest glance from Langford to his master who nodded his head almost imperceptibly. "Very good m'Lady." He reached out his gloved hand and took the glass.

"And, Robert," she added quietly, using his forename to emphasise the trust she was placing in him, "do put plenty of whisky in it. The last one seemed a little on the weak side."

Langford nodded but said nothing and, with a slight bow, left the room.

Lady Blairbuie now sighed. “I don’t know why you had to let these people stay at the house. I mean, doesn’t the RAF have enough accommodation at Turnberry?”

“I’ve explained that to you already, Virginia.” In an accent that was not local but had been acquired at an English public school, Lord Blairbuie continued, his patience clearly wearing thin. “You know how long it would take to get from Turnberry to here. That’s a fifty mile car trip to Gourock, the ferry ride across the Clyde estuary and then fifteen miles from Dunoon to Glenstriven on a minor road. By the time they got here each day, they’d have to leave to get the last ferry.”

“But it’s such an imposition.”

There was now a sharp edge of anger to Lord Blairbuie’s voice. “There are people whose sons and perhaps daughters are dying for the War effort. All we are being asked to do is put up a few people for a few nights while something is tested. You’re always complaining about how isolated you feel here. I thought you would have been pleased to have some new company. There may even be some hunky RAF chaps for you to flirt with.”

“Huh! I doubt there’ll be the chance of that at my age.”

“Perhaps…but I bet you’ll have a damned good try.”

“You are extraordinary! What reasonable husband would accuse his wife of such a thing?”

Lord Blairbuie was about to give an explosive answer but the door opened and Langford entered carrying a small silver salver on which Lady Blairbuie’s drink sat, the evening sun strengthening the golden radiance of the liquid. A hostile silence filled the room until he had nodded his little bow and left. Lady Blairbuie lifted the glass, swinging her long hair away from her face. “Cheers.” She took a long drink. Lord Blairbuie stood abruptly and walked to the window, laying one hand on the grand piano. He could just make out the water lapping on the beach but the view of the loch was dominated by the silent grey monster that lay at anchor a little further north from the house.

The Courbet.

He had watched two days ago as the ship was manoeuvred into position and, using binoculars, he had read the name on the rather battered bow. The hull had patches of rust...clearly a ship that had been retired. He had looked up the name in the Guide to Shipping he had in the library; she was a redundant French warship built before the Great War and now retired to this sheltered backwater. He did not know what her role would be in whatever testing was to be carried out and he was intrigued by the whole operation. She still sported her huge gun turrets, two fore and two aft with two amidships. What destruction had they caused, what horrors had the ship been through?

Perhaps he had been wrong to agree to the testing but he had to confess to a degree of fascination. He would perhaps hate the disruption and the noise of whatever they may be doing but it was too late now and they must do their bit for the War.

And then he saw it again.

Some way down the Loch, a disturbance in the water... something large pushing through it just beneath the surface. Without taking his eyes from the spot, he reached out his hand and lifted the binoculars from the windowsill to his eyes. Adjusting the focus, the bow wave came sharply visible and he followed it for several seconds. What was it? A whale? No, a whale would occasionally blow or show its flukes. Some yards back from the bow wave was a slight disturbance in the water. Something mechanical. What was going on?

His thoughts were interrupted by his wife's sharp voice. "Why did they choose us anyway? There are dozens of lochs they could use."

"Because Jessica suggested us to her boss...and, from what I've been told, our Loch is ideal."

"Jessica suggested it? Is that why she's coming tomorrow? I thought she had some leave which she decided to use to see us....um...her parents."

"What does it matter? If she said she has some leave, then she has some leave. If she chooses to spend it checking up on whatever they're doing, that's her business. It will just be lovely to see her again. She's not had much chance to come up since the War started."

"That's true. Must be grateful for small mercies I suppose. It will be lovely to see her. I'm so pleased she's doing a proper job... not just throwing herself into some marriage to be a show wife."

Lord Blairbuie decided to ignore the barb. He found that was the best way of dealing with Virginia. He turned again to the window and pictured Jessica. She had always been a lovely girl and he had been delighted that her parents, the chauffeur David Hodges and his wife Maureen, had been willing to accept his offer to pay for her education. She was a beautiful young woman, with a calm nature and a warmth that was extended to everyone. He gently drew his hand across the piano and thought of her playing it, concentration furrowing her beautiful forehead. She had no airs and graces, remembering always, he supposed, that she was the child of humble folk; so unlike her younger brother, George. The interest Virginia and he had taken in Jessica had not turned her head and he was glad of that. She was, he knew, the daughter, the child, he had never had and her parents had always seemed happy to allow himself and Virginia to share her. That was precious.

◆◆◆

"So ladies, be ready for a few days away. Not sure how long it will be but come back as soon as you can. Plenty of other jobs for you to do." Commander Trueman smiled mischievously.

"Nice to have a few days holiday though, isn't it Alice?"

"Definitely. Where is this place we have to go?"

Trueman unrolled a map across his desk and weighted the corners with a polygon of polished marble and empty cups. He leant his tall, lean frame over it. "Here it is, Loch Striven, just beyond Glasgow but you fly to RAF Turnberry which is further South on the West Coast. Someone will take you by car to Gourock, here, and you'll take a ferry across the water to Dunoon." He pointed once again with his finger. "One of the staff at Glenstriven House will pick you up and take you to the manor."

"Why can't we stay at RAF Turnberry? It would be easier." There was a slight resentment in Lizzie's voice.

"Because, Lizzie, the Commanding Officer says it's not appropriate to have civilians staying on the base. He definitely wouldn't want a couple of nosy females hanging around his base for a few days....not that he knows you two are coming."

"We're not nosy, are we Alice?"

"Certainly not...may be a little inquisitive but that's a good thing." Alice's smile broke the fine features of her face, softening the rather severe profile created by the way her hair was tied back tightly into a bun.

"Tomorrow morning, good and early, you fly to Brooklands and pick up a Mr Dennis Thorney. He's an engineer in Barnes Wallis's team. There will also be an RAF Police officer – not sure who – flying with you. He'll make his way to Brooklands tonight."

"I'll need to check the route to RAF Turnberry," Alice said nervously.

"Of course. It's a long way and you can't afford to follow roads and so on. That's why I've assigned you a navigator again, Lizzie. I think you and Alice got on well at RAF Cranwell last time didn't you?"

Lizzie and Alice's eyes met. "We made a super team, Sir."

"Good. Just try to avoid upsetting people Lizzie...accusing them of spying...that sort of thing."

Lizzie's mouth opened wide in mock outrage. "Me Sir? I'll do my best but if I see a spy..."

"You report it to the RAF Police officer and let him deal with it."

"Huh. That doesn't sound any fun." Lizzie flicked her ponytail in mock umbrage.

"One day, Lizzie, you're going to jump in and make a horrible blunder."

"I'll keep her under control, Sir. Don't worry."

"Thank you, Alice. Good luck with that!"

Lizzie became business-like. "What aircraft will we have, Sir?"

"I've assigned you a Lockheed Hudson Mk III. It's faster than an Anson and has a good range. Have you flown one before?"

"No, Sir."

"Well never mind. Read the notes as usual…I'm sure you'll get on well with it. It's quite powerful which you'll like."

Lizzie smiled. "Absolutely Sir. I do like a powerful aircraft. Perhaps you could acquire that new jet aircraft…the Meteor. Now I'd love to fly one of those."

"Not much chance of that I'm afraid. Let's hope that before it comes into service, we've beaten Jerry." Trueman sighed. "It's been too long already…so many deaths, so much suffering."

Lizzie and Alice nodded and waited a little while, contemplating Trueman's remark. Anything they could do to play their part in defeating Hitler, they would do, whatever the personal cost. "Is there anything else, Sir?"

Trueman looked up, snapping out of his thoughts. "No. Dismissed. Shall we say no later than seven hundred hours tomorrow morning?"

As they left Trueman's office and returned to the briefing room, Lizzie linked her arm with Alice. "I'm so glad we're on a mission together again. It was very good to have you with me when we went to Cranwell in March."

"I enjoyed it too, though it did have its moments. Seems a long time ago now doesn't it?"

"It certainly does. I suppose having to fly to different destinations every day makes time pass very quickly."

"I wonder if Grainger will be on this job?"

"I hope not. I don't think I'd be able to avoid giving him a mouthful...though I have to admit, I did gain a grudging admiration for him. Can't be easy doing the dirty work."

"No...it can't. I don't want to have a gun pointed at my head again though."

Lizzie squeezed Alice's arm tighter. "I won't let that happen again. We'd better get sorted out for tomorrow. It's going to be a long day."

They climbed the stairs and turned down the corridor that led to the women's quarters. "See you in a bit for some dinner then," Lizzie said, her hand on the doorknob to her room.

"Yes. I wonder who the RAF Police Officer will be?" An impish smile crossed Alice's normally serious face.

"Could be anyone...probably some crusty old chap who'll bore us to death with tales from his very ordinary past."

"Or it could be a handsome young Scotsman who is very definitely struck on you." Alice squeezed Lizzie's arm playfully.

Beneath the rather austere face, Lizzie knew that Alice could be playful and had a gentle sense of humour. She loved her for her calm, reassuring manner, her expertise as a navigator, her genuine warmth and care for others. "We'll just have to wait and see won't we?" Alice smiled and Lizzie watched her walk in her precise small steps along the corridor to her own quarters. "See you downstairs in about ten minutes. I think we should treat ourselves to a drink tonight...we've no idea what we might have to face in the next few days."

"I'll see you in the lounge," Alice called, before disappearing into her room.

CHAPTER 2

Robbie McBane laid his knife and fork on his plate. That was a good dinner, he reflected. His dining companion was chattering about this and that and Robbie had rather switched off. Dennis Thorney had, at first, seemed a classic engineer, absorbed in his own work and studious in appearance…the stereotypical boffin. His fair hair was swept sideways to hide the growing baldness of his pate and his eyes, peering through thick spectacles had an owlish quality. But Robbie was realising with increasing irritation that the engineer's tame exterior did not reflect his personality. Now he was talking animatedly about his expertise on the piano and the music he loved.

"Do you sing as well?"

"I do yes. I have little time for music now what with the work being so pressurised but I was counted a good tenor in the choir. How about you Sergeant?"

"I'm afraid musical talent passed me by."

"Ah well…each to his own. Now where on earth is this place we're going to? I know it's in Scotland somewhere and I can see you're a native of those parts."

"It's a big country is Scotland. I come from Glasgow and the place we're heading is not too far North of there."

"What's your role exactly?"

"Apparently, my job is to keep you safe and also, when the tests are being carried out, I have to keep the people of the house where we'll be staying somewhere they can't see what's going on."

Thorney nodded. "Secrecy is very important. This weapon could win the war for us."

Robbie McBane raised his ginger eyebrows. "That important?"

"Oh yes, Sergeant," Thorney nodded his head slowly, "that

important."

Robbie McBane wondered if the engineer was exaggerating the significance of the weapon – whatever it was – in order to magnify his own importance but perhaps he was right...perhaps this weapon would win the War. "What is it exactly that is being tested on Loch Striven?"

Dennis Thorney leaned forward conspiratorially. "Can't tell you here, old boy, but I expect you'll see something when we get to the site and I can explain it all then. Not supposed to of course...it's top secret... but when there aren't prying ears about, I'm sure I'll be able to tell you something, you being in the RAF Police."

"I wouldn't want you to tell me anything you shouldn't. Don't want you falling foul of the Official Secrets Act."

"No I won't do that."

"Tell me about Barnes Wallis. I guess he must be an impressive man."

"Yes...yes, he is. Very creative you might say but...he's come up with all sorts of things though some of them are frankly crackpot. Of course it takes a whole team to do the calculations, refine the design, that sort of thing. To tell you the truth, I've done most of the work on this weapon. It wouldn't have got to this stage if it had been left to Wallis. Too fanciful really. Likes the big idea but doesn't know how to make it happen"

"Oh. I met a young ATA pilot a couple of months ago who swears that he saved her life. She was attacked by a German raider whilst delivering a Wellington bomber but she said the geodesic construction meant the damage was only superficial."

"Pure genius that was. Such a simple idea. If I remember rightly, I thought of that one." Thorney waved his hand around the mess. "Yes, here at Brooklands, we've come up with quite a few things."

"I think it's an early start for us tomorrow. Our transport will be coming just from White Waltham – the ATA ferry pool – which is only a short hop away so I think we take off at eight hundred hours."

Dennis Thorney's smile had a hint of amusement. "You service chaps do like your twenty-four hour clock. That's eight o'clock to us normal people." Thorney looked out of the window at the evening sky, still radiant in the West but purple darkness gathering in the East. "You know I spend my whole life designing aircraft and things associated with them but I'm not actually keen on flying."

"Oh. Any particular reason?"

"It's just that feeling of being vulnerable. Of course I know it won't crash unless something goes wrong – I've done lots of calculations, understand the science – but it's that sense of having nothing solid underneath you. It seems completely improbable doesn't it that a heavy thing like that could float on the air."

"I suppose so but I've never really thought about it. I trust you chaps to have done all the sums so that it will stay up." Robbie pushed his chair back, the legs scraping on the hard floor. "I'm going to turn in early tonight. It'll be a long day tomorrow. Goodnight."

"Goodnight Sergeant. I'll see you bright and early for breakfast."

◆ ◆ ◆

Lord Blairbuie sat back in his chair and, lifting his glass, sipped some wine. At the other end of the polished mahogany table, his wife took a long draught from her glass and signalled to Langford for more. James Blairbuie looked away, anger rising within him, an anger he felt unable to express. He understood of course that she resented being taken away from London and the parties, the dinners, the shops, her friends, but she had to understand that it was for her safety. German aircraft had of course bombed Glasgow with devastating effect and Aberdeen only the previous month but Loch Striven was far enough away not to be a high risk, especially now that Hitler seemed to have shifted his main focus elsewhere. London, however, was still vulnerable, being in easy striking distance of German occupied Europe. One never knew what that madman Hitler may try again.

When Langford had re-filled Lady Blairbuie's glass, he cleared his throat. "I've had some guest rooms prepared, Madam, for our visitors tomorrow. I believe we can expect five people."

"Guest rooms Robert? They're only RAF ranks, no one important is there? I'd have thought accommodation in the servants' quarters would be more appropriate. After all, we've plenty of space there now we're running on a skeleton staff."

"Ah, I see...I thought..." Langford looked to Lord Blairbuie who shrugged. "Very good Madam, I'll have some of the servants rooms made ready."

"I suggest you ask Mrs Hodges to prepare rooms at the back of the house, Langford. The RAF said that while the testing is happening each day, everyone must be confined to the rear of the house so they can't see anything."

"I assume that doesn't apply to us, James."

"It applies to everyone. It's top secret so no one must see, not even us."

"But that's ridiculous. Do they think we're spies or something, going to telephone Mr Hitler and tell him what's going on?"

James Blairbuie could not resist making a point. "Perhaps they are aware of your friendship with the Mitford sisters. After all, Unity was a friend of Hitler's and Diana married Oswald Mosley so they may have suspicions."

"That is outrageous. I have never had anything to do with Fascism, Hitler or his Nazi thugs."

"I know that Virginia but the authorities have a right to be cautious about us all. 'Careless talk costs lives' as the slogan goes and it's not difficult to let something slip to the wrong person. We have no way of knowing if someone is feeding information to the enemy."

Lady Blairbuie tossed her hair and took another gulp of wine.

She said nothing more.

James Blairbuie opened his mouth to speak again but thought better of it. It was not that he did not trust Virginia but that he did not want to alarm her. It was that curious apparition he and Ferguson had seen on the Loch two days ago, a man apparently standing on the water or just beneath it and moving through it. Even through binoculars, he could not make out what he was standing on. And again that very evening, the disturbance in the water. So strange. He assumed it was something to do with the Courbet, the testing but....He hoped Hamish Ferguson had discovered something from the Police at Dunoon.

Meals were usually taken in silence. It was ridiculous really, he and Virginia sitting at opposite ends of this long table but that was what she wanted. Must preserve standards at all times. When he had met her, she was an unspoilt sixteen year old. Very young of course and much younger than himself, a gap accentuated by his experience serving in the army. They married in 1913 when she was eighteen and he was twenty-three, just before the onset of hostilities; it was a time of relative peace and prosperity though there were strikes and the Irish were being difficult. She was lovely then, with a natural warmth and zest for life. Her prettiness was captivating and he loved the way she looked up to him, physically and metaphorically.

But then the World erupted.

It was not just war that had torn the World apart. A new age had emerged where the old order no longer applied; you couldn't rely on the things you had once trusted. It was the Twenties that spoilt her, seduced by the frivolities of the new Jazz Age. Virginia had been enthralled by the Mitford sisters and their set, although she was older than them. He had attended the parties, the dinners, the concerts but had always felt out of place being older and having been through the Great War.

Even now, he woke sometimes at night with the pounding of guns in his ears, the shrieking of dying men, the stench of blood in his nostrils. Virginia could not understand it, more or less told him he should keep it to himself. It was difficult, he knew, for anyone who had not been through it to grasp the pain of it, the everlasting torment, the sense of guilt that he had escaped physically unscathed when so many had not. Perhaps the mental torment he and thousands of other survivors endured was just, a reasonable payment for retaining life.

After he had finished his sweet, James Blairbuie turned his head towards the butler. "I'll retire to my library after dinner, Langford."

"Coffee and brandy as usual m'Lord?"

"Yes please."

"Couldn't you give up one evening to your wife James? Some company, even yours, would be welcome. I can't exactly go and visit friends can I?"

"Must get on with the accounts…you know how it is."

She raised her eyes to the ceiling and pushed her chair back noisily. "Oh I know how it is. Langford, another Highball in the drawing room please. Thank God for the wireless."

The butler bent his elderly frame into a slight bow and left the dining room.

◆ ◆ ◆

The sun was sliding beneath the hills over the Loch, dappling the light cloud with red and casting long shadows of the trees across the Glenstriven park. Darkness occupied the woodland above the house as it had all day, the sun not penetrating the new foliage. Something moved from the tenebrous trees, gliding silently between the last few trunks and hovering on the edge of the forest like a deer checking the air for any hostile scent. The figure held a rifle in both hands ready to raise it and fire. But nothing suitable had ventured onto the open ground.

With long, slow steps, it moved along the woodland to the drive that snaked down to the house. The drive curved away to the West, hiding in the woodland which obscured the Lodge guarding the entrance to the park. Feet crunching on the gravel, the figure crossed the drive and glided along the belt of trees that ran down beside the drive for a short way and then on to the Loch. It followed this line continuing towards the Loch after the drive had left the shelter belt and turned towards the house. With frequent, rapid glances and keeping in the shadow of the trees, it made its way down to the water. There it paused, looking over the serenity of the Loch, feeling the cool of evening descending, watching the colours of the sky changing.

Still holding the rifle at the ready, it moved along the water's edge, now hidden from the house by the contours of the parkland, until it reached the boathouse, an elderly structure that looked forlornly out onto the waters of the Loch, as if lamenting its former, more glorious days. At last, the figure turned upwards towards the house, keeping low and using what cover was available. Very faintly, from behind the house, the rattle of a generator disturbed the stillness. In the final approach, the figure crawled over the grass on knees and elbows, hands holding the rifle off the dew. It stopped and lay on the grass. The rifle was lifted into the firing position pointing at the drawing room window where soft light from the lamps glowed. The figure looked through the telescopic sight, moving the rifle slowly, so slowly, to the left and then stopping when the sight showed the woman draped on a settee, a glass in her hand.

The unknown person was still, the rifle trained on the target. The trigger hand began to tense.

CHAPTER 3

The last of the daylight streaked the western sky with amber, gold and pink as the half-moon climbed lazily in the darkening expanse, casting through the high, hazy cloud an eerie light over the town of Dunoon. Billy shivered even though he wore his overcoat. It was the clandestine nature of what they were embarking upon. Rory stood beside him and scanned the water for a boat approaching. He did not know where it would come from or if indeed it was already there, moored somewhere in the muddle of craft tethered to the quay.

The church clock suddenly began to strike, the sound making Billy jump. "Must be ten o'clock," he said quietly.

"Aye."

"Where is he then?"

"Give him a few minutes, Billy. He won't come on the dot.

"Ah but he will."

Both boys jumped at the voice until they realised it was Gordon McClaughlin. He smiled at their startled faces. "You're all set I hope."

"Aye. All set. Have you the rifle?"

McClaughlin lifted a long shape wrapped in sacking. "That's the boat down there. Come on." He led the way down the stone steps and pulled a boat closer to them, nudging aside other craft as it was drawn in. It was an open, wooden boat about eighteen feet long. Two oars were stowed inside the gunwales and an outboard motor perched on the stern. "Once we're awa' from the town we can use the motor until we're nearly there but then we'll need to row the final part so as not to give ourselves away. Right hop in."

He held the boat steady as Rory stepped in and they both assisted Billy who was unsure where to place his feet. "You go in the bow, Rory, and keep a lookout for anything. Billy, on the stern seat for now. I'll row out a way before starting the engine."

Gordon McClaughlin took the oars and prodded the boat out from the melee of moored craft until it was clear. Soon they were speeding away from the quay with strong strokes, Billy feeling the jerk in his back as each stroke propelled the boat forward. The water whispering against the hull, the moonlight dancing on the waves and the cool evening air lifting his hair produced a great sense of excitement and adventure in Billy. This was just like the films...a secret mission.

When the town had been left behind, Gordon stowed the oars and changed places with Billy. He pulled a cord on the engine and it sputtered into life. Soon they were speeding through the water, the generated wind causing Billy's eyes to weep a little. He wiped them in case the others thought he was crying. He was far from that. This was thrilling!

It was a long trip in the boat, the land darkening despite the moonlight and the cold creeping into their bones. The boat seemed impossibly tiny in the expanse of sea and the lack of familiar sounds such as the gulls created a great sense of loneliness. Billy's excitement faded but he consoled himself with the idea of the money he could earn, much needed by both him and Rory neither of whom had a regular job; there were none to be had so they picked up what bits of work they could.

At last, Gordon turned the boat to starboard and they entered the Loch. It was some time before they became aware of a huge black shape emerging from the gloom further up the water.

"There she is. That's the French battleship. Now what on earth do they want to bring that here for?"

"Maybe they think the Germans will invade here."

"I shouldna think so Billy but it's here for a reason right enough."

They were still a mile from the ship when Gordon cut the engine and once again switched places with Billy so that he could row. It was suddenly peaceful without the sound of the engine. Billy was not the poetic type but he marvelled at the beauty of the scene. As they drew closer, moonlight gradually revealed the detail of the huge ship, its guns projecting for and aft aggressively, its silence making it somehow more threatening. There were no lights on it, no sign of life and even Rory, usually untroubled by fear or foreboding, shivered.

"Someone just stepped on my grave," he whispered and Billy gulped audibly. Gordon began to pull towards the shore until, at last, the boat scraped on the pebbles. He stowed the oars again and stepped over the side into the water. It was only then that Rory noticed his rubber boots.

"Go to the stern wi' Billy, Rory, and I'll pull the boat up the strand a bit." When that had been done, he added, "Right now you can step over the bow and you'll no get yer feet wet." Gordon handed Rory the rifle and a box he took from a large pocket in his overcoat. "Ammos's in the box. Put it in yer bag and don't waste it." The two boys stood waiting for further instruction. "Stay away from the house and don't be seen. I'll be here Sunday night at ten o'clock. There's a clock strikes on the stable behind the big house so you'll be able to hear it. Right. You need t' head up that way and get yersen into the woods. Night is the time to work. Find somewhere to lie up in the day and watch over the Loch."

"We'll need some kip'" Billy said plaintively.

"Aye. Yous can take it in turns during the day to kip and watch."

Billy jutted his head forward, the thick lenses of his glasses catching the pale moonlight. "I canna see anything much. I'll be no good at watching."

"You have ears don't you? If you hear somethin', you wake Rory. Use your sense Billy."

Rory sniggered. "He don't have much o' that."

Lifting the bow of the boat slightly, Gordon pushed hard so that it slid back into the water. He stepped in, took up the oars and, using one as a punting pole, pushed the boat out further, turning it away to point back down the Loch. He said nothing more, waved no hand in farewell. The two boys watched as the oars dipped into the water, and, with soft clunks, propelled the boat away from them.

In no time at all, it had disappeared against the dark backdrop of sea and hills and they were left alone.

◆◆◆

Virginia Blairbuie sighed as she sat at her dressing table. Another tedious day followed by a dull evening. Even James's company would have been better than the wireless and flipping through magazines. They had separate bedrooms...always had, as it was the custom amongst their class. At least she was spared James's fumbling manoeuvres in bed, the heaving and grunting and the final whimper when he reached his conclusion. She did not regret the absence of marital relations, the truce they had silently agreed, but she still longed for a real man to give her pleasure.

The oil lamps either side of the mirror on the dressing table threw a warm light on her face and she turned it slightly to catch the reflection in her eyes. One day, they would have electricity in the bedrooms as well as the main rooms below. She lifted her head and gently tossed her hair back. She was still a beautiful woman: age had certainly brought a few wrinkles but had also brought an indefinable nobility. She let the silk dressing gown she was wearing slip from one shoulder, revealing the lace of her matching silk nightdress. Slowly, her right hand moved up her body and lightly brushed her left breast causing the nipple to harden and arousing a longing lower in her body, a longing for the gentle touch of a man, for kisses on her neck and shoulders and....

She stood abruptly, tearing herself away from her reverie. In bare feet, she paced the bedroom, feeling the curtains, the bedspread, the pillow, everything that was soft to the touch. She picked up the photograph of their wedding day, trying to distract herself from the desire that was making her quiver.

She had to admit that James looked very smart in his uniform, standing with his army hat beneath his arm, impressive, brave, authoritative as one would expect an officer to be.

And she...she looked so young, her eager face looking up at him in admiration, rose petals falling around them, a moment frozen in time. It was, she knew now, a fairytale she had pursued, a youthful excitement at being selected by James from several other debutantes that year. There was an element of competition. Oh they all laughed together, swapped secrets, discussed who was most eligible and hugged each other when disappointments came but they all knew they wanted to be the ones chosen.

She had felt sorry for some of the girls, those from country stock who looked like farmers, large girls whom elegance had not touched, who, when they danced, looked like baby hippopotami. Virginia smiled to herself. She was being unkind but frankly that was how it was. But she was lucky, she had felt then, to be chosen by James, a dashing young army officer who would become a Lord at the death of his father. Even the Glenstriven country estate in Scotland had been an attraction. She had pictured herself as the lady of the manor - actually in her mind's eye it was a castle - holding parties, commanding a whole array of liveried servants, being *the* lady of the whole area.

Little did she know then!

She replaced the wedding photograph and returned to her dressing table on which sat a photograph taken in her coming out year just months before the wedding in fact. The courtship had been short because of the War. James had been required to rejoin his regiment very soon after the hurried engagement and she did not see him again until he was on leave for the wedding. No time at all. They hardly knew each other really.

Her thoughts turned to happier times, before the engagement. She lifted her debutante photograph and gently ran her finger around the profile of her face as if she could bring her younger self to life. Ah, the glamour of the balls, the dresses, the whirlwind of social engagements, the excitement, anticipation, the sense of being special. It flooded back as it always did when she thought of those times. It was no wonder she was swept off her feet...too young to know better, to make a more reasoned judgement.

But still, that was how it was in those days. She returned the photograph gently to its place on the dressing table. She knew she should not complain. James had been a good husband, though he had never been able to give her children. Would she have wanted that? She knew James did if only to preserve the line and pass on the estate. But she hadn't wanted children when she was younger. She had wanted to be free to continue her social life unencumbered by the demands of offspring.

And by goodness she had made the most of it in the twenties and even into the thirties. She had been a part of the most fashionable set in London with the Mitford sisters when they arrived. She smiled again, remembering those times

Having dispelled the longing she had felt earlier, she doused the lights and slipped into bed. Sleep did not come and she lay thinking still about her former life, 'what ifs' troubling the more pleasant memories. What if she had declined James's offer of marriage, had found a suitor who also liked parties. The 'what if' became a fantasy of a life in high society, travelling to America in a great ocean liner, taking lovers and discarding them when they no longer held any allure.

Suddenly, she was disturbed by what sounded like a shot.

She stood once again and moved over to one of the windows that gave a view over the Loch. Drawing the curtain aside, she looked over the water. No one would be shooting at this time of night. It must have been something else. It was a soft night, very little wind, a half-moon riding through hazy cloud, like a lover teasing her, hiding and then revealing himself briefly only to duck behind the diaphanous curtain. It was a night for romance, for love, for passion...things that had been left behind.

The moon cast a sheen on the water, the French battleship a great, dark, ominous shape in the middle of the Loch, a stark reminder of the War that was raging elsewhere. How could there be love, passion, romance in these dark times? How could there be those things for her, locked like some fairytale princess in this remote house, waiting for the charming prince to ride up on his charger?

It would never be. This was her life now, this is what she had chosen.

Saturday 8th May 1943

CHAPTER 4

Lizzie felt the same thrill of excitement that she always experienced when sitting in an aircraft. The prospect of soaring into the air, leaving behind the frustrations of everyday life, was wonderful. Today was even better because this was a new adventure, a long flight to somewhere she had never been and she was in the company of someone she had come to respect and love: Alice. They had worked together back in March when they had flown some VIPs to RAF Cranwell in Lincolnshire to see the first test flight of the new Meteor jet aircraft. Lizzie vividly remembered the palpitations in her stomach when the Meteor had raced down the runway and shot into the sky at what seemed an impossible angle. And the sound...the massive roar of the twin jet engines. Thrilling!

She glanced over to her right where Alice sat a little behind her in the cockpit of the Lockheed Hudson. Their eyes met. "Ready?"

"When you are, Lizzie."

Lizzie opened the throttles and the twin Wright 1200 horsepower engines roared. The aircraft crept forward, slowly gaining speed down the runway, bumping more vigorously as it did so. Lizzie's arms were shaking with the vibration as she glanced at the air speed indicator. At last she pulled back on the joystick and the great bird lifted into the air, suddenly becoming calm and smooth. Such a relief to get airborne. Lizzie engaged the undercarriage lifting mechanism and the noise of the air rushing around the wheels disappeared.

"Just a quick trip to Brooklands...ten minutes at most," Alice said.

Yep, soon be touching down. Then it's a long, long haul to

Turnberry."

Certainly is."

Their route roughly followed the course of the River Thames but naturally they did not need to track its many twists and turns. In no time at all they could see the great circle of the Brooklands car racing circuit and when they came closer, the banking of some sections. Lizzie had the all clear from the control tower on the radio and lined up with the runway which was hard and hence much smoother than the grass airfield at White Waltham.

She taxied across to the buildings and cut the engines. Brooklands was, of course, very familiar to her having visited several times before to pick up new aircraft for delivery to operational bases. In February, she had flown a new Wellington bomber to RAF Silverstone in Northamptonshire, an eventful flight as she had been attacked by a German Focke Wolf 190. The whole trip was eventful in fact...she had discovered the body of a murdered civilian girl on the base!

Another day, another job; she sighed. At least she could honestly say, her job was never boring.

She and Alice dropped from the aircraft and headed for the reception building. Inside, the air was cooler and they paused inside the door to look around. It was not a huge space. As Lizzie turned her head to the right, her heart suddenly lifted and she broke into a smile. Standing there with a broad smile on his face was a tall, imposing, red-haired man in RAF Police uniform.

"Robbie McBane," she said, walking towards him.

His arms opened wide and she stepped into a big hug. "I hoped it would be you," he breathed and kissed her on the cheek. "And it's Alice too, a double pleasure." He hugged Alice but did not kiss her.

"She wouldn't admit it, but Lizzie was hoping the RAF Police officer would be you, Robbie."

"Alice! That's nonsense...I just didn't want anyone boring."

"Well I'm afraid you've got me and I am very boring."

Lizzie wrinkled her nose at him, her smile dancing in her eyes.

"That's not true, Robbie. But I'm hoping we have an uneventful trip. No more murders or spies."

Both Robbie and Alice looked at Lizzie and laughed at the same time. "Now that's definitely not true, Lizzie. That's exactly what you do want. Something to set your prodigious skills of observation and deduction against." Lizzie flushed slightly and Robbie put his arm around her shoulders, pulling her closer. "Ach, I'm only teasing you."

"We're to take someone else too aren't we?"

"An engineer I think," said Alice.

"Aye, a Mr Dennis Thorney. I had dinner with him last night. I did see him at breakfast but he hasna come down from his room yet. Probably doing some last minute calculations."

"What's he like?"

You don't need to worry, Lizzie. He's... fine. Maybe a little full of his own importance. Likes music...plays the piano and sings. You'll quickly get the measure of him I'm sure."

As if on cue, a door banged on the other side of the reception area and a middle-aged man with slightly wild, receding hair struggled into view with a heavy suitcase and a briefcase. Robbie McBane stepped forward and took the suitcase from him. "Let me introduce you. This is Mr Dennis Thorney who is an engineer and will be observing the testing in Loch Striven...whatever that testing may be." Robbie turned towards the young women. "And this, Dennis, is our pilot and navigator, Second Officer Lizzie Barnes and Navigator, Alice Frobisher, both of the Air Transport Auxiliary."

Dennis Thorney nodded a greeting. "I hope I haven't kept you. Just needed to sort something out before I left."

"Not at all, Sir." Lizzie smiled at the figure in front of her, a typical boffin. He seemed somewhat thrown by the presence of herself and Alice. Not comfortable around young women she guessed, more at ease in the very male environment of an engineering office. "Well gentlemen, it is a long flight to RAF Turnberry so I hope you are suitably fed and watered and that you will not require other...facilities."

Thorney looked confused so Alice stepped in. "It's three hundred and thirty miles as the crow flies from here to RAF Turnberry. Our aircraft is a Lockheed Hudson Mk III which has a cruising speed of two hundred and twenty miles per hour. We aim to fly directly so, allowing time for take-off and landing, it will take us just under two hours. But we don't know if we'll have to slow down for turbulence and sitting in an aircraft can induce...um...a need for relief." She smiled at Thorney.

"Relief, yes of course. I am fully serviced thank you and ready to go." Thorney did not return Alice's smile and seemed a little put out that the subject had been raised.

Lizzie offered to carry Thorney's briefcase out to the aircraft but he declined, clutching the handle more firmly.

"Our route will take us through the heart of England, just East of Liverpool and Manchester and then out across the sea until we reach Scotland. The weather is fair so, hopefully, there'll be some nice views on the way." Alice's gentle voice was very reassuring and Lizzie hoped Thorney would warm to her at least.

◆ ◆ ◆

As usual, James Blairbuie had eaten breakfast alone. Virginia did not make an appearance until after he had finished, not being one for early mornings. He, however, loved the early morning. It was something about the way the day had not yet been sullied by anything, just the natural world in unfettered joy. That morning had continued the fine weather, Spring in the air and a wonderful sense of life bursting forth. Life was good and he had the prospect of seeing Jessica again. He felt a warm glow in his breast when he thought of her but it was tinged with sadness that he could never call her his own. God had not been kind in that respect.

His reveries were interrupted by a soft tap on the library door. "Come in," he called and Hamish Ferguson, his estate manager, walked in for their meeting. They usually had two formal meetings per week as well as numerous passing encounters around the estate. "Hamish. Lovely morning."

"It is m'Lord. Are you well today?"

James Blairbuie loved Hamish's rich Scottish accent. If only he himself had been educated locally and not had the public school voice forced on him at boarding school. Sometimes he was tempted to put an accent on but he felt that was an insult to those who had genuine Scottish accents. "I'm very well Hamish. And you?"

"Aye m'Lord, very well." Hamish always had a rather intense look in his eyes, a restlessness in his bearing, as if he was troubled.

The two men sat in armchairs in front of the unlit fire; James Blairbuie offered coffee as he always did and Hamish Ferguson declined, also as usual. It was one of those polite rituals that kept things pleasant and preserved an ancient tradition of kindness to staff.

"And how are things on the estate, Hamish?"

"The lambing has gone well on the home farm. We had fifty three lambs with only two still born. All the ewes are in fine fettle even those with the still births so that's gud."

James Blairbuie could not resist smiling. It was not just the good news about the lambing, it was the way the word "good" was shortened that he loved. A tiny detail that never ceased to please him. "And the clearing of the Victoria plantation in the forest?"

"Went very well, m'Lord. The contractors have all left now. It'll be a fine crop of timber for the War effort. We've had the assessor from the Forestry Commission already and we should get a good price for it."

"Excellent! It's that we're making a contribution to the War effort that I'm especially pleased about though, naturally, the income is important too."

Ferguson nodded and waited for his Lordship's next question.

"By the way, did you find out anything about that strange

thing we saw in the Loch the other day?"

"No m'Lord. When I was in Dunoon yesterday, I went into the Police station and spoke with Sergeant MacGregor. He seemed very cagey, said he knew nothing about any strange craft. He said he would report it to his superior officer when he next telephoned. But...I think he knew more than he was saying."

"It was very strange wasn't it? I mean you see a man apparently standing on the surface of the water and moving through it. What on Earth was going on?"

Hamish Ferguson leaned towards Lord Blairbuie and his voice dropped to a conspiratorial hush. "He seemed very keen to dismiss it as nonsense, more or less said we'd been seeing things. He made a joke about having too much whisky. I told him that neither you nor I were in the habit of drinking in the middle of the day."

"So you think there is something going on that he knows about. Presumably, if it were enemy activity, someone would be dealing with it." Lord Blairbuie rubbed his chin thoughtfully. "It's probably something that our boys are up to."

"I think you might be right there m'Lord."

"D'you suppose that's what our visitors who arrive later today have come to check on?"

"I've no idea m'Lord. Maybe so...unless they're also testing something else. Perhaps that's what the Courbet is doing moored out in the loch."

"Perhaps. But why is it the RAF who made the arrangements about today's visitors? Curiouser and curiouser." James Blairbuie's eyes narrowed in thought. "It's all very cloak and dagger, isn't it?"

"Aye but I suppose it has to be m'Lord. Can't have Jerry finding out about new weapons. Have to keep the element of surprise."

"Quite so, Hamish, quite so."

The two men sat in silence, each contemplating what might be happening in their Loch, a stretch of water that had always represented the peace, the serenity, the timeless permanence of their home.

At last, Hamish turned to look at his employer, wondering if he should say anything about something else he had discovered. He decided he should; if something untoward were to happen and he had not mentioned it, he would be culpable. He cleared his throat. "There is one other thing I think you should know m'Lord."

James Blairbuie turned his head to look at his estate manager. "What's that?"

"Well it's something or nothing. Ewan McCrae and I went deep into the woodland yesterday after I returned from Dunoon and came across what seemed to be a camp. It was very well hidden, deliberately camouflaged, but it definitely looks as though we have someone living there. The remains of a fire were still slightly warm, and there were a few utensils tucked out of sight under the cover. It could of course just be a tramp who has found a convenient place to live but what with the sight of that man walking on the water, it could be ...perhaps...a spy, someone who wants to see what's going on in the Loch. Ewan seemed unconcerned by it but I think it's very suspicious."

"You were right to raise it, Hamish. Have Ewan do a thorough search of that area and tell him to keep his eyes open...any sign of game being taken and cooked, for example, any traces at all in fact. We do need to report it to Sergeant MacGregor and to whichever of our visitors today seems to be in charge. Presumably, with all this testing, the RAF has security people checking the area?

"I've no idea, m'Lord. Perhaps this person is part of the security."

CHAPTER 5

Lizzie spun her head sharply at the first cough from the starboard engine. She stared at it, looking for any tell-tale signs of smoke but, other than a puff from the exhaust, there was nothing. All the same, she was now on full alert. She knew the aircraft could fly and, if necessary, land on one engine but she had had to do that two months before at RAF Silverstone and she didn't want to have to repeat it.

She glanced at the fuel gauges. Both tanks had plenty of fuel and the starboard one was no lower than the port tank. She waited several seconds for another cough but, as nothing came, she spoke. "Did you hear that Alice?"

Alice remained absolutely calm. "I certainly did. What does it mean?"

"Maybe nothing but there could be a problem."

"Like an engine failure type problem?"

"Maybe. I suspect it will be some junk that's got into the fuel line which caused the..."

Her words were cut off by the starboard engine spluttering, not a single cough this time. Now Alice did look concerned. "We're over the sea at the moment."

"Yep...I can see that. Don't worry, we can fly on the port engine alone if need be but best to take precautions." Lizzie flicked the cabin intercom switch and spoke. "There is no need for alarm gentlemen but the starboard engine seems to be spluttering a bit. I may have to shut it down but don't worry, we can fly quite happily on one engine. As a precaution, however, please take the lifejacket from under your seat and put it on. There are instructions on the front. Help each other if necessary. We are currently over the sea but we will soon be back over land again. Once we are, I'll ask you to take off the lifejacket and put on the parachute."

Moments later, Robbie McBane appeared in the cockpit doorway, pulling the lifejacket straps tight around his body. "Our man back there is terrified, Lizzie. He's as white as a sheet."

"It's just a precaution, Robbie. We'll be fine.

Robbie ducked and peered through the front windscreen. The coastline of Scotland was already becoming visible even though the morning was hazy. "By the time we get his lifejacket sorted, we'll need to take it off and put on the parachute."

"It'll take his mind off things." Alice smiled sweetly, hiding any fear she may have been experiencing and Robbie ducked back into the passenger cabin.

Alice had set a course roughly North by North-West from Brooklands which took them right across the centre of England, East of Liverpool and Manchester and out across the Irish sea though not far from the coastline which they could now see curving in a great, shallow arc to their right. Although the weather was fine, the air was too hazy to pick out any landmarks so Lizzie and Alice had not been pointing any out to the passengers.

The starboard engine seemed to recover but after a couple of minutes started spluttering badly again. "I'm going to shut it down, Alice, in case it causes any damage. Probably just a bit of muck stirred up from the bottom of the fuel tank."

Lizzie again reached forward and flicked the intercom switch. "This is second Officer Barnes again, Gentlemen. I'm going to shut down the starboard engine to prevent any damage being caused and we'll fly on to Turnberry on the port engine. This is perfectly normal procedure. You can now take off your lifejackets and put on your parachutes." She flicked off the intercom and turned to Alice. "Let's hope it doesn't occur to our nervous flyer to ask what happens if the port engine gives up."

"What does happen?"

"Our navigator finds a nice smooth field for me to glide down and land on."

"Right." Alice looked ahead to the rugged and forested terrain of Galloway. "That could be tricky."

"Yep. It could be a rather bumpy landing."

"How can you stay so calm?"

"Because there's no alternative. I can't do anything about it until it happens."

"True."

Lizzie turned and saw the smile playing on Alice's face. She really liked Alice. She was quiet but had a lovely sense of humour and she was utterly reliable, unflappable. It was good to have someone like her with you. To take her own mind off the engine problem, she thought about what awaited them. It was clear from what Trueman had said that they would be staying somewhere quite remote. She did get bored easily and hoped there would be enough to do to keep her occupied.

Her mind quickly strayed back to her two passengers. Thorney would no doubt be in a state of fear; Robbie, like Alice, was calm. He'd cope. Thinking of Robbie brought a warmth to her breast. She was glad of the radio mask that covered her face and hid the blush she felt rising in her cheek. Alice would tease her again if she saw it, not that Lizzie minded a little teasing.

Perhaps, on this trip she may feel able to be more responsive to Robbie. It was clear from the way he had greeted her that he was fond of her and she was fond of him. It was just that... Her hands gripped the joystick with unnecessary tightness. How long could the past destroy one's future? How long would it be before she could come to terms with the events of her childhood and allow a man close to her?

They limped into RAF Turnberry on the port engine but the landing was good despite that. Lizzie cut the engines and sat for a few seconds enjoying the quiet. Taking off her mouthpiece and flying helmet, she shook her hair loose, flicking it with her hand in case it was plastered on her head. "Thanks Alice. You got us here flawlessly."

"What did you expect?" Alice smiled. "Nice flying too. Let's hope our passengers are ok. One of them will be at least." Alice gave Lizzie a knowing look which she chose to ignore. They gathered their bags and went through to the cabin. Ground crew had already brought a set of steps up to the door which Lizzie opened.

"I hope you enjoyed the flight, Gentlemen."

Dennis Thorney was pale but his eyes, magnified by his spectacles, were blazing with anger. "What on Earth do you mean by bringing us on a defective aircraft? Didn't you carry out proper checks?"

"Of course, Sir, but these things do sometimes happen."

"Not if the engines are properly serviced. Remember I design these damn things and I know what I'm talking about. Make sure it gets thoroughly checked before the return journey."

"I'm sorry we had that trouble but..." Lizzie did not finish the sentence as Thorney, clutching his briefcase, was bustling out the door, his head held high in indignation.

"You're flying was, as always, impeccable, Lizzie." Robbie laid a hand gently on Lizzie's arm.

"Thank you Robbie."

She and Alice let Robbie descend first and then followed. The member of the ground crew by the steps looked confused. He mounted a couple of steps and peered forward through the cabin. "Is the pilot in there somewhere?"

Lizzie shook her head. "No. She's standing here." The poor man looked even more puzzled. "I am the pilot, Second Officer Lizzie Barnes, and this is the navigator, Alice Frobisher."

"Oh right...right. Um, well Miss, Group Captain Boggen would like to see you all in his office right away. I'll show you where it is."

"Thank you." As the aircraftman led the way, Lizzie said quietly to Alice, "We need to prepare ourselves for more incredulity. Let's hope Group Captain Boggen is not another one of those men who can't believe that women can fly or navigate an aircraft. I'm getting rather tired of having to justify myself."

"Just stay calm Lizzie, smile sweetly and don't give him the satisfaction of letting him see your anger. He may be perfectly reasonable anyway."

"I wish I had your optimism, Alice."

◆ ◆ ◆

The train was crowded but Jessica did manage to get a seat. A rather gallant young army officer had stood up and smiled at her when she had stumbled with her suitcase along the corridor looking into each crowded compartment. He was in the last one and happened to be looking into the corridor through the open door. He must have seen the weariness on her face, the prospect of standing for hours in the corridor.

"I'm only going as far as Birmingham," he'd said, "and I could do with stretching my legs so please...do have my seat."

He was tall and Jessica knew how cramped those seats could be with insufficient leg room for someone of his height. "If you're sure. I'd be very grateful, I've been very busy the last few days."

He had pushed some bags on the luggage rack along to make room for her suitcase which he swung aloft effortlessly. The only disadvantage was that she felt obliged to converse with him all the way to Birmingham as he stood in the doorway looking down at her. He was pleasant enough but tiredness pulled at her and she would have liked to relax into the seat and slumber.

That opportunity came after Birmingham. Several passengers alighted there and, whilst the train remained crowded, her compartment had two empty seats. Sadly neither were next to her so she could not take advantage of them. She contented herself with sitting back and closing her eyes, hoping the rhythm of the train on the tracks would induce the sleep she longed for.

Thoughts of her home seeped into her tired brain like water slowly creeping across a parched land. She was so looking forward to the peace and quiet, the majesty of the mountains and the Loch, perhaps to playing the piano. A smile played around her lips when she thought of her parents and how pleased they would be to see her. Her mother Maureen was so warm and thoughtful, such a kind person and her father's quiet, unflappable manner was a solace. She was loved, had never had any doubt of that and, in such a turbulent World, that was a blessing.

She was lucky of course. Lord Blairbuie – James he now insisted she called him – was a gentle and caring man who was like a second father to her. It was not just his generosity in funding her education but his genuine regard for her, his warmth. She knew of course that she was the daughter he and Lady Blairbuie had never had. She wondered for the hundredth time why that was and gave her usual answer: some people are not blessed with children. Lady B had an enthusiastic kindness, perhaps a little intrusive, that made her own mother a little uncomfortable she felt, though Maureen had never said anything and had never opposed anything the Blairbuies had done for herself.

And of course George. Her heart was always troubled by her brother. From an early age, he had appeared different, limited, struggling at school and much happier to be out on the hills or in the woods. The Blairbuies had not treated him the same. They had not paid for a private school for him nor given him the support and encouragement that she had had. Perhaps with more help, he may have done better for himself but, then again, he had seemed happy initially to work on the estate. There was a chasm between him and her, though; she suspected an unspoken resentment that she had been to university, made something of herself, now lived in London and he had not.

Working at the ministry was exciting and gave her the certainty that she was doing something important for the War effort. It was always hectic but the last few days had been especially so. Her boss was very anxious that these tests went well and that was why she was now travelling North. She was officially a secretary but...it was much more important than that. She couldn't be classed as anything more than a secretary because the Ministry didn't allow women to be anything else but her boss had found ways to ensure she was adequately compensated financially for what she did.

Loch Striven, her home, was perfect for these tests and she had had no hesitation in recommending her boss contact Lord Blairbuie. The Loch was narrow, lengthy and was not immediately accessible from the sea. Pilots would need to find their way around the Isles of Arran, Bute and the smaller islands that nestled in the area, giving them the kind of experience they would need to carry out the type of missions planned. Flying low to avoid detection was hard enough but to do so around numerous islands and headlands was doubly difficult.

But it could make such a difference.

The train rattled northwards; a change at Crewe brought a compartment that was even less crowded and Jessica could feel the tensions of her London life slipping away from her. She was going to enjoy herself as well as do what she had been tasked to do. Perhaps they could go out on the Loch in the small boat Lord Blairbuie kept in the boathouse for fishing. There was no greater pleasure on a fine evening when only the slightest breeze ruffled the surface of the water to row out into the Loch, watching the sun disappearing behind the hills and hearing the sea birds calling to each other before heading to their roosts for the night. So far away from the War and the bloodshed that so many endured.

She was going home.

CHAPTER 6

The sun was warm on his face, and Billy felt drowsy. It was his turn to keep watch over the Loch but nothing was happening and the sleepless night was dragging him towards a blissful escape. They had found an ideal spot on a bit of a crag some way up the Loch from the big house. The battleship was a silent, grey shape about a mile from where they lay and the Spring sun was penetrating the thin cloud that had made mysteries of the moon the previous night.

Billy had hated the night. He had been cold, tired and hungry because Rory had insisted that they needed to ration their food and water. They had left the shore on the Loch and found a path that, after a short climb uphill, had crossed the lane that led to the main gate of Glenstriven House. No lights had been visible in the lodge that nestled inside the big, iron gates. They had passed on and, as Gordon had told them, found a stile into the woodland. Rory had moved through the trees crouching, holding the rifle ready, his knapsack on his back and Billy had followed, stumbling occasionally on tree roots.

Suddenly a noise had startled them, a twig cracking or a branch creaking, and Rory had dropped down. Billy had nearly fallen over him and Rory hissed into his ear, "Get down for God's sake." They had waited, ears straining for any sound that might suggest what was in the forest with them.

"There must be someone there, Rory," Billy whispered.

"There'll no be anyone aboot, I'm telling yous," Rory hissed, raising himself from his crouched position.

"Well what was that noise then?"

"I dinna ken. Probably a deer or something."

"Don't be daft, deers move about silently. We need to stay quiet for a bit." To emphasise the point, Billy tugged at

Rory's jacket, unintentionally forcing him to topple backwards cracking a twig as he fell.

Clutching the rifle, Rory put his mouth close to Billy's ear. "Now you've done it you bloody idiot." He crouched down in the bracken again his eyes peering through the gloom of the forest, ears straining for any sounds in response to the cracked twig. They waited several minutes before daring to move again and when they did so, they omitted to do anything to restore the bracken they had crushed as they crouched. They moved forward cautiously, crouching low and ducking from bush to bush.

Billy tugged Rory's sleeve and whispered. "Where are we heading? Shouldn't we just wait for something to come past us?"

"We need to be further into the centre of the forest....that's where the game will be."

"I dinna get it, mate. If we shoot things won't that bring a gamekeeper or someone?"

"Unlikely at this time of the night. According to Gordon, the gamekeeper will be safely tucked up in bed and, even if he hears a shot, by the time he gets to the place he thinks it came from, we'll be away."

"I'll take your word for it," Billy said with no conviction. He was beginning to think this was a fool's errand. It had sounded like a great idea outside the pub when McClaughlin had raised it. Take some free game, deer, rabbits, even grouse maybe and pass them on to someone who'd be selling them on the black market in Glasgow. There was no limit to what could be sold there what with rationing and people nearly starving. But now, out here in the darkness with the strange sounds of the forest all around them, it seemed an impossible task. How could you shoot something amongst these trees? You'd never have a clear shot and those animals could move very fast.

Eventually, Rory had agreed to try what Billy had suggested and stay hidden in the bracken on the edge of a clearing. At last, a deer had ventured from the trees, sniffing the air, moving so slowly, stopping, moving forward again. Billy tugged

Rory's sleeve and Rory shook him off. Slowly, without a sound, Rory had raised the rifle to the firing position. Billy had felt excitement grow in him. He could not miss at that range.

But as Rory had been about to squeeze the trigger, he had moved ever so slightly... but enough for his boot to scrape against something on the ground. He had pulled the trigger but the deer had leapt away unharmed.

"Damn and blast it," he swore quietly.

"Maybe we should find a field where the sheep are. They'll be much easier targets." Billy was glad that the deer's flight had not been caused by him. He would never have heard the end of it.

They stumbled on through the woodland for what seemed an age, climbing slowly, until they came to the edge of the trees and the open moor lay before them in the moonlight. The going had been easier, though rocky underfoot, and eventually they had found the flock of sheep, most laying down but a few still standing; there was an occasional bleat from a lamb.

"Dinna go for one that's too big Rory or we'll never carry it down to the water."

"I know, I know, I'm no' stupid."

The flock seemed to ignore them as they skirted round, peering through the half-light to select a victim. Rory had pointed to a young sheep standing slightly apart and nibbling the grass and Billy had grunted his agreement. Again Rory raised the rifle and fired. This time, the sheep did not move but the rest of the flock struggled to their feet making a horrible racket.

The lamb lay where it had fallen.

"You did it. Well done Rory."

They had stumbled over to the dead lamb to inspect it.

"Right. Let's get it down into the trees and find somewhere to stash it until tomorrow night. You pick it up, Billy."

"Me. Why me?"

"Because I've got to carry the rifle."

Yes, Billy was glad the night was done. One more night to get through. The days would be easy as long as the weather held. Lying here on a grassy bank was no problem at all. He looked over to Rory who lay a couple of yards from him, wrapped in sleep. Billy forced himself to sit up; he had to try to stay awake.

◆ ◆ ◆

He had plodded around the woodland all afternoon, looking without enthusiasm for signs of the visitor whose camp he had found deep in the trees the previous day. It was only the thought that Hamish Ferguson might find it too that had decided him to let the Estate Manager know about it. And now, apparently, Lord Blairbuie had asked that he should track the intruder down. Ewan McCrae peered into a clump of bushes and then straightened, putting his free hand on the small of his back.

"I'm getting too old for tramping around like this," he said to a raven that looked down at him with clear contempt. He stared back but the raven did not flinch. "You'd soon move if I took a shot at ye." Ewan raised the shotgun slowly but the bird stared back unperturbed. He lowered the gun and sighed. "A cup of tea would help I 'spect," he mumbled and ambled off through the trees, certain that the mystery camper was simply a poacher.

He stopped abruptly, staring at the ground behind a bush, his forehead creasing. The bracken had been flattened. He bent over, examining the way the stems of the plants were broken. That was not an animal. It was something bigger had done that...a person or maybe even two.

Poachers! He had known it of course. He sighed. Not very good at it either; golden rule of poaching was to leave no trace.

He plodded on, staring at the ground. There were other signs. He shook his head slowly. It would not be his responsibility soon. He had very mixed feelings about that. He was too old and tired to be traipsing about the hills and woods trying to keep the Laird's deer and livestock safe but... it was his life, the estate; man and boy he had worked for the Blairbuie's for sixty years, learning from his father and taking over from him when he passed on. What would happen now that he was being required to hang up his gun? It was not a prospect he welcomed. Without his job on the estate, he would be nothing and, even worse, they were not going to let him continue to live in the cottage as he had hoped; they needed it for whomever they appointed to take over, some stranger who wouldn't know a donkey from a deer!

If George, the Hodges' son, had been of any use, he could have been trained up and taken over eventually. But the lad was simply not up to it. He pictured George, tall, lanky, with very little between his ears. He had tried to teach him things and the boy had at one point seemed keen but he didn't seem able to remember anything, probably couldn't understand things, but he had seemed to love the woods. When he entered his teenage years, he became sullen, brooding, given to sudden outbursts of anger. Eventually, they had fallen out and Ewan had nearly knocked him down because of what George had said. He became a bad'un, no doubt about it, and the whole estate was well rid of him.

Where was he now? Down in Glasgow perhaps but only God knew what he was doing. Such a shame for his parents. A lovely, bright, pretty daughter and then they have a son like that. He was glad that he had never had children. To have a son like that must be devastating.

Ewan emerged from the woodland and headed down to the big house. There was always a welcome from Maureen Hodges, George's mother, in the big kitchen and he had even sometimes visited the cottage nearby where the Hodges lived. He liked the big kitchen though. It was always warm with lovely smells and Maureen was an excellent cook.

He pushed open the back door and slipped off his boots in the small lobby inside before padding into the kitchen in his thick socks. Maureen was at the range, preparing food for the evening meal.

"Good day to ye, Maureen."

She turned and smiled. "Ewan. Have you been out in the woods?"

"Aye...looking for the mysterious fugitive. Someone has built a wee hide deep in the forest and the Laird wanted me to try to find him. There's a body living there alright but who he is or where he is I couldna find."

"Perhaps a cup of tea would cheer you up."

"Aye that it would but a wee dram would be even better."

She laughed. "You won't get that from me, Ewan, as you well know."

"I know, love, I know." He watched her move about the kitchen filling the kettle and putting it on the range. She was a lovely woman, full in the figure now but probably quite a beauty in her youth. There was always a warmth about her, a caring, kindly soul. It seemed so unfair that she had a son like George.

"Are ye looking forward to having Jessie back?"

Maureen Hodges turned to face him and her eyes sparkled. "Oh yes. It's been a long time since she was up here. Can't get away very often you know what with the War."

"Aye, it's a bad business but let's hope it'll be over soon."

"We can hope but there doesn't seem much sign of it."

"So how many are you cooking for tonight?"

"As well as Lord and Lady B, there'll be five visitors and I'll cook some extra for Robert Langford, Jess and ourselves. You can eat with us too if you like Ewan. There'll be plenty of food and I know Jess would love to see you."

"Ach no. It's very kind but I'll leave you to enjoy your daughter without a grizzly old chap like me. I'll be sure to see her tomorrow."

Maureen poured the tea and she sat with Ewan at the big old pine table positioned in the centre of the kitchen. "We're very lucky, you know. We're never short of food out here what with the game you bring and what we raise ourselves. I hear that the rationing is very strict. One egg per person per week. That must be difficult. I couldn't cook a lot of things without eggs. Such a blessing to have our own hens."

"Aye and no bombs falling around our ears." Ewan paused. "I suppose the supply of food will continue when I'm..." Despite his efforts to control it, his lip quivered.

Maureen reached her hand across the table and laid it on his own, squeezing gently. "Now, now Ewan. You'll be fine and you deserve a rest now after so long working."

"Aye, but...you know..."

"I do know, Ewan, I do. There'll always be a welcome here for you, I want you to know that."

He nodded. "Thanks Lassie, thanks."

There was a laden silence for several seconds before Maureen turned the conversation to something more ordinary. "David's gone to Dunoon to pick up the visitors. He's taken the shooting brake so he can get them all in with their luggage. It'll still be a squash but David can put the luggage on the roof rack."

"That should impress the visitors. I dinna suppose they often get to ride in a Rolls Royce."

Maureen smiled and sipped her tea, her thoughts clearly elsewhere.

"A penny for them."

She laughed and shook herself but all trace of humour was absent from her eyes. "Nothing really..." her brow creased... "just wondering about George...where he is...what he's doing."

Ewan reached across the table and laid a hand on her arm. "Now, now lassie, dinna go upsetting yerself. He'll be fine, I'm sure, and when he's finished his wanderings he'll come back to you a proper man."

"I wish I could be so confident Ewan. How I wish I could."

CHAPTER 7

"Joss, Jed, come." Virginia Blairbuie slapped her walking stick against her boot and the two black labradors came hurtling into the scullery, tails wagging and looking up at her expectantly. "Yes it's time for a walk. We can't lounge around all day."

When she opened the door, the dogs burst into life again, charging outside almost knocking each other over, tails swishing furiously. She followed them, closing the door behind her. Walking with strong strides along the house and diagonally across the lawn towards the Loch, she breathed the air, the salty tang of weed and water filling her nostrils. When she had first come to Glenstriven House, the smell had faintly disgusted her, so different was it to the sanitised streets of London. But now, she actually liked it, though she would never admit that to James.

She strolled northwards along the foreshore, her boots causing the pebbles to clink against each other, the promise of the approaching Summer whispered in every breath of wind, every crying gull and every wash of water on the strand. A short distance away, a cormorant standing on a rock by the water's edge, spread wide its huge, glistening, black wings to dry in the sun; strange, primitive looking bird, its carefully tailored feathers fanned out and its slender head held disdainfully high.

Turning to the South, she scanned the Loch, her eye resting on the huge dark shape of the Courbet. Why they wanted to bring an old French warship to this remote spot, she could not fathom. It was clearly well past its working life. She hoped it had not been brought simply to rust away, defiling the beauty of the Loch, gradually falling apart and perhaps sinking where it lay at anchor.

Her eye caught a movement on the surface of the water. It was no more than a slight disturbance but it seemed to be heading up the Loch towards her. She trained her eyes on it wishing she had some binoculars with her. A seal? It must be a seal swimming up the Loch. One did see them quite often. She waited, expecting to see a small head appear above the water, a snout held in the air, checking what may be happening.

But as the ripples on the water came closer, she realised this was something much larger than a seal. Could it be a whale? They did sometimes stray into the lochs around the coast, people said, but she had never seen one. She continued to watch. If it were a whale, at some point, it would blow out air and then take another breath. She watched for several minutes as the ruffling of the surface moved past her and deeper into the Loch. No spray of water burst from it and no sound reached her ears.

A mystery. She would tell James about it and see what he thought it was. She continued her walk, watching the dogs gambolling at the water's edge and chasing each other before stopping to sniff bushes. Such an uncomplicated life, no worries, food provided, a comfortable place to sleep. They enjoyed life here much more than in London but she could never be satisfied with this...a walk each day, drinks in the evening, rarely seeing anyone. She thought of the life she had lived in London, the parties, the dinners, the friends, bright lights, music, plays. God how she longed to be back there. As soon as this damned war was over, she would go back whether James wanted to or not.

She had wandered about a mile North of the house when her reveries were disturbed by a feeling...a feeling of being watched. She raked her eyes across the surface of the water again. There was no disturbance, nothing to suggest anything or anyone was out there. She stopped and listened. The distant cry of a gull, waves lapping on the shore...nothing else.

Suddenly, both dogs stopped, noses in the air, standing at point as if watching a falling game bird. Then Joss started barking and was joined by Jed. Both bolted forward to a clump of bushes just off the shore and stopped, barking furiously. There was something or someone there. The barking stopped and both dogs ambled forward, heads down, whining with pleasure.

A figure stepped out from the bushes and bent to pet the dogs. He stood up.

Oh...it's you," she said. "What are you doing here?"

◆ ◆ ◆

A Tilly arrived with a screech of brakes and Dennis Thorney tumbled out of the front passenger seat. A few moments later, Robbie McBane appeared from the back rubbing his posterior. "My God that thing is uncomfortable. May be alright for a short trip but bouncing around on a thin cushion is not fun."

"I'd have thought you'd have enough padding there, Robbie," Lizzie smirked.

"Aye you'd think so but clearly I haven't."

Boggen had arranged for herself and Alice to travel in his staff car to Gourock whilst Robbie and Thorney were taken in a Tilly. Despite the greater physical comfort of the staff car, it had not been a pleasant journey.

Lizzie distrusted Boggen. He was a good-looking man in his mid forties with neatly groomed, dark hair, receding to reveal a high forehead. One could describe him as distinguished looking but he had a strong sense, she suspected, of his own worth and appeal. She had disliked the way he had eyed Alice and herself as if they were possible prey and the way he had tried to impress them by ordering his staff about, though, she had to acknowledge that could be his normal modus operandi.

When they had first arrived at RAF Turnberry and been shown to his office, he had positively beamed and made some comment about what a nice change it made to have young women on the base. After lunch, he had opened the front passenger door of the staff car for Alice, glancing down at her legs as she eased herself inside and then he held the rear door open for her. She knew the length of her skirt would prohibit any untoward view but, nevertheless, she wrapped it tightly around herself as she stepped in. There was something unctuous about him, his unwelcome attentions, his knowing smile.

But it had become worse. As soon as they had set off, he started making conversation.

"I certainly did not expect to have the company of such attractive young women on this trip. It's very welcome. Tell me, how long have you been with the Air Transport Auxiliary?"

"I joined three years ago, almost to the day, and Alice joined about a year ago, I think, wasn't it Alice?"

"That's right."

"I suppose the War effort requires women to do their bit as much as men. Are people surprised when you say you're a pilot?"

"Of course. Even the airman who brought the steps to our aircraft this morning was looking inside for the pilot…couldn't believe it was me."

"Perhaps he can be forgiven. You're probably the first female pilot he has met…actually, you're the first one I've met. But tell me, are all the ATA female staff as good-looking as you two?"

Lizzie had paused before replying. She had been tempted to give him both barrels but had smiled sweetly. "I suppose you intend that as a compliment, Sir, but actually in the ATA we are judged by the qualities and skills we bring to our jobs, not on our appearance."

He had chuckled. "I certainly meant to pay a compliment and I'm sorry if I gave offence." His hand had moved towards her and he patted her knee. "No need to get uppity when a chap pays you a compliment my dear." Even the memory now made her flesh creep.

Lizzie had very pointedly swung her legs away from him and shifted in her seat to increase the distance between them. He had seemed unconcerned but Lizzie made sure that she said as little as possible and made what she did say as curt and to the point as she could. Even now, she could feel her anger returning. What was wrong with men…some men she should say…that they felt they had a right to touch women? She knew she would have to be very careful around Boggen.

Now they stood on the empty quay, gulls wheeling mournfully overhead as if lamenting the absence of the ferry. Boggen looked out over the sea. "God it's a desolate place isn't it. Not much around here I'm afraid but…needs must."

"I think it's beautiful don't you Alice?"

"Absolutely…so still, so peaceful."

"It won't be so peaceful when our chaps start testing tomorrow I'm afraid."

"Then we'll enjoy it while it lasts."

A taxi came into view from the North. They watched it approach, reduce speed and ease to a halt beside them. An elegant young woman alighted and smiled at the driver as she handed him money through the window. As he drove away, she waved and picked up the small suitcase she had lifted from the taxi. She walked over to their group and smiled, a smile that was both warm and confident. Her high forehead, accentuated by the way her hair had been pulled back into a ponytail, gave an air of nobility and her finely chiselled features added to that.

"Jessica Hodges," she said presenting her free hand to Boggen. "You must be Group Captain Boggen.

"Correct. It's a pleasure to meet you Miss Hodges." Boggen was beaming again. Lizzie turned away feeling her anger returning. Another possible victim? The man was insatiable!

Jessica smiled at Lizzie and shook her hand, then Alice's before doing the same with Dennis Thorney and Robbie McBane. "You're all waiting for the ferry, I guess." Her voice was precise, refined, with the merest hint of a Scottish accent which gave it a lovely, lilting quality. The confident way she had greeted everyone, the genuine warmth in her bright amber eyes, her elegance; Lizzie could not help liking her.

Boggen answered. "We're all heading for Glenstriven House and hoping that someone will be on the other side to pick us up." Perhaps Lizzie was condemning Boggen unfairly but his smooth voice and the look in his eye troubled her.

"That'll be my father probably. He's the Blairbuie's driver

amongst other things."

"We'll not fit in one car surely?" Alice's brow creased.

"He'll most likely bring the shooting brake...lots of room in that."

"So Miss Hodges, you live at Glenstriven House?" Robbie smiled at her.

"Jessica please. Not really. I was brought up there but went away to school and now I live and work in London. At the Ministry of War in fact. I just have a few days leave so I thought I'd come back. Exhausting train journey though...early start." She turned towards the sea and pointed to a boat approaching from the other shore. "Here's the ferry now."

They fell silent and watched the boat being moored to the quay. It left as soon as they had boarded and chugged across the strip of water. Lizzie and Alice sat either side of Jessica.

"What's your job at the Ministry?" Lizzie ventured.

Jessica paused for a second before replying. "I'm a secretary."

"Must be interesting work...knowing about aspects of the War effort."

"Yes, Alice, it is interesting...demanding too. Things happen very quickly so there's constant change." Suddenly she changed the subject. "It'll be such fun to have the company of two women of about my age for the next few days. Not much chance of that normally. There are other secretaries at work of course but there's never any time to chat...long days...too exhausted to socialise after work."

The ferry bumped against the quay and they clambered over the gangplank once more. A man of medium height stood waiting, the faintest smile on his face which broadened when he saw Jessica walk towards him. He held her in his arms for several seconds and then gently kissed her on the cheek. She was a little taller than him.

"Welcome everyone. Lord and Lady Blairbuie are looking forward to meeting you." His accent was definitely not local, probably London, Lizzie guessed. "I'll need to put the larger items of luggage on the roof rack but if you'd like to climb in now, please feel free."

"I'll gie you a hand." Robbie McBane was significantly taller than Hodges and powerfully built; those hours training when he used to play rugby were evident to Lizzie in the way he swung the suitcases effortlessly onto the rack for Hodges to position.

"Come on you two, let's squeeze in the very back." Jessica pulled a rear door open, tilted the seat forward and, ducking her head, climbed into the back. Alice and Lizzie followed.

"If I'm not mistaken, this is a Rolls Royce Phantom Mark II isn't it?" Dennis Thorney's admiring eyes lingered on the contours of the shooting brake and Lizzie noticed the way he stood, pompous, self-important.

"That's correct, Sir. Built in 1930 I believe. Lord Blairbuie bought it from new."

"Lovely motor car."

"You're right there, Sir." Hodges pushed the last suitcase into position on the roof rack and, standing on the running board, began to strap the luggage down. Boggen, Thorney and Robbie McBane watched him do so. When he had finished, he opened the front passenger door and looked at Boggen. "Perhaps you'd care to sit in the front, Sir, or maybe you'd..."

"The front will suit very well. Thank you."

Robbie and Dennis Thorney took the centre row of seats and, glancing around to make sure everyone was in, Hodges started the engine. It purred quietly and the car moved off almost silently.

CHAPTER 8

The sun was still warm; Rory groaned as he was shaken awake.

"Rory, Rory, wake up." Billy shook his shoulder again.

"Canna be time for me yet."

"It is. The clock struck four a while back. But there's something happening down there."

Rory sat up rapidly, suddenly awake. "What is it?"

"Look down there. " Billy pointed with a trembling finger. "Can you see it?"

Rory forced his sleepy eyes into focus. "Aye...something in the water. Looks like a whale or some creature."

"That's never a whale. That's one of them submarines I bet."

"What submarines?"

"You know...the U Boats the Germans have. It's moving slowly."

From the vantage point on the crag, they could see a dark shape moving beneath the water, merely a ghostly shadow, making the smallest of bow waves with the slightest disturbance of the water at the rear. They both watched it move slowly up the Loch but quite quickly the dark shape became indistinguishable from the water surface and all they could see was the small waves spreading in a V shape from the front and rolling to either side until they were lost.

"That must be what he wanted us to see. That's great. We can report that to him and we'll get more money." Rory rubbed his hands with glee.

"Shouldn't we report it to the Polis or someone? I mean it could be a German invasion starting."

Rory chuckled. "Billy, the Germans won't come all the way round the top o' Scotland to start an invasion here. I mean what could they do when they landed? They'd have to go miles to fight anyone."

"Maybe that's the plan."

"Dinna be daft!"

"But even if it's no' an invasion, they must be up to something."

"Aye you're right there. They must be spying. Probably wondering what that old ship is doing in the Loch. Perhaps they'll torpedo it."

"That would be gud to see. A fine explosion to light up the sky."

Rory looked pityingly at Billy. "If they were going to do that, Billy, they'd have done it already. They wouldn't be cruising about the Loch. Anyway, we're not telling anyone because we're going to tell McClaughlin who'll pay us handsomely for the information."

"If we get anything at all. I mean d'you think the guy meant it? He's not goin' ta take the information and the sheep and gi'e us nothing?"

"We'll get the money alright, Billy. I'll see to that even if I have to… make him." Rory bunched his right fist and held it up. "He'll no' argue with this."

Billy shrank back a little even though the threat was not to him. He knew Rory of old; he had a nasty streak. "Right. Well it's your turn to keep watch now. I can have another couple of hours kip and then we can have something to eat can't we?"

Rory stepped forward and ruffled Billy's hair. "Aye, we can do that ma wee man. I won't let you starve."

◆ ◆ ◆

They had been ushered into the drawing room by the elderly butler whom Jessica had introduced as Langford. It was large, elegant, comfortable with a grand piano prominent in the curve of the bay window adorned with, presumably, family photographs. The butler had offered tea which they had gratefully accepted. They all sat except Jessica who, Lizzie noticed, hovered nervously in the room. Her father, the chauffeur David Hodges, was still outside unloading their luggage from the shooting brake.

Langford turned to Jessica. "Would you care to go through to see your mother, Miss Jessica?"

"I'll wait until I've seen Lord and Lady Blairbuie."

"Very good Miss. I'll let them know you've arrived."

But before he had turned to go, a tall man entered the room. He had the bearing of a senior military man but seemed too diffident to give orders. In fact, his features had a gentleness about them, his manner warm with almost a shyness in his demeanour. His eyes scanned the room and then he smiled, moving directly to where Jessica stood. She smiled too and both her hands reached out to him. He took her in his arms and held her, kissing her almost reverently on the cheek; there was real affection in the embrace, a respect on both sides which was touching to see.

He let her go. "So good to see you my dear. Welcome home."

"Ladies and gentlemen, may I introduce, Lord Blairbuie...who has been so good to me..."

"Now, now Jessica...no need to go into that."

Jessica was about to embark on a round of introductions when the door opened and a woman in her late forties walked confidently into the centre of the room, head held high and barely looking at anyone. Her hair was expertly groomed and her make-up applied with great care. She was beautiful and probably knew it! Her features were sharp but delicate like a fine alabaster statue, the bone structure in her face suggesting she would remain beautiful even into old age. She walked with the air of someone used to making an entrance, an assumption of her worth and status.

"Lady Blairbuie, how nice to see..."

"Jessica." The marble face cracked into a smile. There did seem to be warmth in it and certainly the embrace she offered seemed as genuine as her husband's had been. "It is so lovely to see you. Thank you for coming to visit us...or rather your parents of course. You look very well. I hope they're not working you too hard. Now, who have we here?"

Jessica raised her hand towards Group Captain Boggen and announced his name. There was the slightest hesitation on Lady Blairbuie's part before she shook his hand as did her husband. Was it surprise that she would be hosting a Group Captain? Lizzie watched his reaction.

He lifted Lady Blairbuie's hand to his lips. "Charmed to make your acquaintance my Lady." Lizzie could see that glint in his eye which suggested he had just found another possible victim of his desire. She turned away. The others were introduced and Alice and herself last. She knew that Jessica would not be doing that for any reason other than it was the accepted order of things. One day we women will be truly equal she thought.

A girl wheeled in a trolley with tea things and, having introduced her as Isla, Jessica slipped out of the room to see her mother who was presumably somewhere in the back of the house, slaving away. Isla, whose brown hair was tied back, had dark eyes and distributed tea without a smile nor a glance at the guests. She was about sixteen, a curious downturn at the corners of her mouth making her look sullen, though, had she smiled, one would have called her handsome. Lizzie had a strong sense that she resented her position of servitude, was perhaps even angry to be required to wait on others. She tried to catch her eye and smile at her but Isla turned away.

There was one moment which caused Lizzie to smile.

Which room have you put Group Captain Boggen in, Langford?"

He looked somewhat non-plussed. "I've had the rooms at the top of the house prepared as you requested m'Lady. They are all very similar so I haven't assigned your guests to any particular one though it would be helpful if the young ladies were happy to share a room."

"No, no, no, Langford. Group Captain Boggen must be given a room on the first floor. I suggest the Green Room. It has a wonderful view over the Loch, Group Captain, and I'm sure you'll be very comfortable there."

"I will be happy to go wherever you think best, Lady Blairbuie. Us forces chaps are used to making do you know. After all, there is a war on."

"I'll have the Green Room made ready, M'Lady." Poor Langford bowed and left the room. Lizzie was cross on his behalf. Why did the upper classes think it was acceptable to put blame on their servants rather than admitting they themselves had got something wrong? Lady Blairbuie had clearly not expected to be hosting an officer of Boggen's rank... or was there something else that interested her? That slight hesitation when she greeted him. Before her fertile imagination could start to work, Lizzie and the other guests were shown to their rooms by Langford who eventually brought up their luggage.

Lizzie and Alice were in an attic room which Lizzie assumed was designed as servants' quarters. Robbie McBane and Dennis Thorney were similarly housed but in separate rooms a little further along the corridor. Disappointingly, all the rooms looked out over a courtyard at the back of the house and, beyond it, the parkland which rose to the woods. The front of the house would have given a much more interesting view over the Loch.

Once in the room, Alice and Lizzie sat on the beds to test them. "Quite comfortable," said Alice. "Probably much more so than anything we'd have had at RAF Turnberry."

"Agreed. What did you make of Lord and Lady Blairbuie?"

He seemed very nice...certainly loves Jessica...but I didn't take to her. Perhaps too much like my own mother. A lot of what she says and does is for show I suspect, though she did seem very warm to Jessica too."

"I agree. But there was something about the way she greeted Boggen...a slight hesitation before she offered her hand, her eyes opening wider. Not sure if that meant she is as interested in the opposite sex as Boggen is or..."

"Probably pleasantly surprised to have a senior officer. May have thought she would be hosting just the likes of us."

"Not even the likes of us. I bet she didn't expect female visitors."

Dinner was served at seven o'clock. There was some confusion when Langford showed them into the servants' hall. Before they had sat down, a bell jangled harshly in a nearby room and Langford bustled away. He was back within minutes saying her Ladyship had requested they all join her and Lord Blairbuie in the drawing room for drinks and then in the dining room for dinner. It was quite a formal occasion marred only for Lizzie by being placed next to Dennis Thorney who talked endlessly at her about engineering and music. The only consolation was that it saved her from talking to Boggen who sat on her other side next to Lady Blairbuie.

After dinner, she and Alice were taken by Lady Blairbuie back to the drawing room for coffee whilst, to Lizzie's disappointment, Robbie McBane and the other men went to Lord Blairbuie's library for brandy and cigars. Robbie smiled in a resigned way at her as she and Alice followed Lady Blairbuie out of the room. She felt a little stirring in her heart; he was perhaps as disappointed as she not to be able to spend the rest of the evening together.

◆ ◆ ◆

The sun had slipped below the hills on the far side of the Loch some time before, turning the sky at first orange, then red, then purple and they had caught the distant sound of the bell at the big house clanging nine times in the soft evening air. A few last gulls were wheeling and crying over the foreshore, preparing to roost for the night and the light breeze that had cooled the day had died. Everything was slowing to stillness but for the gentle sound of water lapping beneath them; the waves, so mighty in the open sea, now tamed by the sides of the Loch, were yet restless when all else prepared to sleep.

"It's beautiful here right enough," Billy said wistfully.

"Forget the poetry, Billy, we've work to do. Come on."

Rory had refused to let Billy have another sandwich, saying that was tomorrow's breakfast and Billy had grumbled until Rory had snapped at him. Billy reluctantly struggled to his feet.

"We didna bring enough food."

"Food, food, food. Is that all you think about?"

"No, but…just saying."

"God Almighty! I wish I hadna told you about this job. If you're that hungry, ye can have a few bites from that lamb we shot yesterday."

"Could I? We could make a fire and…"

"Billy, when will you learn when I'm being sarcastic. If we make a fire, everyone will know exactly where we are. We may as well go to the big house and say, 'Here we are. We're the poachers. Arrest us now.' Just think will you afore you open your mouth."

Billy said nothing. He hoisted the knapsack onto his shoulders and followed Rory away from the crag which had been their lookout post all day.

"I'm going to get a deer tonight. We'll get more money for that than a sheep I reckon."

"It'll no' be easy to shoot a deer in those woods."

"Aye but I'll no' shoot it in the woods. I've been thinking and remembering what my dad told me. The deer come out of the woods at night to eat the grass and stuff in the fields. We'll wait on the edge of the woods, hidden in the trees, until we see one and then…"

Billy shrugged and plodded behind Rory. One day, he would make a suggestion that Rory would admire. One day, he would be the one in charge.

CHAPTER 9

Langford hovered around the room ensuring all the gentlemen had a glass of brandy and had been offered cigars. Only Lord Blairbuie and Boggen accepted the latter. Soundlessly and unnoticed, he stationed himself in one corner of the room.

"Thank you Robert. You've had a long day. We'll be fine now. We can serve ourselves."

Langford bowed stiffly. "Thank you m'Lord. I'll bid you all a very good night gentlemen." He glided away closing the door behind him with a soft click.

James Blairbuie raised his glass. "Good health to you all. I hope that whatever it is you're doing here is successful and that it brings us closer to defeating that madman over in Germany."

Three glasses were raised in response. "Here, here."

I know it's hush hush but what can you tell us Boggen about what's going on in the Loch. I must say we're rather puzzled by some of the things we've seen."

Boggen's eyes narrowed, making a judgement. "Mr Thorney here knows everything because he is closely involved in the development of the weapon we will be testing over the next few days."

Thorney, who had been slouching in the comfortable armchair, sat straighter. "On the flight up, I did take the liberty of briefing Sergeant McBane here as he is tasked with providing security. He needs to know what he is securing."

Boggen's voice was cold. "I think, Mr Thorney, you should have consulted me first."

"You weren't on our flight old boy. Besides McBane is not going to go blabbing to anyone. He needed to know how important it is."

"Well, Lord Blairbuie..."

"James, please. No need for such formality."

"James...you may as well be told provided you guarantee to keep it to yourself. There will be four of us who know then and no one else needs to." He looked pointedly at Thorney, took a sip of his brandy and set the glass down thoughtfully on the occasional table beside him. "You probably know that Hitler has some battleships anchored in Norwegian fjords. One in particular interests us and that is the Tirpitz. The problem is how to destroy her. The amount of armour plating she carries is formidable, she is heavily armed, protected by anti-submarine nets and our chances of destroying her are minimal. However... perhaps Mr Thorney you can take up the story."

Dennis Thorney stood up, clearly relishing the chance to impress, and looked out of the window presumably to build anticipation. In the fading light, the Courbet lay like a sleeping monster in the Loch. He turned back to face the expectant faces. "We are developing a special kind of bomb. You see, the most vulnerable part of a ship is the underbelly; the sides are protected well below the waterline by armour plating which counters the threat from torpedoes but there is rarely anything protecting the lower regions of the hull. Our new bomb will be dropped from an aircraft flying low at an exact speed and height. It will be spun at a precise speed and will bounce on the surface of the water just like a stone skims the surface." Thorney made the action of skimming a stone. "If we get the distance, the height and the speed right, it will reach the ship and roll down its side. A pistol – that's what we call the detonating device - will explode the bomb at the correct depth and blow a hole in the ship under the armour plating. Then the ship sinks."

Dennis Thorney sat down enjoying the stunned silence that greeted this revelation. It was broken by Robbie McBane. "There seem to be a lot of 'ifs' here. How can you make the detonator fire at the right depth?"

"That's easy. As you know, the deeper an object drops in water, the greater the pressure exerted on it. We know the depth we want and the water pressure at that depth. The pistol is fired by the water pressure."

"So the Courbet is the target?" James Blairbuie offered.

"Correct." Boggen resumed the narrative. "As you will appreciate, this is a fiendishly difficult thing to achieve but Mr Barnes Wallis and his team which includes Mr Thorney are confident it can be done. Some testing off the Kent coast has already been carried out but we need a location that is more like a Norwegian fjord so that the pilots can learn how to drop it."

"So we can expect aircraft to be flying low over the Loch and dropping bombs on the Courbet. I must say that sounds very dangerous. What happens if they miss the target? I mean we could be killed."

"Oh no, " Dennis Thorney cut in, "the bombs used in the trials are dummies – filled with concrete to the exact weight. They won't explode."

"But a lump of concrete dropping can do a lot of damage," Robbie McBane said tetchily.

"You need have no fears on that score either of you. My pilots are flying from RAF Turnberry in Mosquitoes especially adapted for the purpose. They are well used to low flying and will make their approach along the Loch over the water. There is no danger of them releasing a bomb on the land."

Robbie McBane looked deeply sceptical.

"It seems a rather more dangerous thing than I was led to believe." James Blairbuie drained his glass and lifted the decanter to top up his guests' glasses before re-filling his own. "How long each day will this go on?"

"Not long. Three aircraft will fly up on each sortie from Turnberry. The first attempts will start at ten hundred hours tomorrow and there will be one more attempt probably at about thirteen hundred hours. After dropping the bombs, the aircraft will need to return to Turnberry to re-load and then fly up here again. You will not be disturbed for long."

"What about security? I was told I'd have to keep everyone who lives here at the back of the house so they can't see what's going on."

"That's correct, Sergeant, but that is only needed when the aircraft are in the area. Once they've dropped their bombs, there's nothing for people to see."

James Blairbuie's brow was creased. "That isn't the only aspect of security we need to consider. We think we have someone in the woods. My gamekeeper has found a camp with plenty of evidence of someone living there. It may be just a poacher but on the other hand it may be a spy."

Boggen turned to Robbie McBane. "Are you armed Sergeant?"

"No Sir."

"I have a rifle and a couple of shotguns, Sergeant, if that's any use." James Blairbuie liked the look of Sergeant McBane; he sensed he was reliable and trustworthy. "Both Ewan McCrae, the gamekeeper and Hamish Ferguson, my estate manager, have guns too."

"And I have my trusty pistol always on me if it's needed." Boggen lifted his jacket and pulled a revolver from the holster attached to his belt. He laid it carefully on the table beside him. "Can you work with the gamekeeper to find this person and, if necessary, take him into custody?"

"Aye, Sir, but I can't be here ensuring everyone is at the back of the house if I'm away in the woods."

"I'm sure everyone at the house will follow your instructions. You won't need to stay here throughout."

"Ok, Sir. If that's your order."

"The other thing you should know is that we have assistance from the Navy. There will be one MTB – a Motor Torpedo Boat that is – stationed at the entrance to the Loch ensuring there are no seaborne intruders and a second one will be entering the Loch with observers on board to assess the tests. That is of course on top of what Mr Thorney and I observe."

James Blairbuie looked at Boggen, doubt writ clearly on his face. "On a couple of occasions recently, I, my wife and my Estate Manager, Hamish Feguson, have seen something very strange. I saw a man apparently walking on the water. Of course, unless his name was Jesus, that cannot have been. He must have been standing on something that was moving on or just beneath the surface. Is that part of this testing?"

Boggen's face moved quickly from concern to faint derision. "I think you must have been mistaken, James. There must be some other explanation. Perhaps one swimmer being lifted out of the water by another."

"We were not mistaken, Paul, and no swimmer could hold up another for that length of time swimming at such a constant speed. There was something out there and, if you don't know about it, perhaps it is enemy activity."

"I do have a radio set with me and I will make sure the MTB crews are informed. If there is a craft out there that shouldn't be, they will find it with their sonar scanners."

Dennis Thorney, wanting to assert his position as the engineering authority in the room, changed the subject back to the tests. "The MTB that comes into the Loch will anchor flags at the right distance from the Courbet so that the aircrew know exactly when to drop the bombs. You can see that we've prepared for these tests carefully."

No one spoke for several seconds. James Blairbuie sipped his drink meditatively. "I hope you have, Mr Thorney, I hope you have."

◆ ◆ ◆

Lizzie lay in bed unable to sleep, running through the events of the day. It was not uncommon for her to find sleep difficult when she had been flying, despite the fatigue that always accompanied it. It was as if the intensity of the experience, the excitement of it, would not leave her or perhaps she was reluctant to let it go. Also, the people she had met had intrigued her and one, Boggen, had angered her.

Alice lay in the other bed, her breathing slow and peaceful. The sleep of the innocent and untroubled, except Lizzie knew

Alice carried the burden of a mother who was only interested in herself. What had Alice said? Lady Blairbuie reminded her of her mother and certainly Lizzie had recognised a self-centredness in their hostess as soon as they were introduced, throughout dinner and in the drawing room afterwards. It had been trying but she was very glad of Alice's company; it was a shame, but entirely understandable, that Jessica wanted to spend time with her parents rather than join them for dinner.

Lizzie sighed softly. She needed to walk about to still her mind so she slipped out of bed quietly. She did not of course light the paraffin lamp they had carried with them up the creaking stairs to their attic room. It was not a cold night - her nightdress was perfectly adequate – and she tip-toed towards the door, drawing back the bolt and opening it as quietly as she could. Alice did not stir. She glided out into the corridor and closed the door carefully behind her.

There were doors on both sides of the corridor; the rooms at the front of the house she knew were empty. She tried the first handle and the door opened without resistance. Pale moonlight cast a milky half-light into the room. It was similar to their own: two beds, two wardrobes and a dressing table with a chair. She trod softly on the bare boards to the window and looked out.

The scene that greeted her was magical. The moonlight washed the surface of the Loch with a white sheen, brighter where it was in line with her view and weakening either side until the water was quite dark. Even the old ship anchored in the Loch took on a mystical appearance, the light silvering its dull grey surfaces, rendering it dreamlike, mythical, entrancing.

She stood for a long time captivated by the scene feeling it seep into her mind and calm the whirling thoughts therein. At last she turned and left the room. Outside, she stopped and listened to the house. It was silent. The faint call of a hunting owl reached her ears no doubt floating over the park at the rear of the house. Suddenly there was a muffled sound in the distance...a gun shot. Poachers in the woods perhaps?

The silence was restored. She decided to explore a little; the temptation of a big old house sleeping was too much. Carefully, she made her way down the stairs to the first floor. On the landing, she stopped to listen. Muffled sounds reached her ears. It was only the faintest murmur but there were definitely voices.

The corridor housed the main guest bedrooms and presumably Lord and Lady Blairbuie's rooms; she moved along it stealthily. Each door boasted the name of the room, all colours. She passed red and blue, the voices becoming louder. She stopped when she reached the Green Room and knew that the voices came from inside.

She listened intently.

Lady Blairbuie's voice, soft, husky, inviting, teasing and then a cracked reply, urgent, breathing hard. Boggen! She shook her head. So he had found a suitable victim. Lizzie could not feel any concern for Lady Blairbuie. She was old enough to handle herself and perhaps as eager as Boggen. Taking a risk, she very gently leaned the side of her head against the door.

"Oh Paul, that's wonderful. Just like it was. We would have been good together."

"It could never have been, Virginia, you were already married."

"I know, I know, but if only..."

Lizzie suddenly felt embarrassed and moved away as swiftly as she could. She had no wish to eavesdrop on such an intimate moment but the revelation was fascinating.

Sunday 9th May 1943

CHAPTER 10

They had succeeded in shooting a deer, or at least Rory had. They were euphoric but it was a struggle carrying it down through the forest in the dark to hide it in the scrub at the edge of the Loch where they had been dropped on the Friday evening. Rory said they mustn't drag it as it would leave obvious marks. He had also insisted on waiting until the blood from the wound had stopped flowing. "Leave no trace - that must be our motto."

It took them a while to find the place where they had hidden the sheep. It was disgusting. Already flies were crawling around the wound. "No one will eat that surely to God?"

"They will, Billy, when it's butchered, you know cut up into nice joints for the oven. There'll be no flies on it by then."

"Will it no be rotten?"

"Och no! You have to hang meat for a good few days to let it ease. It'll be fine. Here, have a bite." Rory waved a leg in Billy's direction who recoiled.

"I'm no eating lamb ever again."

"Don't be such a baby, Billy. I'm hoping Gordon will give us a nice joint each for home. I love a bit of lamb."

The dawn was breaking when they had finished and Billy was exhausted: the lack of proper sleep, working at night, not enough food. He was glad the worst was done and they would be going home that night. He longed for his bed, a nice cup of tea and a few other home comforts which he'd never take for granted again. Grey light infused the landscape and a few streaks of brightness showed over the hills behind them. The birds were stirring, the new day stretching and yawning into life.

From the vantage of the higher ground, they could see a man down by the edge of the Loch. He was walking along slowly with a folder held tightly under his arm, a smallish, rotund man with a balding head and glasses. He stopped every few paces, checked something on a piece of paper he was holding and looked out over the water. Once he spread his arms as if trying to estimate distance.

"What's that bloke doing I wonder?" but Rory didn't reply to Billy's question.

Billy trudged behind Rory as they made their way back into the woods. They needed to skirt the house staying out of sight and find the crag where they had spent the previous day. They knew what they were looking for now...the mysterious movement in the water, the German sub as Billy confidently maintained.

Suddenly, Rory stopped and put out his arm. Billy walked into it. Rory turned to him with his finger on his lips and then pointed. A figure was gliding through the forest; by the stride, it looked like a man and he was carrying a rifle. The two boys crouched in the bushes and watched as the figure passed ahead of them, moving quickly downhill towards the Loch. He was tall, thin and looked young. They waited for several minutes and then moved forward cautiously.

"Perhaps the gamekeeper," Billy whispered.

"Aye, perhaps."

Some five minutes later, as they approached their lookout crag, a muffled shot rang through the trees and was answered by the faintest echo from the far side of the Loch.

"Strange time of day to be hunting. Maybe not a gamekeeper. Maybe another poacher like us."

"Aye maybe, Billy. We need to be very careful we're not seen."

They crawled out of the bushes onto the grass of the crag and edged forward to see if they could see anything. Nothing... at least nothing unusual... the gulls crying mournfully in the morning air and the water lapping softly below them on the shingles.

◆ ◆ ◆

Robbie McBane followed Ewan McCrae's long, slow strides up the hill towards the woodland. He had tried to engage him in conversation but the old Scotsman seemed one of those not inclined to talk. The ground was a little soft but not so bad as to cause his boots to sink and become muddy. There would be rock close to the surface and on this slope, water would drain quickly towards the Loch. He turned to look at the scene behind him.

It was quiet again. The MTB was moving slowly from the red flag towards the Courbet, sailors on the rear deck feeding a line over the stern. He watched for only a few seconds and then trudged on behind his companion. Robbie could have...would have...walked faster but he had to acknowledge that the older man knew how to pace himself, saving energy for the long climb through the trees. He could doubtless walk like that all day when a more impatient person would tire.

The woodland was, in places, dense with conifers, crowding together and blocking most of the light so that they walked in an eerie darkness, the heady scent of the pines filling their nostrils. In other places, they passed through sections of older forest, large oaks spreading gnarled arms and fingers, their fluttering leaves filtering the morning sunlight onto the undergrowth which seemed to shimmer like sequins on a lady's dress.

They reached a plantation of conifers that had been recently felled and now looked, in the quiet Sunday morning, like one of the battlefields of the Great War, the dead laying silent where they had fallen. The height and slenderness of the trunks around the edge of the cleared plantation were now more obvious, naked and exposed, no growth clothing their lower stems.

Ewan McCrae stopped. "Are ye alright? Not going too fast for ye am I?"

"No, you're grand. All that rugby training you know."

"You're a rugby player?"

"Aye. Was. No time for that now and I'll probably be too old by the time this finishes."

"You've a good few years in you yet, I reckon."

"I'm twenty-six now. I could be pushing thirty by the time the war's over. Too old that is for rugby."

"Aye, probably."

Ewan turned to trudge onwards but Robbie wanted a few more seconds to enjoy the quiet of the forest. "This might be a case of looking for a needle in a haystack. I hadna realised the forest was so big."

"Aye. It is big. It goes right across the hills up to the moorland. But we're nearly there." Ewan McCrae turned and trudged on. The ground began to level off as it reached the brow of the first long hill. Soon they were back in old woodland, picking their way across the knotted hands of roots clutching at the soil. Ewan McCrae plodded onward unspeaking.

At last, he stopped and pointed. Robbie could see nothing at first just a dense mass of undergrowth at the base of a large oak.

"It's a good shelter that. Whoever made it knew what he was doing. Someone used to hiding out in the woods."

"Aye…or well trained."

They dropped to hands and knees to crawl through the entrance which was almost invisible, so well had it been hidden. The space inside was small but served the purpose well. A lattice of branches formed the roof which was spread with large fronds of bracken, layered thickly so that water would run off and down to the ground. More bracken had been spread on one part of the floor with a dark green blanket folded on top. Carefully, Robbie unfolded the blanket and searched for a label. There was none. It did look like army issue, though perhaps not British army. He re-folded the blanket exactly as it had been and laid it on the bracken.

"He's a tidy soul anyway."

"Aye he is." Ewan pointed to a green canvas rucksack in which were some tins of food and a tin opener. "Planning on staying a while." Ewan then led Robbie out of the hide and pointed to a clearing close by where the cold ashes of a fire were in plain view.

"Wouldn't a fire have given him away?"

"No. The smoke would be dispersed by the trees and if he lit it at dusk we wouldna see a thing at this distance what with the hills and woodland in between."

"He knows what he's doing then?"

Ewan nodded slowly. "Aye. He does that."

◆ ◆ ◆

Alice laughed at the look of frustration on Lizzie's face. They had heard the aircraft roaring up the Loch and a great clang after each had passed. Sitting in their attic bedroom forbidden from looking out over the Loch was a punishment to Lizzie.

Alice touched her arm. "It must be hard being so inquisitive."

"Yes it is. I do like to know everything Alice. Perhaps we may see the second test later today."

"How so?"

Lizzie smiled but said nothing. They clattered down the narrow staircase to the floor below, down the next flight to the ground floor and arrived at the rear door which opened from a lobby room next to the kitchen. Boots in various states of cleanliness sat on low shelves and a tall, slim, wooden cupboard nestled in one corner. Lizzie heaved open the heavy outside door and they stepped out into the fresh air.

It was a beautiful morning. Lizzie had been excited by the drama of what had been happening out of their sight on the Loch but she was also open to the joys of natural beauty and she was looking forward to their walk. After the roar of the aircraft, the scene was quiet, peaceful. If one set aside the test, it was difficult to believe in this remote Scottish place that war was raging across Europe.

They walked along the foreshore, heading North away from

the house, stopping frequently to take in the breathtaking views over the Loch. A gull, wings outspread, hovered above them, balancing on the breeze and then flying away with raucous cries. Further away, a cormorant dropped at an impossible speed, plunging into the water to reappear moments later with a fish wriggling in its beak.

"It may be peaceful, but it's a savage world really isn't it?"

"It is Alice, in nature just as in humankind. I just don't think Hitler needs to do what he is doing in order to eat. At least the cormorant is obeying a primeval need to survive."

"True. It's just that we sometimes forget how brutal nature can be. Small fish are eaten by bigger ones who are eaten by birds and seals and they in turn are the prey of other creatures. We sometimes forget those aspects when we see a beautiful scene."

It was Alice who saw it first, what looked like a crumpled heap of clothes dumped on the foreshore. They both went to investigate and, as they drew closer, realised the clothes were occupied. The body was lying face down, arms bent and hands clutching the pebbles of the beach as if to haul himself up. A dark red stain smeared the right side of his face and spread over the nearest stones. Some flies were already crawling on the face.

Lizzie stifled her shock and revulsion and bent down to look more carefully. It was a young man, not much more than a boy really, with dark, matted hair. She could not see the face fully because of his position and she knew that she mustn't move the body until the Police had been called. She looked up and scanned the scene around them. Still the same sense of peace and quiet, the birds behaving as normal, the waters of the Loch still swishing gently in rhythmic pulses on the pebbles of the beach.

"Do you suppose it was suicide?" Alice's voice was tremulous.

"Why suicide?"

"Well you know...where the wound is. Perhaps held a pistol to his head and..." Alice shuddered.

"Perhaps. We won't know until the scene is carefully examined. There's no sign of a gun nearby is there?"

"I can't see anything but it may be beneath him."

"Possibly...but wouldn't it be in his hand still. Unless he dropped it before he fell I suppose."

"But it can't be murder surely...out here in the middle of nowhere?"

"What were you saying about the brutality of nature? It extends to humankind without a doubt."

They stood back, taking in the sight of the body lying in such an undignified manner. "What a way to end a life." Alice's eyes were watering.

But Lizzie's gaze was on the young man's left hand. She stepped close to it and stooped over it. A small piece of paper, probably just a corner from a larger sheet was trapped in his grip as if he had been trying to hold it and it had been torn from his grasp. Why would someone be holding a piece of paper out here? Unless there had been someone else with him.

"Come on Alice. We need to get back to the house and alert Robbie McBane. It may not be his concern but it might be something to do with the tests. God knows if there is any Police presence in these parts. I suppose the nearest place would be Dunoon."

"We need to take careful note of the surroundings so we can find it again. That high crag is what, thirty yards away? We need to look for landmarks as we return so that we know the way back here."

"Lead on Alice. Let's hope the carrion eaters don't find the body before we're back."

CHAPTER 11

"Bloody idiots. They can't have been flying at the right height or speed or something." Boggen replaced the handset on its cradle. He had set up the radio in the drawing room so that he could liaise with the MTBs during and after the tests.

Dennis Thorney was staring out over the Loch his eyes screwed up as if estimating something. "I don't think it's your pilots at all, old man. I think the red buoy may not have been placed at the right distance. Have the guys on the MTB check it. It should be twelve hundred yards."

Boggen lifted the handset again. "MTB One...MTB One...this is shore control...over."

A voice crackled from the speaker on the radio. "MTB One...go ahead, Sir...over."

"Mr Thorney thinks the red buoy may not have been positioned at the correct distance. Kindly check it and let me know...over"

"Will do, Sir. It'll take a while..."

"I realise that. Just get on with it." Boggen didn't bother with the usual signing off courtesies. He dropped the handset back on its cradle with a clatter. "Trust the bloody Navy. We should have sorted it ourselves," he growled.

"We don't know whether that's the reason Group Captain. I just think it's worth checking."

The two men stood together watching the MTB move slowly from the red buoy towards the Courbet, a line being paid out from the stern. Dennis Thorney at last spoke, uneasy in the simmering silence of his companion. "The bomb spun and did bounce which is the main thing."

"We already knew it would do that!"

"Yes but it shows your pilots must have been flying at the

right height and speed. If it is just the distance, it should be possible to put that right quickly."

"What distance should it be again?"

"Twelve hundred yards. It has been precisely calculated."

Boggen was not in a good mood. "How are the aircrew supposed to know when they reach that distance if they are attacking the Tirpitz? I mean we can't send an MTB to put down marker buoys."

"We've got something in mind...a simple device that we think will work."

"Well it doesn't look like the buoys have worked."

The two men fell silent again until Dennis Thorney again spoke to break the tension. "It was quite a clang when the bombs hit the ship."

"And had they contained explosive, they would have done some damage to the superstructure but left her floating. That's no good is it?"

Thorney shrugged. He had tried to cheer Boggen up but he decided to let him stew in it. After some fifteen minutes, the radio burst into life. "Shore Control...Shore Control...this is MTB One...over."

"What's the distance?"

"We have a distance of eight hundred, repeat eight hundred yards."

"It's supposed to be twelve hundred yards. Get the bloody buoy moved to the correct position immediately."

"Will do Sir...."

Boggen didn't wait for the sentence to finish and again dropped the handset onto its cradle. "Bloody idiots," he muttered.

"Your pilots are certainly able to fly low and navigate through all the islands round here."

"So they bloody well should. They've spent enough time training."

Dennis Thorney shrugged. Boggen was clearly determined to be grumpy. He sidled over to the grand piano and drew a hand across the beautifully polished top. He sat on the stool and a smile lit his face as he lifted the lid over the keyboard. He began to play and Boggen turned at the sound, his brow, at first deeply furrowed, relaxed as the music flowed into the room.

"Ah...Mozart," he said.

Dennis Thorney nodded but said nothing, his hands dancing on the keys, rapid though not always precise. Boggen stood in silence watching and listening until the door of the drawing room opened and Virginia Blairbuie entered.

The piece finished as she walked across to the piano, the final chords loud and crashing. "I do love Mozart. I didn't know you played Mr Thorney."

"Yes...yes. I hope you don't mind."

"Not in the least. I'm very glad it's being used. Neither James nor myself play and the piano is only touched when Jessica comes home. She plays beautifully...er, as do you Mr Thorney."

"Thank you Lady Blairbuie."

She turned to Paul Boggen, her face a broad smile and the hint of a blush on her cheek. "I've asked Langford to serve luncheon at one thirty today because of your tests. They'll presumably be over by then and we can eat in peace."

"That's very thoughtful, Virginia. One thirty is perfect."

◆ ◆ ◆

"Did you see 'em? I've never seen anything like that afore."

"Calm down Billy can't you. Someone'll see you prancing about like that. Sit down for God's sake."

Billy dropped to the grass but his arms were outstretched in imitation of an aircraft. He emitted a low sound which grew louder. "Bombs away."

"There was only one bomb on each plane Billy. You saw that didn't ya? For God's sake man, keep quiet. You're like a wee kid."

"That must have been what Gordon was expecting us to see

not the submarine in the water. Mind you that was interesting too. He'll pay us well for this I tell ya. I can't believe the bomb bounced. D'you think it was made of rubber?"

"Billy, I've no idea what it was made of. It just bounced that's all we need to say."

"He'll no believe us mebbe."

"Why would he not? He was obviously expecting something to happen that's why he sent us here."

"It was worth coming just to see it."

"You've changed your tune. All you've done so far is moan about things…'I'm tired, I'm hungry, it's uncomfortable, the deer was heavy'…on and on. So just sit down and stop acting like a kid."

Billy said nothing but turned away. He didn't immediately sit but looked out over the Loch hoping to see the submarine again. He scanned the surface of the water screwing up his eyes behind the thick lenses of his spectacles. Soon he gave up and turned slowly, his eyes roving over the shrubs along the foreshore.

Suddenly he dropped to the ground.

"Rory," he hissed, "there's a couple of people down there walking this way."

Keeping low to the ground, Rory crawled towards Billy and lay down on the rock beside him. Billy's arm pointed. Two women, young women, were walking along the foreshore towards the crag. Suddenly they stopped and stared at something hidden from Rory and Billy beneath the lip of the rock. The two boys waited, not daring to speak, wondering if there was a way to climb the crag from where the two women were.

Rory leaned close to Billy's ear. "Be ready to run if they come up here."

The women walked forward, still staring at the ground until they too were lost from sight. The boys waited until Billy's nerves got the better of him.

"We should go now."

"No! Stay put. If we move now, it will attract their attention."

It seemed an age until they saw the two women again, now

walking hurriedly back the way they had come. Rory laid a hand on Billy's arm until he was sure the women were far enough away.

"Come on. Let's see what they found so interesting."

Billy half slipped and half clambered down the side of the crag arriving at the bottom in a little shower of dislodged stones. He stood up and brushed the dust from his trousers. Rory was already walking warily across the pebbles of the beach, his eyes watching for any movement. He could see nothing.

"Rory...over here."

Billy pointed to a heap of old clothes lying much closer to the edge of the crag. The boys approached it cautiously and Rory gingerly put his toe against it. It was solid. Billy pointed to the end of the heap furthest from them. Two hands were clutching the stones.

"Holy shit! It's a body."

"It certainly is, Billy. He's been shot. Look, you can see the blood on his temple."

"Do you think....did we...we can't have."

"No Billy, I didn't shoot anywhere near here. Remember that shot we heard earlier."

"Is it the fella we saw walking down through the trees?"

"No idea. Could be. He was heading in this direction."

"What do we do? We should get the Police."

Rory let out his breath. "For God's sake, Billy, we can't do that. They'll arrest us for murder. All we've killed are a sheep and a deer. We've got to get out of here. Those two women will raise the alarm. This place will be swarming soon. Come on, let's go."

◆ ◆ ◆

Robbie McBane left Ewan McCrae outside the big house and made his way to the drawing room in search of Boggen. The last chords of the piano died away as he approached the room.

Inside, he found Boggen, Thorney and Lady Blairbuie.

Boggen turned towards the door when he entered. "Ah McBane. What did you discover?"

"We found the camp alright. There's been someone living there…may still be living there…there's food, the remains of a fire. It's someone who knows how to live wild or has been trained to do so."

"Any other sign of the man?"

"Nothing. The woodland and moorland beyond it are huge. Someone who knows what they're doing could evade capture for weeks even with a small army searching. There was a dark green blanket on the makeshift bed but no label on it indicating where it came from. Could be British army issue but may be from elsewhere."

"We must find that man."

"All I can suggest is that we keep watch on his camp probably at night."

The drawing room door opened again and Lord Blairbuie stepped into the room. "Ok for us to come in now I trust."

"Of course, James. Sergeant McBane was just telling us he thinks he'll have to watch the intruder's camp tonight to catch him."

"Good idea. It may be just a poacher but… perhaps take Ewan with you though.... He knows the estate better than anyone but..." Lord Blairbuie shrugged.

"Thank you, Sir. That would be helpful."

The door burst open and Lizzie, with Alice hard on her heels, rushed in. "We found a body…it's a young man…on the beach up that way. " She waved her arm in a vaguely northern direction.

"He's been shot in the temple." Alice's calm voice betrayed no emotion but the unusual paleness of her face conveyed volumes.

"Body…shot? What on Earth?" James Blairbuie looked from Lizzie to Alice and back again.

"Naturally, we don't know who it is. Just a young man with dark hair. He's lying face down on the shingles so we can't even describe him." Lizzie's eyes travelled to each person in turn. They all seemed stunned.

Lady Blairbuie turned her face away. “Shot? By his own hand do you think?”

“Why do you say that Lady Blairbuie?”

“Well, Sergeant, a bullet to the temple is often an indication of suicide is it not?”

"Aye, it can be but we mustn’t jump to conclusions. Lord Blairbuie, can we telephone for the Police? This is probably a civilian matter.”

“I’m afraid we don’t have a telephone. Such things have not reached us as yet. I’ll send Hodges or Hamish to Dunoon to fetch Sergeant Macgregor. He’s the only Police officer we have anywhere near us.”

“I think McBane that you need to take charge of this until Macgregor arrives. Presumably, we cannot move the body but you’ll want to examine the scene.”

“I’ll do my best Group Captain. Lizzie, Alice, are you able to face showing me where the young man is? Perhaps, Lord Blairbuie, we could take something with us to cover the body... not that anyone will see it out here.”

“I wonder if this young man is our mystery man camping in the woods?”

“Could be, Sir, or maybe our mystery man is a murderer.”

“But there are no young men around here.” James Blairbuie’s brow was deeply furrowed. “This is all most strange.”

No one heard the door open nor Langford enter the room. He approached the assembled group still standing in a rough circle in the centre of the room. He coughed politely and James Blairbuie half turned to him.

“What is it Langford?”

“I wanted to return this, Sir. Not sure to whom it belongs but I found it in your library a short while ago.”

He was holding a silver salver on which lay a pistol.

CHAPTER 12

All eyes were locked on the pistol which Langford held out on the silver tray as if presenting a choice cocktail. He stood, his face impassive, waiting for the owner to step forward. At last Boggen did so.

"That looks like mine but I'm sure I didn't leave it in your library, James." He leaned forward and peered at the gun. "Yes it's an Enfield Number Two, 0.38 revolver, the same as mine." He patted his holster which hung from his waistband underneath his jacket. "I've got mine here as usual."

"Perhaps you could show us your weapon, Group Captain." Robbie McBane's voice was even, non-judgemental. Lizzie picked up the detective instinct in his words.

"Of course." He flipped up the bottom of his jacket, unclipped the holster and reached inside. A frown crossed his face and slowly he withdrew something. There in his hand lay an expensive, leather-covered case for a pair of spectacles. Embossed in gold on the top were the initials JB. He stared at it. "How on Earth did that get there? And whose is it? I don't wear spectacles."

"That's my case. Are the glasses inside?" James Blairbuie took the case from Boggen's palm and opened it. He lifted out a pair of spectacles. "These are my glasses...I use them for reading. I keep them in the Library."

"How stupid of me. I must have picked them up by mistake but...but...I'm sure I replaced the revolver in the holster straight after showing you all after dinner in your Library. I am baffled." Boggen took a step towards the tray and his hand reached out to retrieve the revolver.

With a swift arm movement, Robbie McBane's hand hovered over the weapon. "I'm afraid, Sir, this will need to be examined."

Taking his handkerchief from his pocket, Robbie dropped it onto the Enfield and lifted it clear.

"What do you mean examined? Hand it over McBane."

"We have just been told that someone has been shot in the head. You cannot account for the whereabouts of this weapon. It could have been used to murder that young man. I will hold it until it can be handed over to the Police."

"Now look here, McBane. That's ridiculous. You heard Langford. He found it in the Library. How could it have murdered someone who is hundreds of yards away and yet be in the Library?"

"It could easily have been left there after the murder." Lizzie didn't like Boggen's tone to Robbie; it was clear he was about to try and pull rank.

"So now you know it's murder and not some poor chap who has taken his own life."

"Well no…but he might have been murdered."

Dennis Thorney turned away from the group but, as he did so, Lizzie noticed the way his face turned from deep concern to something that might have been relief. The concern she understood but what was the meaning of the expression he had tried to conceal?

Boggen muttered an expletive under his breath. "I want that back as soon as possible McBane. Make sure the Police know that."

"Of course, Sir." Robbie McBane ignored the burst of questions that were being fired at Lizzie and Alice. Lizzie let Alice answer them as she was concentrating on what Robbie was doing. Carefully, using the end of the handkerchief and holding the gun in his left hand, he pressed the barrel release with his thumb and broke the cylinder and barrel open with his right hand. Tilting the muzzle downwards, the rod released the cartridges. When this rod was pushed back down, five cartridges dropped back into the cylinder whilst the sixth stayed up. This he took from the cylinder and examined it. He replaced it and pushed the cylinder and barrel back to click into position.

"Group Captain Boggen. Was this gun loaded fully?"

"Yes. I have to be ready."

"And did you fire any rounds since you last re-loaded it?"

"No."

"One round has been fired." Robbie waited for a couple of seconds to let that sink in. "This gun could have been used if that young man was murdered."

"But who is it? Surely we need to go and get his body?"

"Quite right, Lord Blairbuie. Someone also needs to go to Dunoon to fetch the Police Sergeant. I will go now to see the body if Alice and Lizzie are willing to show me the place. I'll also need to check all the other guns on the estate, Lord Blairbuie, and whether they are stored securely."

"Of course."

"Are the doors to this house locked at night, Sir?" Lizzie, as usual, was thinking ahead.

"No...there's really no need. We are so isolated here there's no fear of intruders unless..."

"Unless the unknown person who has made a camp in the woods came in last night and took a weapon, Group Captain Boggen's revolver or a rifle from your gun cabinet." Lizzie watched the alarm steal over Lord Blairbuie's face.

"That of course is possible." James Blairbuie turned back to Robbie McBane. "I'll ask Hamish, our Estate Manager, to go to Dunoon. I don't suppose Sergeant MacGregor will be too happy about his Sunday being interrupted but needs must."

◆◆◆

Hamish Ferguson was not too happy either about having to interrupt his Sunday to drive to Dunoon but a sudden death in such circumstances was such a significant event, he accepted the instruction without complaint. He could see that Lord Blairbuie was very troubled by it and, valuing the way his employer treated him, he wanted to help. Isla was in the big house helping to prepare and serve luncheon. She would be over there for some time. He hoped she would be spared the details of the death. He was naturally very protective of his daughter since the death of her mother and the trouble they had encountered those months past. Isla had withdrawn into herself, away from him; he felt he was losing her.

The lane hugged the shore of the Loch until it turned East and, a little further on, North where it explored the hills on the way to Dunoon, occasionally running alongside the Firth of Clyde. The weather was much as it had been for several days, perfect for the testing he imagined. There was only a slight south-westerly wind and high, hazy cloud with no discernible shape washed over the sky. It was the harbinger of the Summer to come, longer days with warmth and sunshine. Such a contrast to the bleak news he was carrying to Sergeant MacGregor.

The Police Station in Dunoon was a substantial stone house where MacGregor lived, its granite blocks conveying solidity, reliability, safety. Hamish parked the Humber, which James Blairbuie had told him to take, in front of the house on the road. He walked up to the front door and knocked using the heavy black iron ring. It was several minutes before the door was swung open and the squat figure of Sergeant MacGregor stood before him, in brown corduroy trousers and a green jumper.

"Hamish...what are you doin' here?"

"I'm so sorry to interrupt your Sunday, Sergeant, but I'm afraid we've had a death on the estate."

"A death? Who is it?"

"I canna tell ye as yet. I've no seen the body. A young man it seems. It was found this morning by two of our guests...two young women."

"A young man ye say? So an unexpected death."

"Aye. Apparently shot in the head. Could be suicide, could be an accident, could be murder."

"You'd better come in." Sergeant MacGregor, opened the door wide and Hamish Ferguson stepped inside. There was a wonderful smell of roasting meat wafting along the hallway.

"I'm so sorry, Owen, I'm interrupting your lunch."

"It's no ready yet. Come in here." He led the way into the front room of the building which was in effect the Police Station. A large wooden desk stood imposingly in front of one wall with shelves behind it loaded with files. Opposite the desk, a large window gave a view of the small garden in front of the building and the road. Hamish noticed the two posters pinned to a noticeboard. One he had not seen before. 'Dig for victory' it proclaimed and showed an attractive young woman smiling as she plunged a fork into the soil.

Hamish pointed at it. "I've no seen that one before. Is it new?"

"Aye. Arrived in the post last week. It's the latest campaign. Food supplies are being disrupted because of the U Boats attacking the convoys from North America. We've got to grow more of our own. I'll have PC McDonald digging up the front grass there. He'll no like that. Have a seat and tell me what you know."

Hamish Ferguson knew little of course but repeated in more detail what had been discovered. Sergeant MacGregor's frown grew deeper as he talked. "I've no dealt with a murder before... nor a suicide for that matter. Perhaps it was an accident, someone else shot him or he shot himself. Was there a gun?"

"Must have been but I don't think one's been found as yet. We have a Sergeant from the RAF Police staying with us because of the tests but there is no suggestion that the dead man is a member of the RAF so he said it would need to be the civilian Police who deal with it. I guess that means you."

Sergeant MacGregor gulped visibly. "I'll have to telephone the Inspector in Glasgow but how soon he can get out here, I've no idea."

"Lord Blairbuie would like you to come out today before the body is moved so you can collect any evidence from the scene."

"Today! I don't think I can..."

"We can't leave the body on the beach for the foxes and other scavengers to eat, Owen, and we can't move it until you have given permission to do so. I'm sorry, but you must come today."

"I'll need to try to get hold of the Inspector first. You go on ahead and I'll try to telephone him."

Hamish bade the Sergeant farewell, suspecting that the enticing smell of the Sunday roast was too much for him to resist.. As he drove away, he smiled to himself, knowing that Sergeant MacGregor would not be able to find out what had happened to the young man. That Sergeant McBane seemed much more likely to be able to conduct a proper investigation and he was the one to watch. MacGregor was a good man but he was a rural policeman whose daily Police diet was petty crime and ensuring wartime requirements were followed.

◆ ◆ ◆

Billy and Rory watched from the edge of the woodland at the rear of the house. The two young women they had seen earlier left the house by the back door with a stocky, red-haired man.

"Keep in the trees, Billy. Let's see what they do."

The two boys kept abreast of the party, flitting between the trees, occasionally losing sight of them and sometimes stopping until they could see them again. It was a sombre procession, the two young women leading the way with the man following carrying a sheet and none of them seeming to speak.

Billy was struggling to see any detail. "How old are they?" he whispered.

"Why d'ye need to know that, Billy? It's not like you're going to chat the women up."

"Just interested. I mean, if they're young and strong, they can carry the body back but, if not, they'll need more than the three of them to carry it."

"I think they're going to cover it up with the sheet."

"Why do that?"

"May stop the crows pecking the body."

"Would they do that...the crows?"

"Aye, course they would. It's just meat to them."

Billy's face portrayed disgust. He stumbled along behind Rory, trying to make sure he didn't trip over anything and give them away. It would be just his luck if he did. It was quite exciting, he had to admit, to be spying on the three people but he was starting again to long for the comfort and safety of home. There were still several hours to go before Gordon McCloughlin would pick them up further down the Loch. He hoped they would get paid well for the meat they had shot; it needed to be worth the hunger and discomfort.

"Down, Billy," hissed Rory suddenly. "Can you see them? They've come to the body. Now let's see what they do."

They watched the three figures stand some two yards away from the corpse, one at his head and one either side. They seemed to be talking though it was too far away to hear what they were saying. The man stepped up to the body and crouched beside it. Carefully, he lifted the head and peered at the wound on the temple. He stared at it for several seconds before gently letting the head rest back on the pebbles.

Billy shuddered. "We need to get away, Rory. If they find us, they'll blame us for killing him."

"Then they mustn't find us, Billy."

CHAPTER 13

There was an awkward silence when Robbie McBane left the room followed by Lizzie and Alice. Dennis Thorney shifted from one foot to the other and cleared his throat. "This will not affect the testing will it Group Captain?"

Boggen glanced quickly at James Blairbuie and then at Virginia. "I don't see why it should...what do you think?"

"It perhaps might seem rather callous... young man dead and we still have aircraft dropping balls of concrete into the Loch but..." James Blairbuie spread his hands, "there is a War on and we must win it."

"Quite James. I think we need to go ahead as planned. The pilots and the MTB crews will not know anything about the body of course so, unless I radio them, they'll proceed as planned."

"I will confirm lunch for one-thirty as I had planned then. We normally have luncheon at one o'clock but it will leave time for the tests to take place...as, apparently, we cannot be trusted to see them." Virginia Blairbuie gave a small toss of her head setting her hair swinging.

Boggen looked sharply at her. "It's just the Ministry is very strict on security. If it were my decision, I wouldn't be worried. I mean who is going to know if you see them? Unless of course one of you is a German spy." Boggen chuckled.

"Having fought the Hun in the last war, Group Captain, I hardly think we are going to assist them in this one."

"Quite so. Happy with that Thorney?"

"Yes, yes of course."

"We may as well have a drink while we're waiting. I'll call Langford." Virginia Blairbuie went to the bell by the fireplace and then suggested they sit down while they waited. Langford slipped in and was given instructions to bring sherry. It was a strange atmosphere in the room, the body they could all privately picture lying by the Loch casting a long shadow and preventing conversation. Lord Blairbuie did raise his glass but offered no salutation. They sipped meditatively, each locked in his or her own thoughts. Lord Blairbuie's eyes kept wandering to the windows of the drawing room, as if he might see the corpse being carried past.

At last he spoke. "I can't understand who that dead young man might be."

◆ ◆ ◆

None of them spoke. It was as if they must stand in respectful silence for some time before discussing what had happened. Robbie had lifted the young man's head to look at the wound but he had laid it gently back on the pebbles and stood back saying nothing. Lizzie's eyes flicked up to Alice to see how she was dealing with the sight but she seemed her usual calm self, her face showing no sign of the emotion she was no doubt feeling. The water lapped gently on the shore, a few gulls screamed in the distance as they wheeled over the Loch but, otherwise, there was nothing to disturb the peace of the morning... except of course this dreadful sight.

Robbie McBane coughed. "Looks like a single bullet wound to the temple as you said. If he was right-handed, it may have been self-inflicted."

"If it were self-inflicted Robbie, there would be a weapon in his hand or nearby."

"True. It may be beneath him so we must wait until the Police arrive but we can look around to make sure there's nothing."

Slowly, they walked in a circle around the body as if performing some strange ritual, scouring the ground and even the water's edge. There was nothing.

"Someone who had shot himself in the head, would not be

able to throw the gun away further than the area we have searched. Unless it's under the body, this was not suicide." Lizzie looked at Alice, realising her analysis was correct.

"Murder then," Robbie said simply. "We need to establish who this young man is...or rather was...and then work out why someone wanted him dead."

"What about the intruder that's been living in the woods. It could be him or he could have been murdered by the mystery person."

"There is definitely something strange going on here. Last night, when we gentlemen retired after dinner to Blairbuie's library, we were discussing security and, as well as the intruder in the woods, Blairbuie raised an issue about something strange in the Loch...a craft of some kind he thinks. Boggen seemed to dismiss it rather too readily, put it down to imagination but Blairbuie was insistent that it had been seen by himself, Lady Blairbuie and the Estate Manager, Hamish Ferguson. It could be enemy activity, some kind of spy craft keeping an eye on the tests. Let's say this young man disturbed them – if they had come ashore perhaps – and they wanted to silence him."

"I think we need to alert the Police to all the possibilities we see but first we must identify the body. Are there any distinguishing marks on him, anything that someone might recognise?"

"Good thinking, Alice. Robbie, when you lifted his head, did you get a proper look at his face?"

"Aye. He has a sort of broad face, quite a round head. Dark hair which is a little longer than you'd expect. He looks quite young, just a scrubby bit of growth on his chin. I'd say he's quite tall, maybe six foot and he has a rather gaunt figure. Looks undernourished. Not sure if that would be good enough for anyone to recognise him."

"We just have to hope," said Lizzie. "Shall we cover him over?"

"Aye," Robbie sighed, "we must do that for him at least."

"Just before we do, Robbie, look at his left hand. Do you see the way that little piece of paper is clutched in his fingers and is torn.

It's the corner off a sheet I think. It looks as though someone ripped it from his hand, either before death or perhaps as life was ebbing from him."

Robbie McBane walked around the body to its left side and stooped to look at the hand. He nodded, carefully pulled the scrap from the inert fingers and straightened. Gently, each holding an edge, they spread the sheet over the body and let it fall softly. It billowed a little before settling on the body, smoothing what had been a rumpled figure. They placed stones around the edge of the sheet.

"We must hope that the Police arrive soon. I wouldna want to leave him here too long for the foxes and other creatures to find."

Lizzie shuddered. "Pray God that doesn't happen."

◆ ◆ ◆

A cloud of steam burst from the large pot bubbling on the range and Jessica watched her mother lean back until it had passed, prod the potatoes with a fork and bang the lid back down. Her mother was tense. She could see it in the set of her flushed face, the briskness, almost violence of her actions, so unlike her usual gentle manner.

"Isla, have you got that sauce mixed yet?"

Isla, further down the range stirring a smaller pan with no enthusiasm, seemed hostile, her slender body rigid, her face unmoving. "Not yet." The words were issued with a sullen defiance.

"What in God's name are you doing with it?"

"Stirring it, like you told me to."

"I don't need your cheek today."

"Oh for God's sake, do it yourself then. I'm not some skivvy. I'm supposed to be employed to wait at table." Isla shoved the wooden spoon into the mixture and walked out of the kitchen.

"That girl is no use to anyone."

Jessica said nothing, watching her mother grab the saucepan and spoon that Isla had abandoned and stir it vigorously, muttering to herself. At last Jessica spoke.

"Mum, it may not be him, There's nothing to suggest it is."

Her mother turned her face away and Jessica knew she was fighting back tears. "It's him…I know it…I feel it in my bones."

Jessica went to her mother and put her arms around her. "Now, now. You cannot know. We must just wait until we find out." She held her mother for several seconds until Maureen shook her off and turned her attention back to the saucepan. Jessica waited until she sensed her mother had regained her control. "You mustn't take it out on Isla, Mum, it's not her fault."

"I'm not taking it out on her. I just need her to be more useful, especially when we have so many guests. There's a lot to do. I don't know what's wrong with her today. She's not a great help usually but today she's no use at all."

Jessica spoke as gently as she could. "Perhaps she is troubled by the news of the body too. She is very young, Mum…"

"She certainly is that."

"Can I do anything to help? You know I'd be happy to."

"Stir this sauce until it's thickened. There's not much else left to do…unless you go after Isla and sort her out. She'll be needed when we're serving. Robert can't do everything himself."

Jessica tended to the sauce and when it was done took the pan from the heat. "It's done now, Mum."

"Thank you dear. I'll take it now." Maureen took the pan and spread the contents into a pastry case that was open on the large kitchen table in the centre of the room. She turned to her daughter. "I'm sorry, love, I know I'm all on edge today. It's this body. I can't stop thinking that it's…."

"I know Mum, I know." Again Jessica's arms were around her mother. "We must just hold on until we know and hope it's not."

Maureen sniffed away a tear. "Now go and find Isla and tell her…tell her I'm sorry. Please explain…you know…"

"I will. I'm sure she'll understand."

Isla was sitting on a low wall at the back of the house, arms folded and staring at the ground. She did not look up when Jessica sat beside her. "Mum is all on edge today Isla...the body that was found you know...she can't help thinking that it might be George. She is sorry that she was snappy with you."

"It's not my fault is it?"

"Of course not. She is not suggesting it is but she is not herself." Jessica humphed and turned her face away. "Perhaps you've been upset by it as well. It's not an easy thing to deal with is it? I mean this is such a quiet, peaceful place one doesn't expect something like that to happen."

"Peaceful, with those bloody planes roaring up the Loch."

"Well yes, not so peaceful at the moment." She sensed that Isla was softening, her body relaxing a little and her face again turned ahead of her rather than to one side. "I wonder if...do you think you know who it might be?"

Isla looked at her for a brief moment. "How would I know?"

"I mean do you have any suspicions or perhaps I should say fears about who it might be?"

Isla said nothing but Jessica could tell she was thinking about her answer. She had a feeling that Isla did have an idea who the dead young man might be. Perhaps she had the same fear as the rest of them. Perhaps she thought it was George. If that were it, what might she feel about George? Both Isla and George had grown up on the estate though George was a few years older than her. She was not aware that they had spent any time together. Though a quiet but lovely girl as a child, Isla had become rather withdrawn and sullen as a teenager. She did not seem to have much in common with George whose difficulties tended to repel others.

"How well did you know my brother, George?"

Isla shrugged. "I knew him of course. We both grew up here but I didn't know him that well. Anyway, why all the questions? I need to get back to work."

She stood abruptly and marched off towards the rear door. Well at least she had succeeded in getting her back to work! Jessica sighed. She had no confidence that harmony would reside in the kitchen today. She decided to return there herself and do what she could to keep her mother and Isla from another row whilst trying to contain teh fear that clutched at her own heart.

CHAPTER 14

Robbie McBane found a silent group sitting in the drawing room sipping drinks. He declined the offered sherry. "It's always a disturbing sight...a body, especially of one so young."

"Anything to indicate who it was?" James Blairbuie asked tentatively, his forehead creased.

"A young man...just a little growth on his chin...broad face, tall and looks under-fed."

Lord Blairbuie's face drained of colour but he said nothing. Robbie resumed. "We did not move the body, I just lifted the head to see the wound more clearly. There may be other wounds we cannot yet see but it looks like a single shot to the right temple."

"So suicide then?"

Robbie McBane looked at Lady Blairbuie. She was clearly a woman who liked things sorted out. "We could find no weapon so, unless it is under the body, we have to assume murder."

"Murder!" Dennis Thorney sat upright. "Good God. That suggests we have enemy agents in the area doesn't it?"

"We can't make that assumption, Mr Thorney."

"But...but why else would anyone be murdered here?"

Robbie shrugged. "I've no idea...yet. But I'll do my best to help the Police establish what has happened." He glanced at his watch. "I think there's time before lunch to check your gun cupboard, Sir." He turned to James Blairbuie.

"My gun cupboard? But why..."

"I just need to check that everything is where it should be, Sir. No cause for alarm."

Lord Blairbuie placed his glass on the occasional table next to him and led the way out of the room. He walked along a corridor that divided the front rooms of the house from those at the rear. The kitchen door was slightly ajar and warm smells wafted from it making Robbie realise that he was hungry despite the morning's tragedy. Blairbuie opened a door on the right and they entered a small room which had an adjoining door to the kitchen. A rack of boots stood against one wall with outdoor coats hung on pegs above them. A smell of dogs and waxed coats hung in the air, giving a sense of the routine of country life, the peace, the security.

How that had been shattered!

James Blairbuie turned to a wooden cupboard that stood on the opposite wall to the boots and he pulled open the door which stuck a little at the bottom, making a dull sound. Robbie McBane watched his face carefully. A frown creased his brow but he said nothing. Inside the cupboard were three guns, two shotguns and one rifle. All were standing upright, butts resting on the base of the cupboard and barrels held between pegs at the top. A shelf at the top of the cupboard held small boxes, presumably ammunition.

"Are any guns missing, Sir?"

Blairbuie shook his head slowly. "No, Sergeant, all present and correct."

"Is this cupboard locked usually?"

"No Sergeant, never."

"Is the room locked?"

James Blairbuie shook his head. "No it is not. You must understand, Sergeant, that this is a remote place. The only people around are those who live and work on the estate. There are occasionally other people like the men who were felling trees in the plantation we have just cleared but they would not have been near the house."

"I see there is an outside door from this room. Is that locked at night."

"Again no, Sergeant, for the same reason."

Robbie McBane nodded. Privately, he was appalled at the casual approach to security but he realised that, in a place like this, one would see no reason to take precautions. He stole a glance at James Blairbuie's face again. It wore an expression of puzzlement mixed with embarrassment.

"When you first opened the cupboard, Sir, you seemed surprised by something."

"Oh did I? Yes perhaps. It's nothing really but when I put any of the guns away, I stand it so that the bend of the gun is against the wall if you understand what I mean. But the rifle...the rifle is standing the other way round. Curious. I wouldn't have put it away like that. Perhaps Mrs Hodges has been cleaning the cupboard."

Robbie McBane looked at the dust and grime at the base of the cupboard. There was no evidence of cleaning. "Or perhaps, the rifle has been taken by someone and used."

◆ ◆ ◆

Lizzie and Alice had left Robbie to report back about the body and began to climb the first of the two sets of stairs to their attic room. Jessica was walking along the corridor.

"Did you see it?"

"Yes...we did. Not a nice sight for a Sunday morning."

"You wouldn't know who it is but perhaps you can describe the face."

Lizzie saw the anguish that Jessica was trying to banish from her eyes. "Do you have an idea who it might be?"

"No...but I fear it may be...."

"The body was lying face down," said Alice gently. "We couldn't see any features that we could describe. We'll have to wait until the Police come."

"Of course." Jessica looked lost, so different from the confidence she had exuded the previous day. "I should have come with you but I had to make sure Mum was ok. She's sure it is George."

"We're going up to our room for a bit before facing everyone at lunch. Why don't you come with us?"

Jessica looked up, relief flooding her face. "Would you mind? My mother is sure the body is...George. I've been trying to keep her calm. Isla seems very upset too but she's young of course, never experienced anything like this before. Mind you, nor has anyone. This place is so quiet and peaceful."

The three young women trooped up the two flights of stairs and flopped onto the beds in the small attic room. It was a little shabby, needing a new coat of paint. The sun had moved around so that it no longer shone through the small, grubby panes of the window. For all that, it was a restful place.

"Do you mind talking about George?" Lizzie laid a hand on Jessica's shoulder. "Would it help?"

"Perhaps, but it's complicated. When he was a child, our relationship was good...very good. He had difficulty at school with reading and writing but he was always very loving and I suppose he looked up to me as an older sister. But something happened when he turned about twelve. I was away at school then, in my last year, and when I came home for the holiday, he seemed different...angry, hostile. He was devoted to a dog he had but it died...kept its collar with him always. It can't have been just that though. He didn't want to talk with me or spend time with me. Mum said it was just his age, he would grow out of it. But he didn't. He became worse, arguing with everyone and being really vile to me. I seemed to get the worst of it."

Jessica's mouth twisted as if to stop herself crying at the memories she was evoking. " I suppose I didn't try hard enough but it's difficult when every approach you make is rebuffed."

Lizzie and Alice said nothing, allowing Jessica time to reflect before saying more.

"I'm sure he resented my success and certainly the way Lord and Lady Blairbuie helped me out...you know, paying for my education. They took a lot of interest in me but didn't spare any thoughts for George. I suppose they thought he was not worth taking an interest in. His difficulties at school marked him out as a future labourer in their eyes...not someone the Laird would want to be associated with." She shook her head as if to clear the thought. "I'm being unfair of course. They are good people... James especially...and they did a lot for me but..."

Lizzie sat beside Jessica and put her arm around her. "It may not be George, Jessica. Isn't he living in Glasgow?"

"That's what we all believe but who knows? He may have come back... for some reason." Jessica again fell silent for a short while, her eyes searching the floor as if for some answer. "Of course there is guilt on my part. I didn't do enough for him... ploughed my own furrow...But, if I am being entirely truthful, he seemed to become more and more a burden...perhaps almost an embarrassment. We had nothing in common and his sullen manner irritated me. There, I've said it. I was not the elder sister to him that I should have been."

"You should not blame yourself." Alice's quiet voice caused Jessica to lift her head and look at her. "We cannot put our own lives on hold. You had a future to pursue and George had to find his own way."

"I know you're right but I still feel I should have done more, perhaps said to James that he should not spend so much on me and provide George with something to help him."

Lizzie sighed. "If only we could change the past but all we can do is try and put things right."

The three young women sat in silence until Jessica suddenly looked at her watch. "Oh my goodness! I nearly missed it. Got to go girls. Must see the test." She jumped up from the bed, suddenly brisk and business-like again, with great self-control, pushing more personal thoughts to the back of her mind.

"Where are you going to watch it from?"

"You want to see it, don't you Lizzie?"

Lizzie smiled. "Of course."

Jessica beckoned with her finger for Alice and Lizzie to follow her. She left their bedroom and softly opened a door on the other side of the corridor, the door that Lizzie had opened in the night. The three of them bunched together in front of the window.

"Had you not been with us, Jess, I was going to come in here anyway."

"Not a word to anyone right?"

In the distance, they could hear the faint drone of aeroplanes, the sound increasing every second. Lizzie held her breath as the aircraft approached, fast and low over the water of the Loch towards the sleeping giant that was the Courbet. She could feel Alice and Jessica beside her, all three jammed close together in the attic window. The old battleship lay at anchor very slightly North of the house giving them a clear view of the action that was about to take place. They watched intently. It seemed as though nothing would happen and then the Mosquito reached the red flag anchored at the side of the loch and a ball fell from its belly, spinning, falling slowly as it travelled forward until it hit the surface of the water well short of the ship.

But immediately the spray cleared, they saw it bounce up again, still travelling forward towards the ship and still spinning.

"My goodness," Lizzie breathed and Alice gasped.

The ball hit the surface of the water and again bounced up. Twice more it touched the water surface, each time travelling a shorter distance and then, with a loud clang that rang between the hills either side of the Loch, it hit the side of the ship and sank out of sight.

"Was it supposed to do that?" Alice was wide-eyed.

Jessica nodded. "Yes but it didn't look quite right to me. It shouldn't have hit the ship at all really."

"What's the idea of it…I mean what's the point?"

"If anyone finds out I've let you see it, I'll be in big trouble. So, as I said, don't breathe a word to anyone. Act dumb. I'm not going to tell you any more. When I go back to London, I'll report to my boss. Let's hope the next ones do better."

Two more aircraft approached the ship; the same thing happened with the first bomb but nothing fell from the second aircraft though as it turned away to the West something fell from under it and plummeted into the trees on the far side of the Loch.

"I don't understand," said Alice. "It seems to me that, apart from that one, it's worked. They all hit the ship."

"Yes but look at the ship. It's damaged where the bombs hit but that's no good. The bomb needs to reach the ship and roll down the side without exploding. If they hit like they did, the bomb will detonate on the gunwhale – the side of the ship above the water. That will cause some damage but will not sink it. We need it to roll down the side and explode underneath the hull. If we can achieve that, we'll have a very important weapon."

"What happened in this morning's tests?"

"Pretty much the same thing but worse. The bombs bounced fewer times and hit the ship with more force. They moved the red buoy further away from the ship after the first test but probably not far enough…unless there's another issue."

The three young women left the attic room and returned to Lizzie and Alice's bedroom on the other side of the corridor which looked out over the rear of the house. Lizzie glanced at her watch: thirteen fifteen hours. There would not be another test until the following day. "Thanks Jess for showing us that."

"As you said, you would have seen it even if I had not suggested it."

Lizzie smiled guiltily. "Well I must admit…" She tailed off. " I think you should tell us what you really do at the Ministry."

"I told you…I'm a secretary."

"Secretaries don't report back to their bosses about top secret weapon tests."

Jessica gave a grim smile. "Well this one does." She opened the door. "See you later. Enjoy your lunch."

CHAPTER 15

Lunch was a very subdued affair. Virginia Blairbuie was trying to play the perfect hostess, keeping conversation light, pretending there was no body lying by the Loch within a mile of the house. But no one took her cue and so her voice dominated, dancing among the dishes, her occasional forced laughter tinkling among the crystal glass. Most of what she said was about herself, her life in London after the Great War and she seemed to direct much of it towards Paul Boggen. He smiled appreciatively but his brow was dark, no doubt his mind troubled by the discovery of the murdered young man. It was Dennis Thorney who gave most response, talking about himself in return. Was it a sign of insecurity or solipsism, Lizzie wondered, that some people seemed to be entirely concerned with their own affairs?

"Oh yes, it was such a wonderful time, London in the Twenties," Virginia Blairbuie said wistfully, lifting her glass in elegant fingers to take a sip of wine.

"The Twenties were a special time for me too. I played my first piano concert then and of course was selected from a huge field to work in the team at Brooklands." Dennis Thorney looked around the table in search of an appreciative audience.

Lady Blairbuie, annoyed to have her own memories de-railed by the engineer put her glass down very firmly on the table and gave Thorney a smile of pure malice. "But I don't suppose you had much of a social life out at Brooklands did you? I mean you wouldn't have been mixing with the best class of people."

Before he could retaliate, there was a tap on the door which caused Lizzie to look up from her plate; the Butler, Robert Langford, entered. He gave a stiff little bow and announced Hamish Ferguson.

"Ah Ferguson." James Blairbuie left his seat at the head of the table and walked across to him. "What news from Dunoon?"

"Sergeant MacGregor will be over as soon as he can, Sir. He said he would try to contact the Inspector in Glasgow. I think he wanted his lunch before he came." There was the slightest trace of contempt in Ferguson's last remark.

"That's reasonable."

While the two men talked, Lizzie studied Hamish Ferguson. He was a tall man with fair hair, good looking undoubtedly but there was something about his bright blue eyes that disturbed her. They seemed shrewd, calculating, one might even say hostile. He was the picture of the perfect Estate Manager, composed, with an air of authority but Lizzie felt he was not a man who liked to be crossed. Strange how instinct could sometimes be revealing...if, of course, her instinct was right. She had to acknowledge that she had been wrong before.

Isla was hovering at the edge of the room waiting to clear plates. Lizzie noticed her height, the set of her face but with deep brown eyes. Her father's daughter without a doubt though the eyes came from her mother perhaps. Where was her mother? Was she dead, did she leave? Lizzie's curiosity was aroused. Whereas her father looked in control, Isla seemed brooding, a darkness about her, troubled one might say. When Isla came to clear her plate, Lizzie looked up into her face, smiling encouragingly. Isla met her eyes for the briefest moment and then looked away.

Interesting. There was a story to discover there she was sure. Lizzie knew she must keep her imagination in check but she could not help speculating. What was the trouble that lay behind those eyes? The loss of her mother in childhood? Through death or marital breakdown? She would find a moment to catch Isla on her own and try to unlock that mystery.

Lunch had just finished and the party was retiring to the drawing room for coffee when Sergeant Macgregor was announced. Lord Blairbuie shepherded him into his library and invited Group Captain Boggen and Robbie McBane to join them.

Lizzie bit her lip and turned to Alice. "Why is it that men think women should be excluded from serious things?"

"They think they are protecting our delicate sensibilities."

"Tosh! They want to keep things to themselves in case we show them up. But never fear, I'll get it out of Robbie what they talk about."

"Now go easy on Robbie, Lizzie. You don't want to scare him off."

The two young women watched the door of the library close and, being prevented by the heavy oak door from hearing anything from inside the room, reluctantly joined the others in the Drawing Room.

◆ ◆ ◆

Inside the library, James Blairbuie gestured to the others to sit. There was a slight interruption when Langford brought coffee but then it was straight down to business. "Did Hamish Ferguson give you enough information, Sergeant, or are there questions you have of us before you go to see the body?"

Sergeant Macgregor took a notebook and pencil from the top pocket of his tunic and fumbled it open. "Well, Sir. I understand that two of your guests," he glanced at his notes and cleared his throat," a Miss Barnes and Miss Frobisher found the body – a young man - by the Loch this morning. It appears he has been shot in the right temple." The pencil was being shaken in the Sergeant's hand, as if to cover a nervous trembling.

"That's correct, Sergeant. We have not as yet identified the body as it is lying face down and Sergeant McBane felt it should not be moved until you had examined the scene."

"Quite right, Sir." The Sergeant's chest now expanded with a degree of confidence. "So I'll need someone to show me where the body is and we'll then need to bring it back. It'll be taken to Glasgow for the pathologist to examine. That will take a while as it has to go on the ferry." Macgregor turned to Robbie McBane. "I understand that you are a member of the RAF Police."

"That's correct Sergeant. Special Investigation Branch."

The smile that crossed Macgregor's face was of relief. "Are you…have you dealt with murder before?"

"Yes. Twice and fairly recently. Both cases were unexpected. I was at the locations for other reasons but they happened and I was involved in finding the killers."

"That's good to know. This is of course a civilian matter but I'd be very happy to have your assistance in this case." Macgregor looked at his notebook. "I've not been involved in a murder investigation before. We don't get that sort of crime round here. It's mainly petty crime."

"Happy to help, Sergeant. I'll take you to the scene now if you're ready."

"Absolutely ready."

Robbie McBane turned towards James Blairbuie. "Do you have such a thing as a stretcher anywhere, Sir? And could we ask Ewan McCrae to come to help carry the body?"

"The answer to both is yes." Blairbuie went to the bell beside the fireplace and summoned Langford who was given instructions.

When Robbie McBane and Sergeant Macgregor left the Library, Lizzie and Alice were hovering in the corridor. Lizzie stepped forward. "Are you going to examine the body?"

"Aye, we are, Lizzie."

"Alice and I are coming too."

"There's no need, Lizzie. Ewan McCrae will come with us to carry the body."

"Come on Alice. Let's get our coats." With that, Lizzie and Alice ran lightly up the stairs before Robbie could protest. "Sometimes best not to ask," whispered Lizzie as they started on the second flight.

◆ ◆ ◆

Rory put his arm out in front of Billy. "That's close enough." They were hovering at the edge of the woodland that pointed like an arrowhead towards the Loch where the body lay. Billy felt the new, soft needles of a larch tree brush his face and he ran his hand along the branch to feel the tender new growth. The scent of the dead needles on the ground from previous years perfumed the air, making him feel pleasantly drowsy. Sleep. That's what he wanted now but there were still hours to go.

He could just make out the body; a crow was moving towards it cautiously, tottering from foot to foot like a black-coated old man. "It's no right, leaving the poor bugger there for the crows."

"You're right Billy but I suppose they have to wait for the Poliss to examine the scene."

"Poliss? That's not good for us is it?"

"We'll be fine. We just have to stay out of sight. There'll no be interested in us anyway when there's a body to deal with."

They sat on the bed of needles and Billy leaned his back against the trunk of the nearest tree. Sleep. He could feel it drawing him closer, his eyelids falling despite his efforts to keep them up. What would he give for a nice cup of tea and a cosy sofa to spread his weary limbs on? He must stay awake though. Not long to go before Gordon picked them up and they were on their way home. He smiled as he thought of the money they would get. What would he do with his? Probably save it as there was nothing really to spend it on in Dunoon.

"Billy." Rory's hiss made Billy sit up and open his eyes. "Down there. Can you see?"

Billy peered through the thick lenses of his spectacles. Three men and two women, the same two women they had seen earlier, were walking silently but purposefully towards the corpse the big red-headed guy leading the way. One of the group was a Police officer and the third man was grey-haired and slightly stooped. He was carrying something long.

"That's Macgregor from Dunoon, the Poliss man." Rory breathed. "He'll not know what t'do at all. The man's useless."

"That suits us then."

They watched in silence as the group approached the body. Lifting the sheet carefully, the two women slowly pulled it away, revealing the corpse lying face down as it had been when they had seen it earlier. The big re-headed man then pointed to the head and the pool of congealed blood beside it and Macgregor bent down to examine it more closely. The fair-haired woman gestured in a circle around the body and spread her hands wide.

"She's a bit of alright." Rory whispered.

"So's the other one as far as I can see."

"Aye Billy, but it takes a man."

"A man! You're as much a boy as me."

"Keep your voice down," Rory hissed.

Again they fell silent and watched as a stretcher was laid out beside the body. Carefully, two of the men rolled the body onto it and lifted it into the centre. The old man said something as soon as the face was visible and shook his head. The sheet was once again laid over the body by the two women. Billy was touched by the tender way they straightened it and tucked it around the body. He imagined those gentle hands administering healing to himself on his sick bed. That would be something special. His mind began to wander to pleasant daydeams of being the wounded hero in some wartime drama but the scene playing out in front of him drew him back.

Bending over, the red-haired man examined the ground where the body lay but obviously did not find whatever he was looking for. He pointed towards the South, away from the crag that Rory and Billy had lain on earlier in the day. The group fanned out and moved forward slowly examining the ground.

"They're looking for the bullet casing I reckon."

"You should be a detective, Rory."

"I'd do better than Macgregor that's for certain."

"Shouldn't they look near where the body lay? I mean, if he shot himself, it would be there wouldn't it?"

"Aye it would, Billy, But the big man has already looked there and besides there's no gun there."

"What's that got to do with it?"

"If he'd shot himself, the gun would be lying nearby wouldn't it? I mean, if you shoot yerself through the head, you can't then run round looking for a hiding place to put the gun."

Billy nodded. "Fair point. So someone else shot him?"

"That's right, Billy, so they'll be looking for the murderer or at least someone they can blame."

"Not many people round here are there?"

"No, Billy, there aren't. But we're here Billy and I've got this gun. Come on. We need to hide up. We can't afford to be caught now."

CHAPTER 16

"I'm afraid, Group Captain, that there's something still not right." Dennis Thorney stood in the middle of the drawing room like a penguin, his stomach projecting forward and his head twisting from right to left as he surveyed the Loch. "Yes the bombs bounced and yes the second test was better than the first because we got the distance right but…. We'll see what happens tomorrow but I think we have more work to do on the shape of the bomb. Maybe the indentations are not quite right."

"What do you mean by the indentations?"

"As you know, the bomb is spherical so that it will bounce and the sides are flattened slightly to allow for the mechanism that holds them in the aircraft and which enables them to be released."

"Yes, yes, Thorney. I'm well aware of that."

"We have put indentations in the sphere like a golf ball to help it bounce on the water and keep it spinning. Golf balls are generally hit in such a way as to give them back spin and the indentations assist that. If those are not quite right, the bombs will not bounce as far as they should, even if they are dropped at the right distance, and will not roll down the side of the ship."

Boggen's voice was steely. "Thank you for the lecture. The problem seems to me that they bounced too far. They hit the ship with considerable force. You boffins are supposed to know about all this stuff. Why can't you get it right first time?"

Thorney appeared oblivious to the rebuke and responded with excitement in his voice. "We do know about it but this is cutting edge technology." He emphasised the metaphor by bringing the side of his right hand down with some force onto the palm of his left." It's never been done before. We therefore have to try things out, test things. That's what we are doing here.

I'm wondering if the weight of these trial bombs is correct. We'll need to check that."

Group Captain Boggen turned away, his contempt clear in the movement. However, the engineer was not yet finished.

"There's also clearly a problem with the release mechanism. I did say to Wallis that I didn't think the calipers that hold the bombs in place in the aircraft were engineered with sufficiently tight tolerances but he wouldn't have it. I mean it is critical that the bombs are released at exactly the right moment. The one that failed to drop shows clearly there's a problem."

Boggen turned back to him his face tight with malice. "And I suppose if you'd been in charge, there would have been no problems."

Thorney's eyes narrowed and his cheeks flushed, unable at last to escape Boggen's charge of arrogance. His anger burst out. "I tell you now Group Captain that I have been the lynch pin, the lynch pin, of this project. Oh Wallis gets the credit always but it's me that has done all the important work."

"Really? So it's your fault then that the bloody thing is not working."

"No it isn't. I make my recommendations but sometimes they are ignored."

"I wonder why that is?"

"What do you mean?"

Boggen didn't bother to explain. If the man had such little self-awareness, any explanation would be futile. Instead he said, "It's just as well that my pilots turned to the West after the bombing run. Had they turned to the East, that concrete filled lump of metal might have landed on this house. I assured Lord Blairbuie that there was no danger but, of course, I was working on the assumption that the person who designed this weapon knew what they were doing."

"But it couldn't have exploded."

Boggen did. "No Mr Thorney, it wouldn't have exploded but a lump of metal and concrete weighing nearly a thousand pounds falling on the house would have crashed straight through it, making an extremely large hole and killing anyone unfortunate enough to be near it...including you Mr Thorney, including you!"

Stunned by Boggen's outburst, Thorney stood with open mouth as the Group Captain stormed out of the room, slamming the door behind him.

◆ ◆ ◆

MacGregor was puffing by the time they reached Glenstriven House. McCrae had grudgingly offered to take his end of the stretcher but MacGregor had refused and also declined offers from herself and Alice. She wondered whether he would have been so determined to bear the weight had there not been two young women to impress. She had caught Alice's eye and the look that was returned confirmed her view.

"Let's put him straight into my car," MacGregor wheezed. He was in his mid-forties, of medium height with a generous stomach that suggested a life lacking exertion and someone who liked his food. It was no surprise to Lizzie that he was struggling.

"No. We need to take him into the house." Ewan McCrae's tone stifled any dissent. "Bring him in this way and we can lay him in the pantry. There's a good big table in there."

Alice opened the outer door and Lizzie the one from the lobby area into the pantry as the body was taken through. They stood in respectful silence for a moment when the stretcher had been laid on the table. Ewan McCrae, who had seemed to be in the background whilst walking out to the body, had taken charge of the operation. His connection with the family was clearly strong and no one had objected.

"Right now, you two," Ewan McCrae pointed to the two Sergeants, "can leave for a while. Miss, will you please find Maureen...Maureen Hodges that is. She'll no doubt be in the kitchen."

With a feeling of dread, Lizzie moved slowly through the

lobby and cautiously opened the kitchen door. She was relieved to see Jessica in there with her mother though she knew Jessica would be as distraught as Maureen. Taking a breath, she opened her mouth to speak.

Maureen Hodges turned to look at her and, before she had said a word, sank to her knees with her hands over her face. The wail of anguish she emitted was horrifying. Jessica's arms went around her and the two women crouched on the floor, huddled together. Lizzie said nothing until Jessica looked up.

"Is it...?"

"I'm so sorry."

This brought another wail from Maureen and it took both Lizzie and Jessica to persuade her to rise and half lift her onto a chair. At last, when her tears had subsided a little, Lizzie spoke.

"We have laid him on the table through here...in the pantry. Ewan McCrae said that would be best."

Maureen nodded and, with much encouragement and gentleness from Jessica, rose wearily to her feet. She straightened her back and reached behind her to release her apron. Lizzie recognised the dignity that Maureen was mustering to meet probably the worst scene of her life. She opened the kitchen door and allowed mother and daughter to walk slowly through into the lobby. There was a moment before Lizzie opened the door to the Pantry when Maureen hesitated as if unsure of whether to proceed. At last she set her face in an attempt to control her emotions and Lizzie opened the door. She watched as Maureen and Jessica walked slowly forward like a slow motion scene in a film.

Ewan McCrae stood at the head of the body and Alice at its feet; it was still covered by the sheet. Ewan cleared his throat. "I'm so sorry, Lass. This is not how it should be."

Maureen nodded in acknowledgement and turned to Jessica who stepped forward and took the top of the sheet in her hands. She took a breath and drew back the sheet. The faces of mother and daughter crumpled and tears ran down their cheeks. Maureen stepped forward and laid a hand gently, so gently on

George's forehead.

"My son...my son. What happened to you?" Sobs interrupted her speech. "How did this come about?" She pushed a handkerchief against her face. "You were my baby, my little boy."

Jessica put her arms around her mother and held her tight. The two women sobbed quietly and Ewan nodded to Lizzie and Alice. The three of them left the room, closing the door softly behind them.

Robbie McBane and Sergeant Macgregor were standing outside in the courtyard. Robbie handed a small parcel to MacGregor. "How are they?" Robbie asked.

"As you'd expect. We need to give them some time to grieve before moving the body Sergeant MacGregor." Lizzie's voice was firm.

"Naturally, Miss, but I can't wait too long. I have to get the body back to Dunoon and then on the ferry to go to the pathologist. The sooner that happens, the sooner we may get some explanations."

The door to the house was opened and Jessica, looking dazed, walked past them. She said nothing and headed towards her parents' house. "She'll be going to fetch her father." Ewan McCrae shook his head. "That family doesn't deserve such a tragedy. First having a son like George and now finding him dead."

"And by his own hand perhaps," MacGregor added. "I know you all think he was murdered but we should keep the possibility of suicide alive, maybe even an accident."

Everyone looked at MacGregor. "I think, Sergeant," Lizzie said quietly but firmly, "we discounted that possibility at the scene."

"Ah well, maybe, but we need to keep all possibilities in mind."

There was an uncomfortable pause and Lizzie exchanged looks with Alice. She tried to do the same with Robbie but he was carefully avoiding her gaze.

"Sergeant MacGregor and I have been talking." Robbie McBane spoke carefully, as if worried that what he said would be contested. "He will have to take the body back as he's explained and, in the meantime, I have agreed to start the investigation."

"What needs to be done first, Robbie? Alice and I can help."

"The most likely culprit is the person who has made a camp in the woods. That could be a poacher or someone who has planned to come here for another reason. George may have disturbed them, perhaps challenged them which may have led to his death."

"Do we know when it happened?" Alice's voice was quiet and measured as usual despite the extreme circumstances.

"No. The pathologist might be able to tell us later but it could have been yesterday night or this morning early."

"There is another possibility." All eyes turned towards Lizzie. "Lord Blairbuie is certain that there is some strange craft patrolling the Loch. Remember, it has been seen by Hamish Ferguson and Lady Blairbuie too, heading towards the head of the Loch. If it is an enemy craft, they may have come ashore, been disturbed by George."

Robbie McBane nodded. "That's another lead we must follow, Lizzie. Lord Blairbuie talked about it heading up into the Loch so perhaps we need to go up there and see what we can see."

Ewan McCrae's gruff voice now drew their attention. "The camp I found...it may not be an impostor. It may have been made by George himself."

"Why would he do that? If he was coming back to Glenstriven, surely he would just stay with his family?"

Ewan McCrae looked keenly at Lizzie but she could not read in his eyes what was in his mind. "George was an unusual boy, loved the woods but had some strange notions."

"Ewan, I would like you to take me to the camp again later today. We may find someone there or, if not, we need to search more carefully to find who has been using it."

They fell silent when they saw Jessica returning with her father. David Hodges looked pale, drawn, but his eyes were set firmly ahead and he said nothing as he passed. They entered the big house by the rear door.

Sergeant MacGregor looked at his wristwatch. "I'll give them another minute and then I'll need your help McBane to move the body into my car. I'll go and make sure it's clear."

When MacGregor had walked out of earshot, Lizzie spoke urgently to Robbie. "Why is MacGregor so keen to pursue the idea that George killed himself or that it was an accident? It's clearly murder."

"I'm not sure, Lizzie."

"Perhaps," said Alice, "it's because a suicide is much easier to investigate. He seems rather out of his depth."

"Or perhaps he does not wish to entertain the idea that someone here, I mean from Glenstriven, may have murdered him."

"I think that is jumping too far ahead, Lizzie. Let's follow the leads I've outlined first and see where they take us."

They waited in silence until MacGregor returned. He and Robbie entered the house and some minutes later, the door held open by Jessica, they re-appeared carrying the stretcher. Maureen and David Hodges filed out after it and Lizzie, Alice and Ewan McCrae followed, their heads bowed.

CHAPTER 17

The slightly cloying scent of furniture polish from the beautiful, old, oak-panelled walls infused the air. In the hall, the long case clock ticked loudly and monotonously as it had probably done for generations; its sound easily reached Lizzie and Alice who waited in the corridor close to Lord Blairbuie's library. Inside Robbie McBane was making arrangements with the Laird for the use of the boat. The corridor led to the kitchen and Lizzie's sharp hearing picked up raised voices seeping through the closed door. She motioned with her head to Alice who followed her further along the corridor to a point where the voices were clear.

"You cannot blame me for that, Isla." There was more than insistence in the voice, there was anger.

"Why else would she go? It wasn't natural for Mum to leave me when I was only seven. You drove her away with your nit-picking and nagging," Isla lashed back.

"You're right. It is unnatural for a mother to leave her child and sadly your mother was unnatural. I've done my best for you, I've cared for you, I've protected you which is a lot more than your mother has done."

"Oh, you've protected me alright. Kept me here in the middle of nowhere with no one my age except the few kids I saw at school who live miles away."

"You have one of the most beautiful places in the World to grow up in, Isla. I bet most of the kids in Glasgow would be glad to live out here with the peace and safety...

"Yes, peace and safety but can't you understand I don't want peace and safety...I want to live before I get old."

The voices stopped abruptly but pots and pans were clashed as if deliberately being knocked together.

Alice leaned close to Lizzie and whispered in her ear. "Do you think we ought to interrupt them? Or perhaps better wait further away. I hate eavesdropping."

"Let's wait a little longer...see what happens next."

"Anyway...what's brought this on today? Isn't there enough misery going on without adding to it?" Hamish's voice, trying to be reasonable.

"What's brought it on? What do you think has brought it on? George is dead, someone killed him."

"He may have killed himself Isla, I'm sorry to say."

"Sorry? I expect you're glad."

"Not glad but he was a bad'un, Isla, through and through. Think about what he tried to do, what he would have done had I not intervened."

"Perhaps that's what I wanted," Isla shot back. "That hasn't occurred to you has it? It's always what you want, what you think is best. I'm grown up, I have a mind of my own, a life of my own to live and I don't intend to live it here much longer."

"Isla...Isla...you're still a ch..."

A door slammed violently in the kitchen, probably the one into the lobby. "Should we go after her?" Lizzie whispered.

Alice shook her head. "No, there's no time anyway and this would not be a good moment. She needs to calm down."

Just then the Library door opened and Robbie McBane stepped out. He frowned when he saw Lizzie and Alice. "Have you been listening at the door?"

"No," Lizzie said, her eyes wide with innocence.

Right, let's go. We'll have to row because fuel is so limited."

◆ ◆ ◆

It took Sergeant MacGregor a while to rouse PC McDonald from his Sunday afternoon slumber. He was not a happy man, having to don his uniform and take a trip on the ferry. Whilst he readied himself, MacGregor went back to the station to telephone Glasgow for a car to meet the ferry and transport the body to the pathologist in Glasgow. It would mean the pathologist could start first thing the next morning, Monday, and the pistol could be examined.

Alistair McDonald, muttering about looking for a job that didn't involve working on a Sunday afternoon and feeling the weight of the pistol in his jacket pocket, ambled down to the pier and waited by MacGregor's car. He was a big man, dark-haired and pushing fifty. He should have been given the Sergeant's job some years ago when Sergeant McTavish had retired, he reflected with some bitterness, but there seemed to be no justice in the World. One day...one day, he would apprehend a serious criminal or even a spy and then the powers that be would realise his true worth. A few minutes after he arrived, he saw Sergeant MacGregor strutting along the road from the Police Station, full of his own importance. How did Macgregor get into the Police? Surely he was too short? He watched his boss swinging his arms in military fashion until he reached the pier.

"We'll no be able to lift him on our own, Sarge."

"No, we won't which is why you are going to get Gordon from the ferry to give us a hand."

McDonald, muttering again, strolled down to the ferry that bumped gently against the pier. "Gordon, the Sarge wants you to give us a hand with something. It's got to go on the ferry."

"Is there a drink in it?" Gordon McClaughlin's shaggy beard spoke eloquently of a seafaring life."

"Of course. If ye like seawater. It's part of your job to load stuff on the ferry. So shift yourself and get over to the car."

McDonald turned away before McClaughlin could reply but the latter slowly roused himself. When Sergeant MacGregor opened the rear door of the car, the ferryman whistled softly. "Who's this? What happened?"

"This *was* George Hodges from Glenstriven, you know the chauffeur's son?"

"Oh my God." McClaughlin made the sign of the cross. "He

came over on the ferry a few days ago. When was it? Probably Tuesday or maybe Wednesday. What in God's name happened?"

"Looks like he might have shot himself."

"Poor bastard! He was ever a troubled soul."

"Aye but we need to get him to the Pathologist in Glasgow. There's some sergeant from the RAF Police who thinks it may have been murder."

"Murder? Why would anyone want to murder him? I could understand him taking his own life…I mean he was, as I just said, a troubled soul. Nay it canna be murder…not out there."

"You take his legs and PC McDonald and I'll take the heavy end." Gordon McClaughlin pulled the legs gently and then more firmly until the body began to move out of the car. "Now hold it while we get his shoulders."

They lifted him out and his head flopped backwards as soon as it left the seat. It was a struggle even though he was so thin, stumbling over the cobbles and carrying him down the stone steps to the wooden pier. Fortunately, there were no other passengers for the ferry and they were able to lay him on top of the engine casing, a substantial wooden affair. They spread the sheet over the body and tucked it in so it would not blow off in the breeze.

PC McDonald stood to attention in front of the engine casing looking back over the stern towards the pier. He wondered if he should salute but felt it was unnecessary given the absence of people. It was respectful though to give the dead boy a guard of honour. Gordon McClaughlin started the engine, a cloud of black smoke emerging from the rear of the boat which drifted away and disappeared. Slowly the craft crept away from the pier, picking up speed when it was clear and in open water.

The scene was like something out of a story, PC McDonald reflected. A vague memory from schooldays drifted into his mind, a story about a dead king being ferried across a misty lake to a better place. The memory melted away like the smoke from the engine but it left a strange feeling of sadness, even desolation. He watched the pier and the town grow smaller as they crossed the water, Sergeant MacGregor standing still, watching. Even his boss, it seemed, was touched by this unusual mission.

◆ ◆ ◆

The oars creaked in the rowlocks with each stroke that Alice took. She certainly knew how to row. Each time she pulled on the oars, the boat surged forward and Lizzie, sitting in the bow, felt the breeze stirring her hair. Initially, she had taken one oar and Alice the other but Lizzie's inability to ensure the blade gripped the water meant the craft was constantly trying to turn away from their destination. After a while, Robbie, who was trying to keep the boat straight with the rudder, suggested that Alice row for a while and then he would take over. Lizzie was a bit offended. She knew it was the right thing to do but she did find it difficult to admit that there was something she had failed in.

They sat in silence, lulled by the rhythm of the oars until Robbie called from the stern, "Lizzie, you said there was something you needed to tell me."

Lizzie turned to face him and called over Alice's head. "Whilst we were waiting for you outside Lord Blairbuie's Library…"

"When you were trying to eavesdrop you mean?"

"Absolutely not. We were waiting further down the corridor. Anyway, we did happen to overhear a conversation – a heated conversation at that – between Hamish Ferguson, the Estate Manager, and his daughter Isla."

"Heated you say?"

"Yes and she, after a bit, stormed out of the kitchen, slamming the door behind her. Anyway, we couldn't be sure what the row was about other than Isla accused Hamish of driving her mother away by his nit-picking. She also said the row had been brought on by George's death. But there was something strange about that. I couldn't make out whether she disliked George or had feelings for him. What did you think Alice?"

"Like you Lizzie," Alice exhaled as she pulled on the oars," I wasn't sure but it was clear that Hamish felt he had to protect Isla from him. He said something about George doing something."

"Sounds like something we need to explore," Robbie mused.

"Definitely. The other thing though, was that Isla seemed sure George was murdered but Hamish was saying it may have been suicide. Perhaps Hamish has a reason why he wants to promote the idea of suicide. Perhaps he..."

"Now, now, Lizzie. Don't let your imagination run away with you again. Evidence, that's what we need, evidence."

"I know, I know, but you have to explore possibilities as you've just said."

They fell silent again and Lizzie leaned forward over the bow to watch the way it cut through the water, surging up on both sides when Alice pulled on the oars. The afternoon was calm, a sun made occasionally hazy as the wisps of cirrus clouds, like strands of hair, drifted over it. It was beautiful, a promise of Summer in the warming air and the trees on each shore boasting new growth of fresh green leaves. A gull screamed as it flew low over the water ahead of them and then soared upwards, wheeling round and diving again. Lizzie felt the thrill of it, imagining the joystick in her hands and an aircraft lifting off the ground. How she longed to be flying.

After about an hour, Robbie took over the oars and Alice sat in the stern operating the rudder. Robbie took a few strokes and then started putting real pressure on the oars. The boat surged forward with every stroke.

"Feel the strength, look at the muscle. It's all that rugby playing, Alice." Lizzie laughed.

"It must be yes. We'll be at Ardtaraig in no time at all."

Suddenly the boat lurched to one side and Robbie nearly fell off the thwart. A spray of water flew up from the starboard oar. "You seem to have missed the water that time, Robbie."

He settled himself and began to row again but with not

so much force. "Aye well, it happens sometimes. You see, you sometimes get a hole in the water so the oar canna grip."

Both Lizzie and Alice burst out laughing. "Or maybe, the oarsman is just incompetent."

"I think, Lizzie, after your performance, you should perhaps be a little kinder." Alice smiled at Lizzie, leaning over so she could see past Robbie.

"Touché."

Loch Striven was long and slender. On a map, it looked fairly straight but there was a small headland that projected into it near the top end. Lizzie scanned the water ahead. They had seen nothing of the strange craft that the Blairbuie's had seen and there was no sign of anything that might explain such a sighting. As they approached the headland, they could see a large house on the hill overlooking the Loch. It was not an elegant mansion, its grey walls rather forbidding, but it was larger than Glenstriven House. Lawns sloped gently in front of it down to the Loch and the hill rose sharply behind it. It seemed to nestle in the shelter of the woodland, almost as if it were hiding.

Suddenly, a motor boat came into view from around the headland. It was travelling fast, the bow wave forming great sprays either side and the craft seeming to be leaping out of the water. The roar of its engine grew louder and louder and it seemed to be heading straight for them.

"Shall I wave? They may not have seen us," shouted Lizzie and, without waiting for a reply, she stood precariously in the bow of the dinghy, waving her raised arms in the universal signal of distress.

The launch kept coming without reducing speed and without wavering from its course.

"Oh my God. It's going to hit us!" Lizzie screamed.

CHAPTER 18

"What are they doing? I mean going for a row on the Loch after moving a body is strange don't you think, Rory?"

"It is, but ours is not to reason why."

Billy and Rory watched the boat until it was a mere dot on the water leaving the faintest swirls behind it where the oars had dipped the surface. They had returned to their lookout post on the crag when Rory had judged it safe to do so.

"She's a lovely woman that fair-haired one though isn't she?"

"She may well be, Billy, but what's that to you?"

"I'd like to meet her...maybe she'll have a walk in the woods when they get back and I can chat her up."

"You enjoy your fantasy, Billy. If you do meet her what do you think she's going to say to you?"

"Well I dunno...just talk about the weather and things you know."

"She'll ask you what the hell you're doing here. She'll then go on to ask you whether you killed that bloke they moved earlier. The big guy with the red head will probably then grab you and take you to prison. For God's sake, Billy, you've no sense at all." Rory turned away signalling the end of the conversation but then turned back for a final shot. "She might have a face like the back end of a bus. With your eyesight, you wouldn't know would you?"

"I can tell...by the way she walks and her hair. Anyway, you think she's alright, you said so."

"Yep she is alright but she's not going to be interested in a four-eyed boy like you, Billy."

The two of them sat in hostile silence for a long time. Billy closed his eyes and let a lovely fantasy play out in his mind. He saw himself standing by the Loch with the sun just starting to go down. She was walking along the shoreline in a bit of a dream, her fair hair blown back from her face by the gentle breeze, looking out over the water until the last minute when she saw him standing there. She smiled, a dazzling, warm smile and looked into his eyes. He could see she was attracted to him and he stood close to her, returning her gaze. The delicate scent of her perfume entered his nostrils and slowly he slid his arm around her waist, gently pulling her closer…

"Billy," Rory hissed, "there's someone over there. Get down low on the ground."

Billy was desperate to hoist himself up on his arms to have a look but he didn't dare. He lay on his stomach as flat to the ground as he could but a stalk of some kind was pressing into him. He wriggled sideways to avoid it.

"Keep still!" Rory's voice was just a whisper but Billy could hear the anger in it.

"Who is it?" he mouthed back.

Rory did not reply but very slowly, he lifted himself on his hands, peering through the grass. He watched for several seconds and then lowered himself back to the ground. "It's a bloke, middle-aged, quite tall. Could be a gamekeeper or something. I think he's having a look at where the body was found."

Billy felt a stab of fear. "He might be the killer."

Rory nodded his head slowly and a glum expression spread across his face. Holding the rifle in one hand and keeping it almost on the ground, he slid closer to Billy. "We can't move now. We've just got to hope he doesn't come up here. As soon as he's gone, we've got to get back into the woods where there's less danger of being seen."

Billy nodded. "Can you still see him?"

Again Rory lifted himself cautiously off the ground and looked through the grass. "No. He must have gone out of sight like the women did."

"Why would he be looking at the place?"

"I don't know, Billy, but they say murderers often re-visit the scene of the crime."

Billy stared at Rory in horror.

◆ ◆ ◆

"What is McBane playing at? I mean what's the point in going up the Loch? What's he expecting to see?"

James Blairbuie stared back at Paul Boggen. He was a mild-mannered man but he did not take kindly to being berated in his own library for a decision that was not his. "I think, Group Captain, that he has made a perfectly reasonable decision to borrow our boat and carry out a search of the upper reaches of the Loch. They may find nothing but on the other hand, they may find an explanation for the strange sightings we have made over the last days and indeed weeks. Something is going on and you of all people should be worried because it may be enemy activity. They may be spying on the tests."

"And if it is enemy activity, what are McBane and those two young women going to do about it? I mean if they are confronted by armed spies, they are in trouble. Did he think of that? Of course not. He's just a sergeant after all."

James Blairbuie was finding this man intolerable. He summoned all the superior values of his breeding and spoke with a cold calm. "I'm sure he did think of that and decided that, if they are confronted, as you put it, he can claim to be having a pleasant Sunday afternoon row on the Loch. Had he taken a gun, he could not have maintained that with any credibility."

"I wish you had not agreed to let him take your boat, James."

"Why are you so concerned about it? If, as you say, there is nothing going on in the Loch and that what we have seen are merely the figments of our over-fertile imaginations, there is no cause for concern. And yet, you seem to be extremely concerned as if you know something you are not telling me."

Blairbuie looked hard at Boggen who returned the stare. The

two men stood facing each other for several seconds before Boggen turned away at the sound of the library door being opened. Virginia Blairbuie strolled in, smiling warmly at Paul Boggen.

"Ah, there you both are. Tea is being served in the drawing room. I hope you have time to join me. Everyone else, except Dennis Thorney, seems to be off somewhere, goodness knows where." She then sensed the hostility between the two men. "Oh, have I come in at a difficult moment? Perhaps you two would like to have tea in here, though I could do with saving from Mr Thorney who seems intent on telling me in great detail what a successful little man he has been in everything he's ever done."

James Blairbuie looked at her blankly but Paul Boggen forced a laugh. "Yes, he is rather full of himself isn't he? One wonders how it can all have been fitted into one life."

"I'll take tea in here please Virginia. Would you have Isla bring something in for me?"

"Of course, James. Now," she linked her arm with Boggen, smiling sweetly into his eyes, "come and save me from the ogre."

James Blairbuie watched them go. "He definitely knows something," he whispered to himself.

◆ ◆ ◆

The motor boat was speeding towards them, its bow still lifting high on its own wave, spray cascading out on both sides. "It's going to hit us," Lizzie screamed. She sat down heavily on the thwart as the boat was rocked violently by the motor vessel which, at the last second, veered slightly to starboard and stopped surprisingly quickly beside them, sinking back to its normal level in the water. Suddenly she was staring into the barrel of a rifle.

"On your feet," The order was shouted by someone beside the rifleman, someone in uniform who appeared to be in charge.

Another man dropped a short rope ladder over the side.

"Wh...what's going on? We're just out for a..."

"I said on your feet. Give me your hand, put one foot on the middle rung of the ladder and then step straight up onto the gunwale of the launch." Lizzie felt her hand being grabbed and she was pulled roughly onto the boat. She only just managed to put one foot onto the gunwale before she was pulled on board. Stumbling, she would have fallen had she not been grabbed by another person who spun her round and held her hands behind her back. She watched in horror as Alice and then Robbie were similarly treated.

"Get them down below."

Protesting uselessly, they were bundled down the companionway into the cabin of the launch and pushed onto rudimentary seats. The engines roared and the boat tilted to starboard as it surged through the water. It was clearly turning to head back the way it had come. One guard stood at the bottom of the steps holding a rifle and staring at them with steely calm.

"Who are you?" Robbie demanded, his voice indignant.

"You'll find out soon enough."

"This is ridiculous!" Lizzie exclaimed. "We're having a row on the Loch on a Sunday afternoon and you kidnap us. I demand to speak to the person in charge...now!"

The rifleman looked at Lizzie and a smile slowly spread over his face. "You *demand* that do you? Ha, you can demand all you like Miss. Just sit quiet."

It was only a couple of minutes before the launch bumped against a pontoon. "On yer feet." Lizzie, Alice and Robbie stood up, though Robbie had to bend his head to avoid hitting the cabin roof. Rudely they were herded onto the deck and then told to step onto the pontoon. There were other guards with rifles waiting to escort them away from the water. Lizzie was aware that their own boat had been tied behind the launch. It bobbed forlornly in the gentle waves. They followed a path that sloped up to the large grey house they had seen from the Loch. Taken in by a back door, they were pushed along a corridor and into a bare room. There was just a wooden table and four plain, wooden chairs. The walls were untroubled by pictures or signs and the floor was boarded. It felt cold.

"Sit down. Don't get any ideas about leaving this room. I'll be outside with this." He patted his rifle and smiled again. The door banged behind him.

"Who are they?" Lizzie looked at Alice and Robbie.

"They're British anyway or, if they're foreigners, they've picked up very convincing accents."

"I agree," Alice said quietly. "Their uniforms are strange. They look as though they might be British Navy issue but plainer, without anything that might indicate name, rank or country."

The three of them looked at each other. All were wearing elements of their own uniforms though not the entire outfit and certainly not dress uniform.

"We just need to explain who we are and what we're doing," said Lizzie "and then insist they tell us who they are and what they are up to."

"It's a bit difficult to insist, Lizzie, when they have the guns and the numbers." Alice showed no sign of any fear she may have been feeling.

Lizzie reached over and squeezed her hand. "Are you okay, Alice?"

"Oh yes, I'm fine." The smile that often played in her eyes lit her face. "I'm getting very used to this sort of thing Lizzie. In your company, such events seem to occur with regularity."

"You can't blame me for this, Alice. It wasn't even my idea."

The door suddenly flew open. "Right. Up you get. With me."

They were again herded along a corridor but seemed to be going deeper into the house. After turning a corner, the guard knocked on a door and they heard the command to "Enter" from within. It was a very different room to the one they had left, large and comfortable, rather like Lord Blairbuie's Library but bigger. An older man, alone, sat at a desk and stood as they were shepherded in front of him.

"Who are you?" he barked.

"My name is Sergeant McBane and I'm with the RAF Police Special Investigation Branch. This is Second Officer Elizabeth Barnes who is a pilot in the ATA and Miss Alice Frobisher, who is an ATA navigator. Now I want to know who you are and why we have been taken from our boat?"

Their questioner smiled. "Is that right? Well I am happy to tell you that I am Commander Perry of the British Navy and you are in an area where you should not be. You will therefore be treated as spies until we can establish who you really are."

"This is outrageous, Sir. We are staying at Glenstriven House in connection with tests being carried out by the Royal Air Force. This morning, the body of a young civilian man was discovered and I need to find his killer. What you are doing here, I do not know, but perhaps one of your men is responsible for this death." Lizzie was proud of Robbie, the way his broad shoulders were squared and his chin jutted forward. He was not going to be cowed by anyone, especially not someone purporting to be in the Navy.

CHAPTER 19

The tension tightened his chest and he breathed with unusual depth to try to calm himself. Teenage children! He really did not understand his daughter. Why couldn't she see that he had brought her to a beautiful place where she was safe? She had been able to grow up in a serene landscape untroubled by the dangers and temptations of city life. He stabbed the walking stick he was carrying into the shingle of the foreshore, his teeth gritted. He knew without looking in a mirror that his face would be disfigured by an ugly snarl. Damn that woman! Why had he ever married her?

Hamish pushed down the swelling of anger in his breast and gazed out over the Loch hoping the calm waters, the beautiful sky, the calling of the gulls would soothe his mind. What was done was done and regret was useless but...how could she leave her child at such a tender age? How could she destroy his life and Isla's? It was pure selfishness, an abdication of responsibility for the child she had brought into the World.

He sat on a small group of rocks not far from the crag and tried to think of something else. But he couldn't. Memories crept into his troubled mind, memories of her when they first met. Victoria. She was certainly a good-looking girl, with her dark hair tied behind her and a devilish spark in her eyes made all the more evident by her rather heavy, dark eyebrows that seemed to draw one's attention to them. They were hazel, a gorgeous colour, as if they were gem stones and when she laughed he had felt a little explosion in his heart. It was at a dance in Glasgow ... 1927...and he had been captivated.

The band was playing swing and jazz and the evening was alive with excited young people. The Great War was a distant memory and Hitler was unknown in Britain. Life was a huge party, people, especially young people, determined to enjoy every minute of the life they had been given. He managed to dance with her a few times but she was in demand. As the evening drew to a close and the band played some gentler tunes, he had secured her hand for a waltz.

Holding her close, he breathed in the delicious scent of her perfume, felt the occasional wayward strand of her hair brush his cheek, the warmth of her body next to his own, the softness of her dress and her slim figure moving inside it. Bliss. He knew then he wanted her to be his. He wanted to keep her to himself, treasure her, build a life with her.

Hamish shuddered. He supposed it was his own naivete, inexperience. Had he been in relationships with other young women beforehand, perhaps he would have seen warning signs but... hindsight is a great thing. He never doubted her until the arguments started, the unexplained times she was out, the increasing refusal to accept what he was saying, the defiance. Yes, that's what it was, defiance.

And now Isla. A sensation like cold water crept down his spine. Had she inherited her mother's nature as well as her hazel eyes and that curious downward tilt at each end of her mouth when she was not smiling? And it had been a long time since he had seen Isla smile. Certainly in the last year or two, he had seen plenty of her Mother's defiance, a refusal to do what she was told, a questioning of everything he stood for. And now this. What should he make of it? Was it merely the teenager's natural desire for independence as had been suggested to him or was it something more? Had he done the right thing with George?

He regretted the boy's death, of course he did, but what else could he have done? Protecting Isla was his main purpose in life and George had damaged her even if she did not realise it herself. Actually, he admitted to himself, he did not feel any guilt or regret about George. What he had done was what any caring father would have done. He had simply made sure that George would not trouble Isla again.

But what he did not understand was Isla's feelings towards

that troubling, wayward boy. Surely she could not like him after what he had done? Did she like him or did she hate him? He had gained no certainty about her feelings in their recent argument.

Slowly, Hamish rose to his feet and walked further along. He realised that he was in the place where George had been found and he looked around to see where he might have lain. Why he did so, he did not know; it was just some compulsion, perhaps a rather ghoulish interest in the place where a life had passed. He was not responsible for investigating the death and he did not believe that the RAF Sergeant would be able to find the culprit. It would just remain a mystery, an unknown intruder whom George had disturbed.

◆ ◆ ◆

They had been escorted back to the bare room and now sat in silence. The one window was high on the wall and, though they could see sky, there was nothing else in view. Lizzie was still seething and could not maintain silence for long. "How dare he say we're spies!"

"Put yourself in his position, Lizzie. It's wartime, this is perhaps a naval base and hence there has to be some secrecy about it, some security. We blunder into their secure waters so it is not surprising they have to treat us with suspicion until they can establish our credentials."

"They could at least treat us with some degree of respect, Alice. It must have occurred to that Perry man that we might actually be who we say we are. I just hope he feels thoroughly foolish when he is told who we are and what we are doing." Lizzie folded her arms as if the gesture would somehow reach Commander Perry and register her protest.

Robbie McBane sat still, He was thinking and did not seem particularly troubled by their detention. "Surely you're angry Robbie?"

Robbie crossed one leg over the other and took a long breath before speaking. "I'd rather not be treated like this Lizzie, but Alice is right. If I were Perry, I'd do the same. He is responsible for security and he knows that the Germans are clever enough to impersonate British personnel. There are also people in this country who are happy, for reasons best known to themselves, to assist the Germans. Think about Lord Haw Haw."

"Well let's hope that Perry can get through somehow to the RAF or Boggen or someone. It is annoying that the Blairbuie's have no telephone."

"It would mean bringing a line all the way across from Dunoon, Lizzie. Very expensive for one house." Alice as always spoke in a kindly way, understanding Lizzie's anger and frustration.

"While we sit here, the murderer could be getting away."

"Aye Lizzie, he could but we have no choice."

They subsided into silence, watching the light in the sky change as the sun continued its daily motion without them. Lizzie frequently looked at her watch and saw the time creeping towards seventeen hundred hours. How much longer would they be kept here? She began to think about refreshment. They could at least have brought some tea. Just as that thought entered her head, the door opened and a man bearing a tray clumped into the room and put the tray on the table with a clatter. He said nothing and stomped out closing the door noisily behind him.

"Ah, tea…and look there's some cake. That's more like it."

"I admit that tea and cake is very welcome, Alice, but it's not going to diminish my anger at our treatment."

Alice handed Lizzie and Robbie a mug of steaming tea and then a plate each with a slice of cake.

"Yum, Fruit cake. My favourite." Robbie took a huge bite from the cake and sat back in his chair munching happily.

"I almost feel like refusing to eat and drink as a protest."

"You mean a hunger strike, Lizzie?"

"Yes…but, on the other hand, I could do with some sustenance."

Robbie smiled at Alice. "She's easily bought is Lizzie."

"Not at all. It's just right and proper to feed captives."

Soon after they finished their tea, the door opened and they were escorted back to Perry's office by the same guard still carrying his rifle. His attitude seemed rather different, however, almost deferential, showing them the way instead of herding them as before. He knocked on the door and again waited for the command to enter.

Perry was on his feet. He smiled but the apology that Lizzie expected was not made. "It's taken us some time to make contact. I had to radio our other base who were able to contact someone in the RAF. That person confirmed that you are named as being part of the test team. I did then manage to speak to Group Captain Boggen who confirmed that you had gone on, as he put it, a wild goose chase. He was very apologetic and clearly pretty angry with you."

"Why would he be angry? I'm pursuing a lead in a murder enquiry and I'm entitled to do so." Robbie was again defiant.

"But I think Group Captain Boggen told you that the things that some of the Glenstriven House people had seen were nothing to be concerned about."

"I am not answerable to Group Captain Boggen but my own chain of command in the RAF Police. In the Special Investigation Branch we do not take orders from any officer outside our command whoever they are. Two months ago, I was on an assignment with Air Chief Marshall Sir George Stanley and he understood that I would make my own decisions about what to investigate. If he understands that, I think Group Captain Boggen should do so."

Perry raised an eyebrow but said nothing.

"I assume we are free to go now." Lizzie made sure her words were a statement not a question.

"Yes...soon. I just need to check what you think has been seen."

"Lord Balirbuie and his wife as well as the Estate Manager, Hamish Ferguson, have at various times over the last week or so seen something moving just on or just below the surface of the water heading this way up the Loch. On one occasion, both Lord Blairbuie and his estate Manager saw a figure standing upright and moving through the water – not walking – just moving, as if he were standing on something hidden from view. Whatever it is creates a small bow wave if on or just below the surface. These things are not figments of their imaginations. There is something going on in the Loch and I am determined to find out what it is in case it is enemy action or has some bearing on the murder I am investigating."

There was a degree of amusement in Perry's voice. "That's quite a speech, Sergeant, but I can assure you that it is not enemy action."

"You know about it then?"

"I do indeed...and I can see from your facial expression that you expect me to tell you about it. But that I cannot do, Sergeant. It is top secret and you do not need to know about it." Perry became suddenly serious. "I understand why you felt you must investigate it but you must now rule it out of your enquiry. Your victim was not killed by any of my men and what we are doing here is absolutely essential to the War effort...probably even more essential than the tests you are securing near Glenstriven House." Perry gave his patronising smile again. "You see, we do talk to each other, the Navy and the RAF, even though we are, of course, the senior service."

There was silence in the room for a few seconds before it was broken by Alice's quiet voice. "Sir, it is quite a long way to row back to Glenstriven House and your keeping us here has rather delayed us. Perhaps we could have a tow from your patrol boat back..."

"Of course my dear. That's a very reasonable request." He returned to his desk and pressed a button. The door opened and he had brief words with the guard who left the room. "Now that you have found this lead to be a false trail, Sergeant, what is your next line of investigation?"

"We believe there may be an unknown person staying in Lord

Blairbuie's woodland. We've found a camp. We need to find that person as he or she may be an enemy spy." Robbie McBane smiled sweetly at Perry whose face had fallen at the mention of a spy. "We'll be on our way now, Sir. Thank you for the tow home."

With that, Robbie turned and indicated to Lizzie and Alice that they should leave.

CHAPTER 20

Boggen's face was an ugly mixture of triumph and contempt. "Well McBane, you made a right fool of yourself...as well as making me look foolish."

"Not in the least, Sir. Every lead has to be followed. If I had been told that there was naval activity, whatever activity that is, in the Loch, I would not have wasted my time but, in the absence of that information, I cannot be accused of folly."

Robbie moved away from Boggen before he had a chance to respond and joined Lizzie and Alice by the piano where Dennis Thorney was attempting to play a piece by Haydn; his face at moments expressed rapture and at other times concentration but the music he produced did not live up to the theatrical nature of its performance. All the guests and their hosts had assembled in the drawing room for drinks before dinner.

James Blairbuie sidled over to them. "Did you find out anything useful this afternoon, Sergeant?" As he spoke, he frowned and moved the position of two photographs on the piano, returning them, Lizzie realised to the position they had been in before. Presumably they had been moved in cleaning... but on a Sunday?

"Not really, Sir. All we can say is that whatever it was you saw, was something the Navy are up to. I think we can discount it as enemy activity and I am certain that it has no bearing on the investigation into George's death."

"Boggen was furious that you had gone, you know.

"I've just spoken to him and told him very plainly that if he had been more forthcoming, I would not have had to waste time...although it was a very pleasant afternoon until we were, how shall I say...?"

"Kidnapped!"

"That's a bit strong, Lizzie."

"It's not strong at all. They forced us at gunpoint from our boat into their patrol vessel and kept us against our will for well over an hour. What else can one call it?"

Alice stepped in. "I'm afraid, Sir, that Commander Perry would not tell us what they are doing in the Loch. Top secret he said so my guess is they are developing another weapon. I just hope they know when the bomb tests are being carried out or someone may get a very rude shock."

"I expect our friend Group Captain Boggen has liaised with the Navy…though I think there's no love lost between those two services."

"The Navy regard us in the RAF as upstarts." Robbie McBane lifted his glass and drained its contents. "I needed that after this afternoon."

The sound of a gong interrupted them. Langford stood near to the door with a small, brass gong hanging by a thin leather strap from his right hand and a beater in his left. "Ahem, my Lord, m'Lady, dinner is now served if you would care to enter."

Virginia Blairbuie took Boggen's arm and led the way to the dining room. Lizzie was pleased when Robbie offered her his arm and, very graciously, Lord Blairbuie escorted Alice.

When seated, Langford poured wine and Isla brought in the first course, a delicious salmon paté with toast. "Caught in our very own Loch, the salmon," James Blairbuie said proudly.

"Delicious, James, delicious." Dennis Thorney beamed across the table at Lord Blairbuie who smiled but said nothing.

Robbie McBane, sitting at the Laird's left hand, leaned closer and spoke softly. "After dinner, m'Lord, I intend to go up into the woodland to see if anyone turns up at the hide we found. May I take Ewan McCrae?"

"You can if you can persuade him. He should not be working on a Sunday evening and, to be frank, he is not as co-operative as he used to be."

"Alice and I will come with you to make sure you don't get murdered…or captured by hostile British army types."

“Speak for yourself, Lizzie.," said Alice with uncharacterisitc firmness. "I’ve had quite enough drama for one day. I’ll stay here if you don’t mind.”

◆◆◆

The sun was dropping towards the horizon though there was still plenty of daylight left outside the woods. A pale ghost of a half-moon was rising behind them, struggling to shed its light through the hazy cloud. Amongst the trees, it was growing dark and the sounds of the forest seemed to grow louder. It brought back for Billy all the unpleasant aspects of the previous two nights, the cold, the dark, the strange noises, the lack of food.

Billy had just finished his last mouthful of sandwich. That was all they had left until they reached home. “Soon be time to meet Gordon won’t it?”

“Patience, Billy, patience. It’s another couple of hours yet.”

“Can’t come soon enough. Just hope he gives us a good price for the meat and for the information. You know, Rory, we may be the only people who saw what happened in the Loch, the enemy sub and those bombs, apart from the people involved. That’s exciting. I bet we could get some free drinks and things by telling people back home.”

“I’m sure we could, Billy...provided, that is, you don’t mind being arrested and flung in prison for poaching and giving away secrets.”

“But we’ll be giving away secrets to Gordon and to whoever he might tell.”

Rory sighed. “Yes, Billy, but no one will know that it was us told them except Gordon himself. God, I wish you’d think before you open your mouth.”

Billy fell silent thinking of the comforts of home and then his mind strayed to the fantasy that had kept him going during the long day...meeting that fair-haired young woman. She was classy and there was no chance of meeting someone like that in Dunoon. He knew she was too old for him but in your daydreams, nothing is impossible.

The rising moon reminded him of the film he had seen a year or so ago in the little Dunoon cinema. *Dangerous Moonlight* it was called, quite a thriller, about a Polish composer who was also a fighter pilot. He fell in love with an American newspaper reporter called Carole. It was great the way she was loyal to him until they could eventually be together. He remembered the scene when the pilot - Billy wished he could remember his name - had crashed his aircraft into a German plane to destroy it. He was, of course, badly injured but Carole, played by Sally Gray was by his side. She was beautiful, slightly mysterious, a bit like that young woman they had seen earlier.

Scenes began to play in his mind like a film, he, the hero, doing something very brave like foiling an attempt by German agents to invade Scotland. She would be captured but he, using his considerable ingenuity, would rescue her and she would fall into his arms, relieved, happy and swearing undying love to him.

Billy sighed deeply, his eyes closing.

◆ ◆ ◆

Alice was restless. She could not face another evening in the company of Lady Blairbuie and the pompous Boggy, as she referred to him in her own mind. The two of them, she knew, would be having a cosy chat while Dennis Thorney would no doubt play the piano badly as if he were a World class pianist. Either that or he would bore her to tears with the wonderful achievements of his past. She shuddered. A walk would be a much better option so she excused herself.

The evening was fine but hazy cloud was spreading over the pale blue of sky like the coating on a sick person's tongue; it was a sure sign of a change in the weather, rain approaching from the

South West.

She decided to head North along the Loch, keeping away from the woodland where Lizzie and Robbie would be. She smiled to herself. Her decision not to join them was of course to give them space and, besides which, she was rather tired of playing gooseberry. Lizzie was a strange creature. It was obvious that she really liked Robbie but something held her back, prevented her from making a commitment. She said it was that she did not want to give up her role in the ATA until the War was done but Alice was sure, from things Lizzie had said, that it was more than that. Perhaps a walk through the woods on a fine Spring evening would allow them both to overcome whatever barriers prevented the development of their relationship.

She stopped some two hundred yards short of the spot where they had found George and gazed over the still waters of the Loch, serene in the evening light. It was beautiful. Lord Blairbuie clearly thought so but she was not convinced that Lady Blairbuie enjoyed living here. She obviously wanted society, people, parties and Glenstriven House did not afford her those things. But the peace! Who would not trade the insincerities of fashionable London for such a setting?

Suddenly, a chill ran down her spine as she felt the presence of someone else nearby, a strange sensation, completely inexplicable. Slowly she turned first towards the house and then to face Northwards. She drew in her breath sharply. A figure was standing close to the spot where the body had lain. She had not seen it before as its dark clothing blended into the foliage of the trees behind. Who was it? She could not even make out whether it was male or female as the face was turned away and it stood absolutely still.

Should she investigate or make a hasty retreat?

◆ ◆ ◆

Lizzie linked her arm through Robbie's; his other hand held Lord Blairbuie's rifle. "I hope you don't have to use that."

"So do I, Lizzie. I'm not at all sure it was a good idea to bring it but Blairbuie could be right, there may be an enemy agent about, certainly George's murderer. But now Lizzie, we must go as silently as we can. We're getting close to the camp. We'll walk separately from here."

Lizzie felt a small pang of disappointment. She had to admit that she had liked the physical proximity of walking arm in arm with Robbie. She knew though that she must not allow personal feelings to hamper the investigation. They trudged on through the gloom of the woodland. Lizzie started to imagine sinister creatures hovering in the shadows but she dismissed the thought. She was not given to fanciful notions and the only thing they were likely to find was some poor tramp trying to keep body and soul together out here miles from civilisation and help. Robbie signalled her to stop and put his finger to his lips.

They crept forward, Lizzie following Robbie and both crouched so they would be at least partially concealed behind the scrub. This was a broad-leaved forest, not the tightness of conifer plantations nor the openness and uncluttered ground of beech woods. Plenty of scrubby bushes grew beneath the canopy of giant and gnarled oak trees.

Robbie put one knee on the ground and Lizzie followed suit. He pointed ahead to a clump of bushes. Very cautiously, they moved forward from one bush to a wide tree trunk then to another bush. At every point of cover, they stopped and listened. There were no sounds and no telltale smoke rising from a fire. They moved even closer and both peered through the dim light seeking any sign of movement. There was nothing.

Robbie signalled Lizzie to stay where she was. Holding the rifle at the ready, he rose to his full height and moved forward stopping at the entrance to the hide. Suddenly he darted forward, dropped to one knee and pointed the gun ready to fire. Then he relaxed and called to Lizzie, "No one here. Come on."

It was a sad sight, the few possessions piled neatly exactly as Robbie had seen them earlier that day. "Nothing's been touched. Perhaps our mystery man has left now that he has murdered George."

"Perhaps, Robbie, or perhaps it was George staying here. Look there, under that small pile of clothing. It looks like a collar."

"Or maybe just a strap."

Lizzie bent and picked up the object; it was indeed a leather dog collar. "I bet this is the collar from George's dog. Jessica said he was always with his dog. He was heart-broken when it died."

"Bring it and we'll ask Jessica to identify it."

Robbie was rifling through the pockets of a pair of trousers. He pulled out his hand and showed Lizzie what he had found: some ten pound notes. "Fifty pounds," he said with astonishment. "Where did he get fifty pounds?"

They began to return through the woodland, unconcerned about disturbing anyone now that they were sure it had been George using that camp. They had covered about half the distance to the house when Lizzie held Robbie's arm and pointed between the trees. She was sure it was not merely her imagination: two figures appeared and disappeared as they passed behind trees and bushes.

Robbie lifted the rifle and signalled for Lizzie to follow. They moved swiftly, not worrying about the occasional crack of a twig, heading to a point ahead of the two figures so they could intercept them. Robbie gently pulled Lizzie behind a large trunk. She could feel his alertness, the controlled breath which matched her own.

Suddenly, Robbie stepped out from behind the tree, rifle in the firing position and yelled, "Stop right there, drop the weapon and raise your hands."

The two young men froze for a moment and Robbie shouted again, "Drop the weapon…now."

The rifle was dropped onto the ground and its bearer raised his arms but the other, wearing thick spectacles, turned away and tried to run through the trees. He did not get very far as he tripped on a tree root and fell headlong onto his stomach. Lizzie was with him in no time and dropped onto one knee on his back. “Who are you? What are you doing here?”

He squirmed and twisted his head to look at her. His face turned bright red, the deepest blush Lizzie had seen.

CHAPTER 21

Alice stood transfixed. Should she get away swiftly or challenge the figure who stood some one hundred yards away from her? She decided she must do the latter even though this may be the killer. She would act relaxed and naturally as if she were just out for an evening stroll, which is of course exactly what she was doing. Nevertheless, she could feel the tension in every muscle and was ready to run if she needed to, though running would not be easy over the pebbles of the shore.

When she had covered about half the distance, she coughed. "Lovely evening, isn't it?"

The figure wheeled around to face her and Alice exhaled deeply with relief. It was Jessica wearing a large, dark cape with the hood over her head. "Alice. What are you doing here?"

"Just having a walk – I needed to get out of the house. Lizzie has gone with Robbie to see if anyone is using that camp that was found." Alice waited for Jessica to speak.

"It was here wasn't it…that you found George?"

"Yes."

"Thought so. The ground here looks stained. I had to see where he died, try to understand what may have happened."

"How were things between him and your parents when he left?"

"Not good to be honest. As I said earlier, George had become very difficult. My Mother was always very understanding but my Father…you know how it is between men and their sons."

"Was anything said…anything in particular…did your Father throw him out?"

"I wasn't here of course but I know there was a row between them and I suppose Dad may have told him to go, but not meaning it of course."

"Perhaps George took that literally and felt he couldn't come back to the house though that still leaves open the question as to why he came back to the Glenstriven Estate at all."

"It does." Jessica looked out over the Loch and nudged a stone with the toe of her shoe. "I feel very guilty you know."

"Yes, you said earlier but you have nothing to feel guilty about have you?"

"I did nothing to improve things for George and..." Again Jessica fell silent. What was it she was about to say? Or was it that she was turning over in her mind events of the past, how she might have been a better older sister. Alice knew what that was like. She would be thinking through all the things she did or did not do and wondering whether, if she had acted differently, George would have had a better life and indeed still be alive. She decided to change the subject.

"Lizzie and I, just before we went up the Loch in the boat this afternoon, inadvertently overheard a heated conversation between Hamish Ferguson and his daughter Isla. We couldn't make out whether Isla liked George or the opposite and Hamish referred to something that George had done to Isla. Do you know anything about that?"

Jessica looked at Alice and her brow furrowed. "No...I'm not aware of anything." She thought for a few seconds. "Do you think Isla might have something to do with George's death? Surely a young girl would not be capable of murder?"

"Perhaps not Isla...maybe Hamish."

◆ ◆ ◆

"Let me interview the one with glasses, Robbie, while you question the other one. I've a feeling I'll be able to get more out of him. I think he's afraid and there's something about the way he's looking at me. As we walked them back, his eyes kept flicking up to me and he looked away sharply when I saw him."

"Probably a bit overwhelmed by the sight of a beautiful woman."

"Well thank you, Sir. I'll accept the compliment." Lizzie smiled coquettishly and headed towards the room where Billy had been secured. It was a store room beyond the pantry and the other boy had been put into another room beside it. Both were locked in, the keys remaining in the lock on the outside. They had decided immediately to keep them separate – divide and rule was the strategy – play them off against each other.

Lizzie made some tea and cut a slice of sponge cake from what was left from that afternoon. She smiled warmly when she entered the room, feeling that a friendly approach was likely to produce a fuller response, and placed the tea and cake in front of Billy. His eyes lit up.

"I thought you might be hungry. Do tuck in." Billy needed no second invitation and bit into the cake hungrily. "My name is Lizzie. Just so you know, I am not from the Police. I'm actually a pilot with the Air Transport Auxiliary."

Billy swallowed what was in his mouth. "A pilot? I didn't think women were allowed to fly."

"They're not allowed to fly in the RAF – that will hopefully change soon – but the ATA is not part of the armed services. It's a civilian organisation. Our job is to deliver planes from factories to air bases and to ferry important people around the country. I've just done such a task and am here for a few days. So you don't need to be worried about what you tell me."

Billy said nothing for a few seconds but relaxed in his chair and blew out. "So are we in trouble?"

"Well that depends on what you're doing. Why are you here?"

"We just..." Billy stopped and looked around the room clearly wondering what to say..." we're just having a weekend in the country, you know bird spotting and things."

"How lovely. What birds have you seen...anything rare?"

Billy blushed. "We saw some seagulls and..."

Lizzie let Billy struggle for several seconds. "Where are you from Billy?"

"Dunoon. It's not far away."

"Yes the ferry we took landed at Dunoon. I think there are seagulls there too aren't there? No need to come here to see seagulls."

"No, no...but...we thought we might see something more interesting."

"Were you planning to shoot them...the birds?"

"No..." Billy then realised the point of the question. "...the gun was just for protection...you know in case we came across enemy agents."

"Enemy agents? What out here in the middle of nowhere?"

"You never know."

Lizzie paused a moment, looking at Billy pityingly. He sat up and pushed out his chest. "The posters say you have to be on the lookout. We want to do our bit. We're not old enough to join the army."

"Are you brothers?"

"No, just friends. Our Dads are both off at the fighting."

"And how old are you?"

"I'm sixteen, Rory's a bit older."

Lizzie looked down and then, looking up, said more sharply, "How did you get here from Dunoon?"

Billy looked flustered again. "By boat...we came on a boat."

"Where is it, the boat? Where did you leave it?"

"We haven't got one ourselves. Someone brought us."

"And who was that?"

Billy squirmed on his chair. "I can't say."

"Oh dear. Are you afraid?"

"No...not afraid, but...we were told..."

Lizzie stood up and slipped off the jacket she had been wearing. She stretched her shoulders back and turned sideways to Billy so that her fine figure was very evident. She could see from the corner of her eye how Billy blushed. "You know, Billy, I really thought you would be the kind of young man who would have more courage. You seemed at first to me to be someone who would understand the need to co-operate." She sat down again, leaning forward and looking at him full in the eyes. Her face became earnest and her voice as silky as she could make it. "I am not the enemy, Billy. I do hope we can come to an... understanding."

The chair creaked as Billy shuffled in embarrassment.

"Now let's stop beating about the bush. Why don't you tell me what you are really doing here and then we can let you go?"

Billy wriggled on the chair avoiding her eyes. At last he said, "We've been asked to get some meat."

"So you've been poaching?"

Billy nodded slowly, reluctantly.

"Who asked you to get the meat and what have you managed to kill?"

"I can't say...I'll be I trouble. He said we mustn't get caught. We just got one deer and one sheep...a smallish one."

"When did you arrive?"

"Friday night."

"So you've been here since then? Have you seen anyone else while you've been here?"

"Not until today. We saw an older man this morning down by the Loch, bald, bit of a paunch and another bloke who looked younger walking down through the woods towards the Loch. Then we saw you and the other woman and that red-haired bloke find the body and pick it up later with Sergeant MacGregor and an old man."

"Tell me more about the two men you saw this morning."

"The younger one had a rifle with him. We thought he must be a gamekeeper."

"What did he look like?"

"I couldn't see his face...my eyes," he pointed at his spectacles, "but he was tall and thin."

"Was it the same young man whose body we found this morning?"

"I don't know, Miss. I couldn't see well enough."

"This next question is crucial, Billy. Please answer it honestly even if you think it will get you into trouble. Did you or Rory shoot that young man, even by accident?"

Billy looked up, horrified. There was no doubting the expression on his face. It could not have been acted. "No, Miss. Rory just shot the two animals. Anyway, Rory wouldn't let me use the gun 'cos of my eyes."

Lizzie paused and pointed to the mug of tea. "Were you asked to do anything else while you were here?"

Billy hesitated and took a couple of large gulps of tea. "We had to look over the Loch and let him know if we saw anything unusual."

"And did you...see anything unusual?"

"We saw the German sub in the Loch – or at least a bit of a wave it made – and we saw the planes bombing the ship."

"Billy, it's really important that you tell me who asked you to come here. That person may be working with the Germans. You'd like to help uncover an enemy spy wouldn't you?"

"Enemy spy?" Lizzie watched Billy's mind wrestling between the instruction for secrecy and the prospect of being the hero in a spy story. "It was Gordon McClaughlin...but he's not a spy. He can't be. He's the ferryman from Dunoon."

"And when has he arranged to collect you or are you supposed to walk back to Dunoon?"

"Ten o'clock tonight. He'll bring the boat to the point a few hundred yards down the Loch from the big house. We've hidden the carcasses near there."

"Thank you Billy."

Lizzie left the room and locked the door. She took a few steps along the corridor and tapped on the door of the room in which Robbie was interviewing Rory. Instead of hearing a call from Robbie, the door was opened by him and then shut and locked.

Lizzie could see the frustration on Robbie's face. "How are you getting on?"

"Nothing at all. Denies anything, shrugs his shoulders. He's obviously either too frightened to tell me anything or he fancies himself as a tough guy. Won't even say why he has a rifle with him."

"Well, our strategy has worked. Billy was eventually quite forthcoming after a cup of tea and slice of cake. They are not our killers, Robbie, I'm certain of that. Billy is sixteen he says and does not have the gall to show violence to anyone. They are just boys."

Lizzie gave Robbie an account of the conversation with Billy and the details of when they were expecting to be collected. "We need to lay in wait for this Gordon character. I remember him vaguely from the ferry, big sailor's beard. Do you remember?"

"Aye but I didn't take much notice of him. Too worried about my numb backside."

Lizzie glanced at her watch. "It's twenty-one fifteen now. We can leave the boys locked up and wait down by the point under cover. When he arrives – if he arrives I should say – we can apprehend him. Best take Lord Blairbuie's rifle."

"Aye, that's what we must do. So poaching and passing information. Presumably, this Gordon McClaughlin is working for the enemy, either directly or through someone else."

"Looks like it."

"I've just got time to let Lord Blairbuie and Group Captain Boggen know about the poaching and what we're going to do."

CHAPTER 22

Lord Blairbuie was not in his library but they found him in the drawing room with his wife, Group Captain Boggen and Dennis Thorney. Lizzie sensed an atmosphere in the room. Thorney was, as usual, holding forth, this time about his proficiency as a sailor. He looked decidedly put out when the attention of everyone in the room turned to herself and Robbie.

"Ah Sergeant McBane and Miss Barnes. How did you get on?"

"Miss Barnes managed to get what we think is the truth from the lad with glasses; Billy is his name, but the other lad, Rory, would say nothing at all. The long and the short of it is that they came here on Friday night, dropped off in a boat by a character called Gordon McClaughlin who is apparently the ferryman at Dunoon."

"That's correct. Does a bit of fishing too I believe. And for what purpose were they dropped off...as if I can't guess?"

"Poaching m'Lord. They have killed two animals, a deer and a sheep which they have hidden near the point below the house in readiness for being picked up at twenty-two hundred hours...ten o'clock that is...tonight. The worrying thing is that they were also asked to see what was going on in the Loch and report that to McClaughlin."

Boggen sat up. "So we have got some enemy activity?"

"Perhaps so, Group Captain. But we do not think they are George's killers. They haven't got it in them." Lizzie wanted to state that view early so Boggen and the others did not think it was all solved. "George may have disturbed them but they don't seem capable of murder even if surprised. Rory made no attempt to challenge Robbie when we picked them up earlier, even though he was holding a loaded rifle."

Virginia Blairbuie uncrossed her legs. "You know, I thought I heard a shot very late on Friday night but I couldn't be sure."

"Almost certainly them, Lady Blairbuie." Robbie turned back to James Blairbuie. "We need to keep the two boys until tomorrow, Sir. Can we make sleeping arrangements for them please? They do not now need to be separated."

"They can have one of the attic rooms near where you are Sergeant. All the doors have bolts on the inside but I'll ask Langford to have Hodges screw a bolt to the outside of one." Virginia Blairbuie smiled ironically. "We seem to be getting quite crowded. I'll also ask Langford to make sure the beds are made."

"Thank you m'Lady. We may have McClaughlin too."

Goodness me! It's just as well we've got not servants to house up there."

Robbie addressed Lord Blairbuie again. "What I don't understand, Sir, is why Ewan McCrae has not picked them up before we did. He knows these woods better than anyone, he must have noticed some trace of the animals they had killed."

"Yes you would think he might have been more observant but..." Lord Blairbuie sighed, "...I'm afraid Ewan has very much lost his commitment to the job. He will be retiring in about two months. He feels he is being unfairly treated because we are not letting him stay on the estate. I understand that's hard for him but Hamish does not want him hanging about and getting in the way of the new game-keeper we appoint. He has lived here most of his life but we do need his cottage for that appointee so he must move away."

"Does that in some way give him a motive for murder?" Dennis Thorney was clearly keen to be part of the conversation.

James Blairbuie frowned. "I don't see why. What would he gain from murdering George? I know they didn't get on but that seems rather a stretch."

"Does anyone know why George left the estate, Sir, and more particularly why he came back?" Robbie looked from Lord to Lady Blairbuie who both shook their heads. "Well we can explore that tomorrow. We must now prepare to apprehend Gordon McClaughlin when he arrives in his boat."

"Do you want me with you, McBane?" Lizzie smiled to herself. Boggen clearly did not want to leave the comfort of the drawing room and presumably the charms of Virginia Blairbuie. The relief and pleasure on his face when Robbie confirmed he would not be needed was almost comic.

"We can manage him on our own, Sir, but I'm wondering if he'll be picked up by one of the MTBs. And actually, Sir, how did they not get picked up on Friday night?"

"The MTBs are stood down at about twenty hundred hours. The risk after that is minimal. When they sweep the Loch with sonar early next morning, they would pick up any enemy submarine then. If you want them to pick up this McClaughlin character, I can radio over but, by the time they have a craft out in the Loch, he perhaps would have gone."

"No, Sir. I don't want him picked up. I want him to come right up to the rendezvous point so that he incriminates himself. If he's taken earlier, he'll just say he was out fishing."

"Good thinking, McBane. Carry on."

In the corridor, they found Jessica. She looked distressed. "Sergeant McBane, I need to have a conversation with you."

"It will have to wait until morning, Jessica. We have to go and intercept the person who is supposed to collect the two young men we arrested earlier."

"I would prefer to have the conversation tonight..." Her voice faded; she was staring at Lizzie's hands. "Is that a dog collar?"

Lizzie offered Jessica the collar. "We were wondering if this was for George's dog."

Jessica nodded and then turned her frantic eyes back on Robbie.

"I really need to tell you something now."

Alarm suddenly filled Lizzie. "Is Alice alright? Where is she?"

"She's fine. I think she's gone to your room."

Robbie was keen to get out, anxious in case they miss the arrival of Gordon McClaughlin. "Where will you be when we return?"

"I'll wait in the kitchen."

◆◆◆

Lizzie shivered.

"Are you cold, Lizzie?" Robbie's arm slid around her shoulders but she shrugged it off.

"Not cold, no. It's just the atmosphere, the place, the task we have in hand."

"You're not to put yourself in danger. My plan is to stay hidden until he comes off the boat...hopefully he will do that...and comes right up to the place where the carcasses are hidden. We'll be a short distance away so that when I leave hiding, I can cover him with the rifle and challenge him from the side. We need an element of surprise."

"Will he be armed do you suppose?"

"May be, but he supplied the rifle to Rory and Billy so, unless he's got another gun, he may not be."

They fell silent and walked close beside each other across the lawn where they passed through a gap in the hedge and took a path that straggled along the edge of the Loch. The moon in its first quarter was high but veiled in hazy cloud, an eerie half-light over the scene. A light breeze ruffled the surface of the water, causing tiny waves to lap rhythmically on the pebbles; the sound of their feet on the shingle seemed to play a counter-rhythm. No birds were calling and nothing seemed to be moving. The Courbet, a great, grey leviathan, lay silent, silvered here and there with the moon's light. At another time, it would have been a scene of great beauty but now Lizzie felt it was filled with foreboding.

Robbie pointed silently to a place where a short shingle spit projected into the Loch. "We'll hide ourselves in the bushes over there," he whispered.

When they had reached the bushes indicated, they made themselves as comfortable as possible sitting on the ground; they could peer between the taller strands of the shrubs to see the Loch and so could not miss any boat coming to the shore nearby.

Lizzie found it hard to concentrate and could feel tiredness dragging her attention to more pleasant thoughts. She could hear Robbie's slow breathing beside her, his form large and reassuring. She was tempted to nestle closer to him, lay her head on his shoulder, feel his arm gently slide around her shoulders again. She was weakening, there was no doubt about that. She had, so far, been very certain that she would never entertain the idea of a relationship with a man until the War was over. But she knew, deep down, that it was a stalling tactic, a way of persuading herself that she did not need to risk opening herself to anyone for another year, two or maybe more. Alice had said that not all men were only interested in sex, that there were lovely and loving men such as Robbie and she knew that to be true. But then, Alice had not perhaps experienced the childhood trauma that she herself had endured. It was not easy to open oneself with that still lurking in one's mind.

She sighed.

"Are you ok?" Robbie's whispered voice was close to her ear and the temptation to turn, perhaps to kiss his cheek…his lips… was overwhelming. But she did not of course. A lifetime of distance and restraint could not be overcome so easily.

"I'm fine. I hope he comes soon though." She tried to read the time on her watch but there was insufficient light.

As if on cue, she saw a movement out on the water. She strained her eyes to see more clearly, focusing on the spot. Definitely a movement. After some thirty seconds, it was clear that a small boat was approaching, being rowed. The creak of the oars in the rowlocks reached their ears accompanied by the soft plop as the blades entered the water. Robbie lifted the rifle and they both waited.

Nearer and nearer. It seemed an age but, at last, the boat turned into the shore. The oarsman lifted the blades clear of the water and looked around at the shore, presumably hoping to see the two boys. He waited for several minutes, scanning the shore and then very gently eased the boat into the bank. The hull scraped on the pebbles and the skiff came to a halt. The figure shipped the oars and stood up, facing the shore.

They recognised him immediately as the ferryman.

He stood silently, watching and waiting. Then he raised his hands to his mouth and the sound of an owl drifted over the pebbles to their ears. It was very convincing. He waited again, scanning the shore for movement. The owl sound came towards them again, even more ghostly than the first time. He watched and waited again.

Leaning on the gunwale, he stepped out of the boat, his boots splashing softly in the shallow water. Slowly he began to walk up the beach. Lizzie noticed he did not have a weapon in his hand, though he could have one concealed in his coat. She could feel Robbie tensing beside her. Very slowly, without making a sound, he moved into a crouched position, ready to spring.

They waited. The ferryman's boots crunched on the pebbles, one slow step after another until he was at the line of scrub. He stopped, sniffed the air, took two steps in their direction and stepped into the scrub. Any moment now, he would see the carcasses and perhaps start looking for the boys...or he would load them onto the boat and leave the boys behind.

Lizzie and Robbie watched him emerge from the scrub, carrying a small sheep. Retracing his steps to the boat, he dumped it unceremoniously into the hull. They both held their breaths. If he clambered into the boat, they would have to move very quickly because otherwise he would be away in no time. But he turned again and walked up the beach. Robbie nodded to Lizzie. This was it.

As soon as McClaughlin had entered the scrub, Robbie was on his feet and, with rifle in the firing position, ran lightly across the ground ready to intercept the ferryman on his return trip.

When McClaughlin re-appeared from the scrub, Robbie shouted. "Stay right there. Don't move. Put the carcass on the ground and then your hands up."

McClaughlin looked startled but did not drop the deer which

he carried across his shoulders. "Who are you? What d'you want?"

"I'm arresting you on suspicion of being an enemy spy and of poaching. Drop the carcass and put your hands up."

Lizzie realised that Robbie could not shoot an unarmed man. Slowly she crept through the scrub as the conversation continued.

"Enemy spy? Are you out of your mind?" As he spoke, McClaughlin walked slowly forward towards Robbie. He let the deer slide around his body until he was holding it in front of him. "I need to get this in the boat. Lord Blairbuie asked me to pick these carcasses up. Someone's shot them."

"At ten o'clock at night? Pull the other one."

"I work all day even on a Sunday. I had no time 'til now." By now McClaughlin was only yards from Robbie.

"Stop right there or I'll shoot."

"You wouldna shoot an unarmed man now would you? Who are you anyway?"

Lizzie saw her moment. She rushed forward and threw herself at McClaughlin as hard as she could. She felt his body tumble forward and she fell on the ground. But when she looked up, Robbie was on his back with the deer on top of him and McClauglin was running with surprising agility to the boat.

"Stop him," yelled Robbie as he struggled with the carcass.

"They both scrambled to their feet and began to run, their feet sinking in the shingle. But McClaughlin was at the boat; pushing it back into the water with a vigorous shove, he hopped into it, grabbed the oars and propelled the boat out further by pushing against the ground. The oars were shipped with alacrity and the engine burst into life. The craft surged away into the night.

"Damn and blast!"

CHAPTER 23

"You bloody idiot, Billy. Why did you tell her that?"

"What was I supposed to say? If I hadn't told her, they would be blaming us for the murder of that bloke."

"You should have said nothing at all, like I did. They're going to try to pin the murder on us anyway."

"I don't think so. That woman seemed convinced by what I told her and yes it's against the law but it's much less serious than murder."

"Sweet talk you did she? I bet you were all gooey-eyed. 'Yes, Miss, no Miss, three bags full Miss.' You are a bloody liability Billy. Why ever did I bring you?"

"Well I didn't get us caught. That was just one of those things." Billy sat hunched on the bed. "Anyway, at least we've had something to eat and we've got a bed for the night."

"And we'll have a bed for many nights…in a prison."

They said no more for a while, Billy staring at the floor and Rory pacing the small space between the beds like a caged lion. Billy wanted to climb into bed and sleep. They had given them food and water, a very nice helping of casserole but no pudding. A nice slice of apple pie would have gone down very well but the casserole was very welcome. For the first time that weekend, he felt comfortable and strangely safe. He knew next morning would see them transported to jail but now he would enjoy the small creature comforts they had. So much better than the last two nights.

The clock on the outhouse chimed ten. They looked at each other, both realising the significance. Gordon would be at the rendezvous and would leave without them.

Billy stood and dropped his trousers. He pulled his jumper over his head and dumped it on the floor on top of the discarded trousers. With a deep and satisfied sigh, he pulled back the blankets and climbed into bed.

"What are you doing now?"

"Going to sleep. What do you think?"

"Get up, you idiot. We've got to escape. We've got to get right away from here."

"What's the point? They know who we are. If we do get away where are we going to go? Back to Dunoon? They'll just come and arrest us at home."

"Gordon will get us across the water on the ferry and we'll head for Glasgow. You can hide in a city easily – they'll never find us. And in six months, it'll all be forgotten. They'll have the murderer in prison and won't be worried about a sheep and a deer."

Billy was sitting up in the bed, his legs beneath the blankets. "You may not realise it, but we are in a locked room in the attic of a tall house. How are we going to get out? And if we do, how do we get back to Dunoon to the ferry?"

"What did we see those two women – you know the one you fancy and the other one – and that red-haired bloke doing this afternoon?"

"Rowing on the Loch."

"Exactly. Rowing on the Loch... in a boat. That boat must be here somewhere." Rory crossed to the small window and opened the sash. He leaned out his head for a while and then pulled it back inside before closing the window again. Without a word, he went to his bed and pulled back the blankets. He tugged the two sheets from the bed and sat down. Rolling both sheets lengthwise, he tied one end of each to the other. He handed one end to Billy.

"Hold that." Pulling the other end out, he wrapped it around the rickety chair that was against the wall beneath the window. He then paced the distance to the chair and back to Billy. "Four yards near enough. So with your two sheets, that will be eight yards which is...twenty-four feet. We can drop from the end which means we can lower ourselves another six feet and drop the rest, say another six feet."

"What do you mean?"

"I mean we'll tie the end of the sheet rope inside here somehow, then climb down and get away. We need to wait until everyone is asleep."

"I canna do that. I'm not very fit or strong."

Rory gave a short laugh. "I thought you wanted to be a hero... impress that woman." His face changed and he leaned close to Billy. "You'll just have to do it. We are not staying here."

"But we've got to find the boat."

"I've found it. Down by the edge of the Loch is a boathouse; that's where it'll be."

"I think we should just stay here. They've treated us well and we need sleep. We've just got to accept the punishment for the poaching."

"You really think that's all it'll be? They'll pin the murder on us, Billy. Nice and easy for them. Two blokes with a rifle. We had the means and the opportunity even if we have no idea who that murdered chap is. Now get some sleep and I'll wake you when it's time."

◆ ◆ ◆

"I'm sorry, Robbie, but what else could I do? I knew you could not shoot an unarmed man."

"But he was carrying a deer. I could have overpowered him. After all, his arms were not free."

"But he would have done what he did whether I had jumped him or not. He was deliberately getting closer and closer to you so he could throw the carcass at you."

"Well it's done now."

They were trudging back towards the house, both feeling they had failed. "Anyway, Robbie, we know who he is, we know where he lives and we know that he is involved because he lifted both carcasses and we saw him. He can't deny his involvement."

"That's true. Perhaps I could borrow a car from Lord Blairbuie and get over to Dunoon before he arrives. I can arrest him there."

"You could try, Robbie, but my guess is he will assume that's what we'll do. He'll come ashore somewhere away from Dunoon and creep back to wherever he lives or somewhere else. I think we may as well wait until morning. We can drive over to Dunoon, see MacGregor and have McClaughlin arrested. Even if he has already disposed of the sheep, there will be blood stains in his boat."

"He'll slosh plenty of seawater around it to make sure there's no trace. But, you're probably right, Lizzie. We may as well pick him up in the morning. He may think he's got away with it and drop his guard. And now I must find out what Jessica wants. She looked very upset."

Jessica was waiting as she had said in the kitchen. She was sitting on a chair, deep in thought, holding the dog collar in her hands. Lizzie thought she may have been crying but her face, though drawn and pale, was now dry.

"I see you have the collar."

She nodded. "It's George's certainly. He never got over the death of his dog." She laid it on the table beside her. "Did you catch him?"

"I'm afraid he got away but we'll pick him up in the morning in Dunoon. We know who he is and we saw him take the carcasses...well one of them anyway." Lizzie did feel some guilt that she might have messed things up but she was sure it was a temporary setback.

"What do you want to tell us?" Robbie made an effort to keep his voice pleasant, putting behind him the frustrations of the last hour.

Jessica looked at Lizzie. "I'm sorry Lizzie, but this is for Robbie's ears only."

"Oh...right...I'll head off to bed then. I'll come with you to Dunoon in the morning, Robbie...if you want me to that is."

Robbie said nothing, so Lizzie, feeling re-buffed, left the room.

When the door closed, he pulled a chair closer to where

Jessica was sitting, wincing at the scraping sound it made on the flagstones. "What did you want to say?"

"I think I may be responsible for George's death."

"Do you mean you think you killed him?"

"Goodness no! I could not do that to anyone let alone my brother."

"Please explain."

"I need to start at the beginning. Lizzie and Alice were pushing me earlier to tell them exactly what my job is. They could not believe that I am just a secretary because, as they correctly said, a secretary would not have been sent to keep an eye on a top secret test. In one sense it's true. Government ministries do not have any other grade for women except secretary. So that is what officially I am. But I work for a department within the War Office. I do not usually work in the field...my job is a desk one, analysing information and advising my superiors about threats and how to counter them."

Robbie McBane's mouth opened and his eyebrows rose.

"I can see you perhaps don't believe me but, you can, when you can find a telephone, call my boss, Mr Ian Grainger at the War Office who will confirm everything I am about to tell you. Actually, we work at the Directorate of Military Intelligence Section Six. I can give you the number."

"Ian Grainger...is he a rather arrogant man, at least at first meeting?"

Jessica smiled. "I'm afraid so. He can be very over-bearing too but he is absolutely committed to the security of this country and drives himself very hard. He has earned my respect. How do you know him?"

"In March this year, I was on an assignment at RAF Cranwell in Lincolnshire and Mr Grainger was also there. He caused me a great deal of trouble until he finally revealed what his real role was. It was not a successful first meeting."

"Yes, I can see how that might be. But please take my word for it. He is as straight as you would want someone to be, a touch ruthless perhaps, but he makes very carefully calculated decisions. Things are not straightforward in times of war."

"So I gathered."

"We have been concerned for the last two months that there may be leaks from the Brooklands team developing the weapon being tested here and its larger sister. We have taken steps to check everyone. Last week, we gained intelligence that suggested Dennis Thorney may be supplying information to a German agent."

"Thorney? But why on Earth should he do so? He's been telling us how much the weapon's development is down to him."

"Yes, but you will also have realised that he feels his contribution is not acknowledged. He is a disgruntled member of the team and that is just the kind of person an enemy agent would target."

"That certainly comes across clearly."

"We needed to find out whether that intelligence was true or not. The problem was that Thorney was due to come up here and we had no way of testing him out beforehand. I thought this may be a way of helping George out. I suggested we ask George to offer Thorney money in exchange for information about the weapons. George would not need to obtain the information, just test out whether Thorney would take the bait."

"But how did you contact George? I thought no one knew where he was."

Jessica smiled. "We have agents throughout the Country and we can find things out very easily. Actually, I had already established where George was to make sure he was alive. One of our agents made contact with George, told him what he had to do and gave him one hundred pounds in cash to offer to Thorney as a token of faith."

Jessica suddenly seemed to choke and she coughed to cover her distress. When she looked up at Robbie again, her eyes were pleading. "So you see, I put George in danger. I suggested he make contact with Thorney and I even suggested through our agent that he did not make his presence known to my parents or anyone else at Glenstriven."

Robbie said nothing for several seconds. “So what you are suggesting, Jessica, is that George met Thorney at some point, offered him money and that Thorney killed him.”

She nodded. “I think that’s what must have happened. If Thorney has one hundred pounds in cash, it proves he met George and accepted the money.”

“We found fifty pounds in ten pound notes in the camp that George had made in the woods. He clearly had decided to take a cut.”

Jessica shook her head. “Yes, I feared that’s what he might do.”

“But why would Thorney kill George? How would that help him? Surely, if he is corrupt, he would want to obtain more money? Killing George would be like killing the goose that laid the golden egg.”

“I know, I know. But something must have gone wrong. Perhaps he took the money and decided that George then knew too much. I don’t know, Robbie, I don’t know but I may as well have put the gun to George’s head myself.”

Robbie again said nothing for several seconds. He laid a hand gently on Jessica’s arm. “Thank you for telling me but, Jessica, I have learnt to keep an open mind. It may be nothing to do with Thorney at all but I will of course pursue it.”

CHAPTER 24

Lizzie opened her eyes. The room was in darkness. She had heard the clock on the old stable block strike two hundred hours, the very witching time of night. She listened for any sounds that might indicate someone else was awake but heard nothing. Then there was a muffled thud. It sounded as though it came from nearby.

Throwing back the blankets, she swung her legs out of bed and reached for her dressing gown. As carefully as she could so as not to wake Alice, she turned the door handle, slipped through and stepped into the corridor. The room opposite theirs, the one from which they had seen the test earlier, had been used to house Rory and Billy. The door was secured from the outside, the additional bolt still in place. She listened at the door. Nothing...and then a groan, someone making an effort. This was followed by a clunk of wood on wood.

They were up to something. Should she wake Robbie? That might be too late. She unlocked the door and burst in, knocking on the door as she did so. Only the light from the moon penetrated the room and that was partially blocked by a chair which somehow was held against the open window.

Swift glances at the two beds revealed they were empty, though one had definitely been slept in. She crossed to the window and through the legs of the chair could see a figure on the roof, clinging to what looked like a rope made out of sheets.

"Billy," she hissed urgently, "what on earth are you doing? Come back here. You'll kill yourself!"

Billy looked up and, seeing her, whimpered. He glanced behind him and let himself further down the roof. Suddenly, his feet slipped and he disappeared over the edge though still clinging desperately to the makeshift rope. Faintly, she heard his stifled cry of fear and moments later a soft thud. Then there was a real cry of pain and another voice.

"Get up, for God's sake, Billy. We've got to get away from here."

The boys were escaping.

Dashing out of the room, Lizzie dived into their own and found her shoes which she slipped on, stubbing her toe on the floor before she found the opening. Then she rushed along the corridor and, hoping she had found the right door in the darkness, knocked. She did not wait for an answer but crossed to the bed which she could only dimly see and shook the sleeping figure by the shoulder.

"Robbie, Robbie, wake up."

"Uh...what's the matter? Who is it? Lizzie?"

"Sorry to wake you, Robbie but you've got to get up. Rory and Billy are escaping. I'm going out there now. Get to the front of the house as soon as possible."

She rushed from the room and, trying her best not to make a dreadful noise on the stairs, clattered downwards. Breathing hard, she tore around the house to the front and saw Billy on the ground outside one of the drawing room windows clutching his ankle.

"Billy, are you alright?"

"I think I've broken my leg."

"Where's Rory?"

"He's gone."

"Where's he gone? What was the plan, Billy? Were you going to walk back to Dunoon or what?"

"He's gone for the boat...you know the one you went rowing in this afternoon."

"Damn," Lizzie said softly, frantically trying to decide what she should do...look after Billy or try to catch Rory. "You'll be alright for a bit won't you, Billy?"

"I can't...it hurts, Miss."

Just then Robbie McBane came panting up beside them. "Where's the other one?"

"Gone for the boat. You get after him and I'll sort Billy out."

"Can you manage?"

"I'll get Alice."

"Right." Robbie turned away and ran off into the night.

"Billy, you need to sit up. Lean against the wall and I'll have a look at you."

Pushing himself upwards slowly and moaning softly, Billy sat on the ground and dragged himself the yard or so to the wall of the house where he leaned back with a huge sigh.

"I'm going to check your leg. Where does it hurt?"

"It's mainly down the bottom, by my foot."

"Ok. I'll need to feel your whole leg to see if it's broken. Tell me if it hurts more when I press but don't shout out...you'll wake the whole house."

Lizzie felt Billy's leg, starting with his thigh. It was not until she reached his ankle that he jerked and drew in his breath. "That hurt, Miss."

She felt his ankle carefully but could not feel any bones moving out of place. "I think you've sprained your ankle, Billy. It will hurt and you'll need to go easy on it but it will heal itself in a few days probably. If not, you'll need to see a doctor."

"Are you a nurse, Miss?"

"No Billy, I'm a pilot but I have had some first aid training. Now we're going to get you on your feet and then I'm going to help you move inside. It'll take us a while to get up all those stairs but we'll just go steady and rest if you need it." She crouched beside him. "Put your right arm around my shoulders and push yourself up against the wall with your left leg...the good one."

Lizzie smiled to herself at Billy's struggle to lift himself. He was rather chubby and not an athletic-looking youth. When he had stood more or less upright, she said, "There now, done like a true war hero." In the dim light, she could see the smile cross Billy's face. As they moved off, she supporting him, she thought he was perhaps leaning on her more than strictly necessary.

◆ ◆ ◆

The pale moonlight reflected on the water and put the old boathouse in shadow. Robbie stopped and listened. Sound of movement inside the structure confirmed that someone was inside. There would be some light entering the window and if Rory had already opened the outer doors to the Loch, there should be plenty to see what was happening.

He pushed open the door at the end of the building furthest from the water and strode inside. Rory, struggling to open the second of the two large doors that allowed the boat into the Loch, turned at the sound, his face full of alarm. He turned back and continued wrestling with the door, at last dragging it open. There were walkways on either side of the water and the craft nestled in between. Rory was at the end of one of these walkways and he half stepped, half leapt into the boat which rocked violently. Within seconds, he had the oars in the rowlocks. With both large doors to the Loch open, Robbie had enough light to glance around the boathouse swiftly, taking in the scene.

"Going somewhere, Rory?"

"Going home. You can't keep me a prisoner here. You're not even proper Poliss."

"Well now…you were in a room in the big house with a full stomach and a comfortable bed. Hardly what a prisoner would have been given. So, I assume your desire to get away is an indication of guilt. Perhaps if you had been more forthcoming, we would have let you go. As it is, we still need to find who murdered that young man and, frankly, you are the prime suspect."

Rory looked at Robbie and a humourless smile gashed his face. "It wasn't me and I'm not staying around to talk to you." With that he took the oars and pushed the blades against the sides of the berth. The boat moved forward. "Good luck with your investigation." He grinned and pushed harder.

Robbie smiled at him. "You don't seem to be going anywhere, Rory."

Rory did not reply but pushed with all his might.

"I suggest you come out of the boat now, Rory, before you make a complete fool of yourself."

"I'm leaving now." Rory continued to struggle and the grin on Robbie's face broadened.

"You might get further if you untied the stern line." Rory looked at where Robbie was pointing and his face fell. "I can come in the boat and lift you out or you can come quietly. You should bear in mind that I'm a lot bigger than you and stronger...all those years rugby training!"

Rory flung the oars into the bottom of the boat and stood up. He stepped onto the side and put his hands forward as if to receive handcuffs. Robbie moved towards him and grabbed his arm.

"Ow. You don't need to grip that hard."

"I just want you to know that you're not going anywhere, whatever you try."

◆ ◆ ◆

Although Billy did not resist in any way, it was a struggle to get him up two flights of stairs without waking the whole household. Lizzie had only just got him to the room when Robbie arrived with Rory. Lizzie took the precaution of removing the sheets...not that Billy was going to go anywhere now. The blankets would be rough but they had brought that upon themselves.

Billy had sunk onto his bed with a soft sigh. "Thank you, Miss. I'm sorry to be so useless."

"You're not useless, Billy, you're just not cut out for that kind of escapade. Don't let Rory talk you into things you don't want to do." Rory had looked thunderously at her but said nothing.

She and Robbie left the room and bolted the door. He touched her arm and, as she turned towards him, he whispered, "Well done, Lizzie. Had you not been so alert, they would have got away...well Rory would have done. Billy's not in a fit state to go anywhere."

"They're an unlikely pair."

"That Billy's got a soft spot for you though."

Lizzie smiled. "Of course...most men have."

"Lovely that you are so modest too. Lizzie, on a serious note, I need to fill you in on the conversation I had with Jessica but she told me something in confidence so for goodness sake don't let it slip."

"You can trust me, Robbie. Let's go somewhere we can talk without disturbing anyone."

They crept down the two flights of stairs again and along the corridor where the old long case clock relentlessly marked time. Robbie opened the door into the drawing room, crossed to the bay window and pulled open the curtains; the pale moonlight cast dim shadows of the piano onto the floor. They sat on the nearest sofa, side by side.

"As you suspected, Jessica is not just a secretary though apparently that is what all women in her department are classed as. Do you remember Ian Grainger from our time at RAF Cranwell?"

"Grainger? How can I ever forget him?"

"Jessica works for him. They have suspicions about Dennis Thorney. We've seen that he is disgruntled, quick to anger. Anyway, they needed to test his loyalty so arranged for George to come and offer him money in return for information. He obviously did not offer him the full amount as he had kept back fifty pounds. George was not expected to get the information immediately, just give him a sweetener to see how he would react."

"Why George? Everything we've been told about him does not suggest someone reliable."

"Quite, but they had no time to arrange something else and Jessica wanted to try to do something for George."

"It's that guilt she carries isn't it?"

"Yes, but added to that now is the fear that she has caused

George's death. She thinks Thorney might be responsible."

"He might be of course but...what a strange thing to do!" A thought struck Lizzie. "I hope this is not Jessica throwing us onto a false scent. Perhaps she..."

"What possible reason could she have for killing her brother?"

"Perhaps he knows something about her that she did not want revealed. Perhaps, she is working for the enemy."

"Now, now, Lizzie. You'll be seeing spies and enemy agents everywhere. Jessica has given me the telephone number of her Department so I can verify what she has told me. When I go to Dunoon tomorrow, I will telephone and speak to Grainger. We didn't trust him but he turned out to be above board. I'm sure he will have checked Jessica out fully."

"It was just a thought...must keep our minds open to all possibilities."

"I agree but within reason. I think this case is going to be as difficult as the last. I don't think Rory and Billy are our murderers and we can rule out the strange sightings on the Loch. That means it must be someone from Glenstriven itself, someone who is here amongst us. I want to bring everyone up to speed after breakfast and then I will interview Thorney. While I do so, I want you to get into his room and see if you can find fifty pounds, the other half of the money. If he has it, he will, no doubt, argue that he brought it with him. After that, I'm going to head to Dunoon."

"I'll come with you shall I?"

"No Lizzie, you stay here and keep those lovely eyes and ears open."

Lizzie smiled. "Spoken like a character in a film."

Monday 10th May 1943

CHAPTER 25

Lizzie looked around the assembled group, sitting at the large table in the dining room. All the staff had been invited in for the meeting. They sat in silence, clearly uncomfortable in these elevated surroundings. Jessica was not daunted by the gathering but she looked troubled, wrestling still no doubt with her guilt over George. Lizzie's eyes travelled to Jessica's left. Her face swollen with the tears she had shed and her eyes dark from lack of sleep, Maureen Hodges seemed distant, as if she were in another World. Her husband, David, was stony faced, revealing nothing of the terrible thoughts that must be troubling his brain. She could not read Ewan McCrae or Hamish Ferguson; their faces were blank, perhaps deliberately so. Isla, looking as sullen as always with her eyes on the floor, stood awkwardly at the edge of the room with Robert Langford the butler. Lord Blairbuie seemed troubled, the events of the previous days casting long shadows over his peaceful life and Virginia Blairbuie, whose morning routine had been interrupted, scowled with contempt on the proceedings, probably fuming inwardly about the staff being allowed into the room.

"Thank you, Ladies and Gentlemen, for making time to attend this meeting. And thank you Lord Blairbuie for allowing this room to be used. It is important that I let you know where things have got to. I will be as brief as possible."

Lizzie and Alice had drawn their chairs back from the table so as not to block the view of Robbie for others, Lizzie had said, but in reality it gave her a better view of most of the assembled group. Seeing how they reacted to various pieces of news could be very revealing.

"You all know that we apprehended two boys yesterday

evening who have been on the Estate since Friday night. They are here to poach and were persuaded to do so by one Gordon McClaughlin, the ferryman at Dunoon. The younger of the two, Billy, has been very forthcoming and I am certain that they are not responsible for George's murder. The older of the two carried a rifle but it seems unlikely that was the weapon that killed George. To shoot into his temple would have required the gunman to be close unless he was an expert marksman. A rifle bullet at such close quarters would have caused more damage. I'm sorry Mr and Mrs Hodges and Jessica to have to be so direct and detailed."

David Hodges looked up and gave the faintest shrug; the detail of how their son was shot was unimportant alongside the fact that he was dead.

Robbie continued. "The boys did attempt to escape last night but that was foiled by Miss Barnes."

"Surely attempting to escape indicates guilt?" Dennis Thorney sat back in his chair, hands on his rotund stomach.

"Yes, Mr Thorney, it does but guilty of poaching rather than murder I think. They know they will be in court for killing two animals. We discovered from Billy that they were to be picked up last night by this McClaughlin so we tried to arrest him when he arrived. Unfortunately, he evaded capture but I will go to Dunoon soon to alert Sergeant MacGregor and have him arrested."

"I thought you said you would be able to handle it McBane. Made a mess of it though didn't you?" Boggen drawled.

"We failed in the attempt, Group Captain, that's all that can be said."

Lizzie could see that Boggen's comment had riled Robbie. She felt for him. While Boggen sat around in comfort, Robbie had been working. As well as the events that had disturbed his night, he had checked the boys that morning, escorted them to the toilet and arranged for Isla to take them some breakfast. What right did Boggen have to sit in judgement when he had clearly been unwilling to leave the company of Virginia Blairbuie and the comfort of the drawing room?

"Doubtless, you did what you could." James Blairbuie seemed as irritated by Boggen's remark as Robbie. "Perhaps we should all have come out with you. But, as you say, it should be easy enough to arrest him and, as you saw him with the carcasses, he can hardly deny it."

"Thank you m'Lord. I agree."

"The camp that was found in the woods was being used by George. We can be confident of that because we found a dog collar amongst the few possessions there and Jessica has confirmed it belonged to George."

Maureen Hodges sobbed and put her hand to her face. Her husband laid his hand on her arm and said, "He was very fond of that dog...desperately upset when it died so he always kept the collar with him."

"Our trip in the boat yesterday afternoon established that the strange sightings on the Loch are not enemy activity and nothing to concern us. We have therefore ruled out those things which suggested George's murder may have been an intruder or spy. We must allow for the possibility that there *is* someone unknown to us lurking about but we have no further leads to explore on that front."

Hamish Ferguson was frowning. "Are you suggesting, Sergeant, that someone from the Estate was responsible... someone in this room now?"

"I am not suggesting anything, Mr Ferguson, but it is important that we now establish everyone's movements late on Saturday night and early yesterday morning."

Lizzie could feel the atmosphere in the room change. People were looking at others and the thought in everyone's mind, despite Robbie's attempt to fend off the suggestion, was that George's killer was sitting amongst them.

"I will make a start now but then I must get to Dunoon. May I borrow a car m'Lord."

"Of course. Do you want Hodges to drive you?"

"No thank you, Sir. No need for that."

"Whilst I am away, Miss Barnes and Miss Frobisher will talk to some of you to discover what you might have seen."

"But they're not members of the Police force...and neither are you actually."

"No Mr Thorney, they are not but, as you know, I am a member of the RAF Police Special Investigation Branch and I have investigated murders before. I do so now with the permission, indeed a request from Sergeant MacGregor. Miss Barnes and Miss Frobisher will simply gather what information they can while I am away. Now, Ladies and Gentlemen, I will let you go."

Paul Boggen stood up. "Just before you do leave, the tests planned for today at ten o'clock and one o'clock will go ahead. Please ensure you are at the back of the house as previously instructed. Thank you." Boggen smiled at Virginia Blairbuie and they walked out together. Lizzie looked out of the window. Dark clouds were rolling over the Loch from the South West, scraping the hills on the other side of the water. It was not yet raining but no doubt soon would be.

The assembled group, still looking at each other with suspicion, left the Dining Room. Dennis Thorney stood up but, before he could leave, Robbie took a few steps towards him and said, "I would like to ask you a few questions, Mr Thorney."

◆ ◆ ◆

"This does not seem right, Lizzie. I mean searching someone's room is an intrusion into their privacy."

"I agree, Alice, but sadly needs must. We'll be careful not to leave any trace. We're looking for a sum of money, probably fifty pounds. It may be in an envelope or it may be just in a pocket somewhere."

"Or he may have it on him. If he did accept the money from George, surely he would keep it somewhere absolutely safe and that would be on his person."

"That may well be the case, Alice, but we certainly can't ask him to turn out his pockets."

Alice giggled. "Actually, Lizzie, I suspect you would be happy to ask him to do just that!"

"I'm not that bad am I?"

"I won't answer that." Alice smiled at Lizzie who returned it, warmed by the relationship she and Alice had developed.

Swiftly and deftly, Lizzie checked the wardrobe while Alice went through the chest of drawers. It did not take long as, naturally, Dennis Thorney had not brought much with him for this short trip. They found nothing that would incriminate him. Lizzie checked the bedside table...nothing that raised suspicions of his loyalties but...Lizzie pulled out a magazine and her mouth opened wide. She lifted it up for Alice to see and opened it. Inside were pictures of young women in very scanty clothing posing, lips pouting with 'come and get me smiles'.

Lizzie felt her anger rising towards Dennis Thorney. "If it had been Boggen's room, I would not have been surprised to find this but perhaps all men are just the same."

"You've got to get out of the habit of assuming all men are the same Lizzie. They're not. Robbie isn't is he?"

"I hope not." Lizzie placed the magazine back in the bedside cabinet.

Alice pointed at the bed. They bent over each side and ran their hands between the bedstead and the mattress. Lizzie stopped when her hand felt paper. Lifting the mattress with one hand, she peered underneath and her free hand closed over something. She pulled it out.

It was a brown envelope. She held it up and they both read the name on it...no address...just a name: 'Mr D Thorney'. The envelope was not sealed so Lizzie opened it and took out several notes. She laid each on the bed in a slow ritual. Fifty pounds in ten pound notes, just as they had expected.

"It looks as though we may have our man," Lizzie said.

"Perhaps, but the fact he took the money does not mean he killed George. Why would he? How would he gain from doing that especially if he thought he would be able to get further pay outs?"

"True, but maybe George said something to him, threatened to turn him in. After all, George was a difficult character, falling out with people."

"What do we do now?"

"We take it down to Robbie and give it to him."

◆ ◆ ◆

"Why are you starting with me? I don't have to answer your questions, you know."

Robbie McBane smiled and indicated a chair. He had been given permission to use Lord Blairbuie's library and had led Dennis Thorney, protesting all the way, into it. He waited until Thorney had slumped into the indicated chair before speaking. "I realise Mr Thorney that you do not have to answer any of my questions but it might indicate you are hiding something if you refuse to co-operate. As I said, this discussion is merely about finding out what your movements were and what you might have seen."

Thorney sat in his chair, hostility radiating from his rotund body. "Get on with it then but I can tell you now, I've seen nothing suspicious or out of the ordinary."

"Please start by telling me what you did on Saturday night after you left this room."

"I went into the Drawing Room to join the ladies for a short while but didn't stay long as I was tired. I think that was true for the ladies too. Sunday was important and I needed to be fully refreshed and alert."

"Did you leave your room at all during the night."

"No, of course not. Why would I?"

"It was just a question Mr Thorney. Did you hear anything, a gunshot for example, in the night?"

"No, nothing. As I said, I was tired and I slept soundly."

"Early Sunday morning, that is before breakfast, did you leave the house?"

Thorney answered immediately. "No."

"I ask you to think very carefully, Mr Thorney. Are you sure you didn't go out…for a walk perhaps?"

"I've already answered." Thorney leaned forward, his eyes hard and his voice an aggressive monotone. "I did not go out on Sunday morning."

"Ah…it's just that we have a witness who said they saw a man fitting your description walking along the side of the Loch beyond the house…heading Northwards."

"Witness? What witness?"

Robbie McBane did not answer but waited. Thorney sat back and looked around airily. "Perhaps I did go out…just to look at the scene before the tests. Yes, come to think of it I did."

"How far up the Loch did you walk?"

"Oh not far at all, a few hundred yards at most."

"Did you meet anyone or see anyone?"

Thorney shook his head slowly and pushed his lips out from his puffy face. "No…no I saw no one."

There was a knock on the door.

CHAPTER 26

When Robbie opened the door, Lizzie and Alice were standing there. Lizzie beckoned him outside and he closed the door behind him. She thrust a brown envelope towards him.

"We found this in Thorney's room, hidden under the mattress. As you can see, it's addressed to him and there's fifty pounds in ten pound notes inside. It all adds up."

"So he must have met George at some point."

"Yes...and perhaps he's our murderer."

"What I don't understand," said Alice, "is why he would want to murder him. It doesn't make sense. In fact, I can't see why anyone here would want to murder George."

"I'm wondering if George gave him the money and then threatened to report Thorney. Perhaps George wanted some of the money back that he'd just given him." Lizzie wanted to make sure that this theory was planted in Robbie's brain. "We know that George was a difficult boy."

Robbie nodded slowly. "Perhaps...we have at least caught Thorney in a lie. At first he said he had not been outside yesterday morning, then, when I said we had a witness, he remembered that he had been for a short walk."

"One can understand why he wouldn't want to admit meeting George because that would involve a mention of the money and an admission that he was willing to accept it in exchange for information."

"You're right there, Alice. And if I confront Thorney with this envelope, he will deny it came from George. Is there any way we can verify it is the same envelope given to George with the full one hundred pounds?"

"Jessica might be able to do that."

"Can you find her and ask please?"

"Of course...always at your service, Sir." Lizzie grinned and whisked away followed by Alice. Robbie went back into the room where he found Thorney pacing about.

"Please accept my apologies for that Mr Thorney. Can we resume?" He pointed to the chair.

"You've got a bloody cheek, McBane. Surely you realise I'm a very important scientist and engineer. I'm crucial to the War effort and to the success of this weapon which could bring the War to a quick end. And what are you doing? Delaying me by asking ridiculous questions and, more than that, implying that I'm a murderer."

In his most innocent voice, Robbie said, "And are you Mr Thorney?"

"Of course not! Are you an idiot? Why on Earth would I murder a boy I do not know and have never met. My God, McBane, your superiors will know about this from me and from Group Captain Boggen I shouldn't wonder." Thorney turned to the window. "This is outrageous."

"I just have a few more questions, Mr Thorney, if you would be good enough to sit down again."

Thorney, his lip curled in a snarl, sat heavily on the chair, bolt upright, his stomach bulging over his thighs. "Get on with it."

"Could you please tell me as accurately as you can what time you went for your walk yesterday morning?"

"I don't know. Probably about seven o'clock, maybe a bit later."

"And did you see anyone inside the house before you left?"

"No. I went out the back door and I could hear movement in the kitchen. Probably Mrs Hodges preparing the breakfast."

"Thank you, Sir. I think that will be all for now but, please, if you think of anything else, anything at all, do let me know. Often these cases are solved with the most insignificant details."

Before Thorney could get up and leave, there was another knock at the door. Robbie McBane put out his hand as a signal to Thorney to stay where he was. "I must just see who this is if you would be good enough to wait a moment longer."

"I've been here long enough," Thorney barked but he did sit in the chair again. Robbie strode over to the door, opened it and was relieved to find Lizzie and Alice there.

Lizzie's eyes were open wide with excitement. "We've got him, Robbie. Jessica said that all the notes had been marked – standard procedure – with a tiny pen squiggle in the bottom right hand corner. It's not something you would notice. See." She fanned the five notes and Robbie peered at the corner of each. He smiled, took the notes and returned them to the envelope.

"Thanks, ladies. Let's see how he wriggles out of this one."

Robbie returned to his seat and Thorney, who must have sensed a change in him, looked at him apprehensively. Robbie produced the envelope, holding it face down. "Have you seen this envelope before, Mr Thorney."

"I've got no idea. It's just a brown envelope; there are dozens of them about."

Robbie turned it face up. "This one seems to be addressed to you."

"So what? Anyway where did you get it?"

"In your room, hidden under the mattress."

"You've been in my room? How dare you?" Thorney stood up and glowered at Robbie. "You've gone too far now McBane."

"Have you seen it before?"

"Of course I have...it's got my name on it."

"Do you know what's inside?"

"Yes, some money which I put under the mattress to make sure it did not get stolen."

"How much?"

"Fifty pounds."

"That's a lot of money, Mr Thorney."

"It may have escaped your notice, McBane, but we are hundreds of miles from my home and if something goes wrong, I may need to buy a train ticket back, I may have to stay overnight somewhere. Anyway, what the bloody hell has it got to do with you? It's my money and, if I choose to bring fifty pounds, that's my choice."

"Where did you get it from?"

"Where d'you think? A bloody bank."

"Ah. It's just that each of these notes has been marked. Look here in the bottom right hand corner. They were marked by a member of our security services and given to George with instructions to offer them to you. I put it to you Mr Thorney, that you did meet George this morning, had a conversation with him and he gave you this money. What have you to say?"

Thorney said nothing. He sat staring at Robbie McBane, his face twisted in a vicious snarl. At last he said, jabbing his finger at Robbie, "I'm saying nothing more McBane but you are not going to pin the murder of that young man on me." He stormed out of the room.

◆ ◆ ◆

Lizzie and Alice had agreed that they would start with Isla and be as gentle as possible with her. Lizzie had suggested Alice begin as she herself was inclined to be too direct. Isla was as wary as a wild fawn and would bolt at the slightest sign of threat. They found her in the kitchen finishing the washing up after breakfast. She was alone.

"Hello Isla, we wondered if we could talk with you briefly."

Isla turned towards Alice but her eyes darted to Lizzie and back again. She then turned back to the pile of plates she was drying. She shrugged. "If you want."

"I hope you won't think it intrusive of us but we are a bit worried about you. You seem very unhappy."

Surprise opened Isla's eyes and lifted her face. "Why?"

"You never seem to smile. That's unusual for someone serving guests but also for someone your age." Lizzie took a risk making the observation, hoping it would not offend the girl.

"What's there to be happy about?"

Alice nodded. "I suppose there's not much at Glenstriven for you. There's no one of your age."

"That's about it." Isla clattered the last dry plate onto the top of the pile and lifted the whole lot over to a cupboard.

"How well did you know George?"

"Quite well when he was here though we were never... what you'd call close friends."

"His death must have upset you."

Isla looked sharply at Lizzie. "Of course. You don't expect someone you know to be shot out here."

"Did you know that George had returned to Glenstriven?"

Isla did not answer for a while, busying herself drying cutlery. "Maybe."

Lizzie needed a straighter answer. "I need to press you on that Isla. Either you did or you didn't."

Isla faced Lizzie and there was anger in her voice. "What's it got to do with you?"

Alice stepped in, calm, soft-voiced, conciliatory. "We're trying to help Sergeant McBane find out what happened to George. He's had to go to Dunoon. We're not being difficult, Isla. I don't know if you liked George or not but I hope you feel able to help us."

Isla answered more calmly. "Yes I did know but I had met him only twice since he came a few days ago. I took him some food. And yes I did like him, even though most people didn't."

"Do you know why he came back, or why he didn't stay with his parents?"

"He said he had a job to do but he didn't say what it was."

"That's helpful. We also need to try to find out why George left Glenstriven in the first place. Do you know why?"

Isla hesitated. "I'm not sure. There could have been a few things." She turned away from them and continued with her work though Lizzie noticed her shoulders were shaking. She guessed that one or two tears had escaped from her eyes.

Lizzie took a deep breath. "Isla, yesterday afternoon, we were waiting in the corridor for Sergeant McBane and we could not help overhearing a conversation between you and your father."

Isla whirled round. "You were listening to a private conversation?"

"No Isla. We could not avoid overhearing it. Your voices were raised."

Isla was fighting to stop herself crying. Both Alice and Lizzie could see it. Alice said as gently as she could, “Isla, please sit down and tell us about George and you.”

Isla put down the tea towel and slowly sat on the chair that Alice had pulled out from the table. Lizzie and Alice also sat down so that the three were in a small group.

“If I had been living somewhere else, George would probably not have been someone I would choose as a boyfriend but, as my Mum used to say, 'beggars can’t be choosers.' We were never really courting but I liked him well enough. We did become, you know...close because we were the only young people here. George was getting very frustrated and angry ‘cos people kept having a go at him...his Dad, Ewan McCrae. But one day, we were...you know...”

“Kissing perhaps?”

Isla nodded. “That and a bit more...but not the whole thing,” she added anxiously. “My Dad interrupted us. He was furious. He wants to control everyone, especially me. He did the same thing with my Mum. He threatened George. I think he may have told him to go away and maybe threatened him with violence if he came back. I tried to tell my Dad that I was happy with what was happening but he wouldn’t listen. He wants to keep me as his little girl...can’t deal with the fact that I’m growing up.”

“Do you think...do you think that your father may have done something to George when he discovered him on the Estate?”

Isla nodded and now her tears came freely, running down her face. Alice crouched beside her and put her arm around her shoulders, pulling her close. She held her until she had reached into her apron for a handkerchief and the tears had subsided. When she had regained her composure, Lizzie pulled her chair forward and held her hands in her own.

“You mentioned that George did not get on with Ewan McCrae.”

Isla sniffed. “Yes. He was always criticising George, whatever he did was never right. George would get angry and answer back and Ewan would shout back at him, making threats. He probably never intended to carry them out but he made George's life here a misery. That's one reason why he wanted to leave. George's Dad used to nag him all the time too so it was not surprising George wanted to go."

"From the conversation we overheard, it sounds as though you want to leave too."

"I do and I will. When George left, he told me he would find my Mother. When she left, she was heading for Glasgow. George said he would try to find her and then come back for me. He'd help me get away and I could go and live with my Mother. My Dad would not like that at all. He couldn't face losing me to her. He wants to come out on top in everything. He wants to be the winner. I'm afraid he would do anything to stop me leaving."

"So you think that your Dad..."

"...may have killed George," Isla finished.

The faint drone of aircraft engines reached their ears. The test was beginning.

CHAPTER 27

It was approaching eleven hundred hours when Robbie McBane found the Police Station. He parked the borrowed Humber on the roadside, reflecting on how good it was to drive a superior car, and walked briskly to the door of the building where he rang the bell. The door was opened by a large constable who looked him up and down inquisitively before allowing him to enter. Robbie was wearing his uniform and was a little offended by the scrutiny.

"I've come to see Sergeant MacGregor. Please tell him I'm here."

"Sergeant's out at the moment. He won't be long though. You can either take a seat and wait or you can talk to me."

"You are?"

"PC McDonald. And who are you?"

"My name is Sergeant McBane from the RAF Police Special Investigation Branch. I'm staying at Glenstriven House where we discovered the body of a young man."

"Ah yes, George Hodges. Tragic. I accompanied the body across the water yesterday."

"Thank you. I need to update Sergeant MacGregor with events from last night."

As he spoke, MacGregor's heavy tread was heard on the steps and, moments later, he joined them in the office. "Ah McBane. Hello. How are things at the big house?"

"Do you know the ferryman, Gordon McClaughlin?"

Both police officers nodded. "Aye we do. What of it?"

Last evening, we apprehended two boys, Rory and Billy, who were poaching on the Glenstriven Estate. They'd been there since Friday night. They say that Gordon McClaughlin took them there in his boat, provided them with a rifle and told them he would pay them for any animals they were able to take. Apparently, he was going to sell them on to someone in Glasgow. It sounds like a nice little black market racket he's got going on."

"Gordon McClaughlin? Well I didn't know he was up to that. Did you McDonald?"

"Why would I know, Sarge? He's not about much as he's on the ferry."

"We tried to catch him last night but he gave us the slip. However, we did see him load one carcass into his boat and he would have loaded the other if I had not stopped him. He can't wriggle out of this as I'm a witness. This is a civilian matter, so could you please arrest him?"

"Aye, we can do that."

"But I need to interview him because the boys said that he had also asked them to see what was going on in the Loch and to tell him. He said he would pay them for any information. That means he is supplying someone else with that information, perhaps an enemy spy. That is very serious."

MacGregor blew through his teeth making a whistle. McDonald lifted a pair of binoculars from the desk and went to the window. He scanned the sea. "I can see the ferry starting out now to come back here. We can go down to the pier and pick him up when he arrives."

"Please do that Constable."

McDonald picked up his helmet, placed it carefully on his head and left the building.

"When you come over to Glenstriven, Sergeant, you'll also need to arrest the two boys. The older one Rory seems as hard as nails...wouldn't say anything , but the younger one, Billy, was very forthcoming. He's not cut out for that kind of work. Seemed more keen on getting inside and being fed."

"Aye that would be right. I know both of them. Daft pair! I suppose it was the prospect of earning some money. There's not much work around here even with many of the younger men off at the fighting."

"My view is that the boys are not responsible for the murder of George Hodges. They did have a rifle and used it to shoot the animals but the shot to George's forehead looked as though it was close range. A rifle would have made much more mess at close range and you'd have to be a good marksman to hit the temple from a distance."

"You still think it was murder?"

"I do, aye. We've ruled out an intruder on the Estate. The camp was being used by George and the strange sightings on the Loch can be discounted. That's the Navy doing something. We've got one suspect at Glenstriven. I just need to pursue this spy link with McClaughlin."

◆ ◆ ◆

Lizzie and Alice made their way up the stairs to their own room in silence but as soon as the door was closed behind them, Lizzie burst into shocked speech. "Hamish Ferguson. Goodness. That's another suspect for Robbie. Isla was very forthcoming about him wasn't she?"

"She was. The word that worried me was 'controlling'. He obviously drove Isla's mother away and if he is as Isla portrays him, he would not think twice about threatening George to stay away. He is so protective of Isla."

"That's one word for it." Lizzie paused. "I don't think we should tackle him though. We should leave it to Robbie. He may want to go a particular way to work with him."

"I agree. We mustn't do anything to compromise the investigation."

"Group Captain Boggen?"

"I know you dislike him, Lizzie, but what motive would he have for murdering George. I mean he's probably never even met him."

"True. What about Ewan McCrae?"

"He could be a tricky customer. He obviously didn't like George, probably was instrumental in driving him away whatever anyone else did. I think we should start with the softer targets, try to get more information about why George left."

"I agree. I can't see any reason why Jessica, Maureen and David Hodges would want George dead. I mean, even if George and his father did not get on, I can't see a father murdering his own son."

"There's plenty of boys of that age don't get on with their fathers and girls with their mothers for that matter."

Lizzie looked at Alice. She was frowning and Lizzie knew she was thinking about the relationship with her own mother, a woman who seemed to have no interest in either of her children. "What about the Blairbuies?"

Alice looked up sharply. "What possible reason could either of them have to murder George? James Blairbuie does not have that degree of malice in him and I suspect that Virginia Blairbuie would regard George as being beneath her notice."

"She is an arrogant woman, bitter too at having to live here away from London society. I don't feel there is much point in questioning her. She would tell us nothing, probably even refuse to meet us. James Blairbuie would be more helpful but I'm not sure he would really know much about how the staff got on with each other."

"Let's see if we can talk with Maureen or David Hodges. Together or separately?"

"Together if we can. Come on then, let's go." Lizzie stood up.

Alice had a sudden thought. "The two boys. They will have been able to see the test from their window."

"They will. It doesn't matter. They can't tell anyone for a while and, besides, I'm pretty sure they saw at least one of the tests yesterday."

Before Lizzie could open the door, they heard a heavy tread on the stairs. Hamish Ferguson, puffing a little, appeared in the corridor. "Which is the room the boys are in?"

"It's this one here? Are you visiting them?"

"Hardly visiting. I've agreed to check on them and escort them to the toilet if they need it."

"Oh good. I hope they're still there. Billy will be...he's in no state to climb out of the window again and he's got no stomach for it anyway."

"Is he the one with the glasses?"

"That's right. He's a nice lad really."

"Yes," added Alice, "so go easy on him."

"Easy. That pair of little b...were stealing his Lordship's deer and sheep. I've a mind to give 'em both a good hiding."

"I think you should let the Law deal with them."

"The Law? They'll be given a slapped wrist and told not to be naughty. In my day, we knew where we stood...proper discipline."

"Well," Lizzie looked hard into Ferguson's eyes, "we'll expect them to be alive still when we come back."

◆◆◆

The rain had just started, a soft drizzle, not unpleasant, when PC McDonald began to walk down to the harbour. The sea and the air above it had turned grey, the one almost merging with the other. He stood in the lee of the passenger waiting area and watched the ferry chug closer. It bumped against the pier and Gordon McClaughlin stepped nimbly onto the side with a rope in hand. When he had secured the ferry, he helped two older ladies and a gentleman out. All three were Dunoon residents and known to Alistair McDonald.

He stepped into view and waited for McClaughlin to look up. "Now then Gordon."

"You here again? Not another body I hope."

"No...nothing like that. When you've made everything fast, you'll need to come with me. We've a few questions to ask you."

"Me? Well dinna make them difficult ...I was never clever you know."

"I think maybe you believe yourself to be more clever than us."

Gordon looked at him under lowered lashes. "I dinna ken what ye mean by that Alistair but I'll do my best. I'm ready when you are. Fire away."

"No, up at the Station."

"Oh I see. Like that is it? I hope I'll get a cup o' tea."

"I'll see what I can do." McDonald began walking and McClaughlin caught up with him.

"Gie us some kind of clue can you, Alistair? What's this about?"

PC McDonald turned to look at him. "It's about last night, Gordon. It's about young Rory and Billy."

They walked the rest of the way to the station in silence. When they entered, the two Sergeants were waiting with serious faces. MacGregor nodded at McClaughlin but said nothing, showing him to a chair in the office. The three officers took seats and Robbie McBane started.

"Mr McClaughlin, we meet again. My name is Sergeant McBane from the RAF Police." McClaughlin didn't lift his head but Robbie could see his eyes darting around looking at the three pairs of shoes. Crafty. "I suppose you are not going to deny that you took a sheep from the Glenstriven Estate last night and would have taken a deer had you not thrown it at me to get away."

His voice was gruff. "Like I said, the Laird asked me to collect them for him."

"If that was the case, why on Earth did you need to escape?"

"I didn't know you. Could have been a German spy or something."

"Naturally, I checked with Lord Blairbuie. He has not asked anyone to remove carcasses from his Estate."

McClaughlin's eyes darted to Sergeant MacGregor. "Well it wasn't himself who told me, obviously. It was one of his staff."

"Which one?"

"I canna say."

"No of course you can't because, either no one asked you to do it, or you are working in league with one of the staff there."

McClaughlin said nothing so Sergeant MacGregor took up the questioning. "You took the two boys to the Estate on Friday night, didn't you?"

"They asked me to take them there, I dinna know why."

"So you were happy to take them over fifteen miles in your boat, late at night and you didn't ask them why."

Robbie McBane had heard enough. "You're just wasting our time. You organised for them to go there to poach animals and, on Sunday night, you were picking up what they had killed. You were supposed to pick them up too but we had them under lock and key. The thing that worries me is that you asked them to see what was happening on the Loch during the day. They said you were going to pay them for information. So who's your contact, McClaughlin? Who is the spy you're working for?"

McClaughlin shuffled in his seat. PC McDonald intervened, his voice calm, reasonable. "Gordon, you were best to tell us otherwise it'll be you on a charge of espionage. You know that carries the death sentence." McClaughlin looked up suddenly, fear in his eyes.

The telephone rang, its harsh jangle a sudden intrusion into the tension of the scene. Sergeant MacGregor walked across to the desk, picked up the handset and, after confirming his name, listened carefully. The others were still and silent like statues, frozen. At last, he slowly returned the handset to its cradle.

"That was the pathologist in Glasgow. As you suspected, Sergeant McBane, the bullet that killed George Hodges was fired from the pistol you sent over for examination."

CHAPTER 28

Lizzie gently pushed open the kitchen door from the corridor where they had stood the previous day listening to Hamish and Isla arguing. She put her head around it. Maureen Hodges was standing facing someone who was out of sight in the lobby. Maureen's voice, laden with anxiety, was directed at the unseen figure.

"The letter gone? But it can't have. Who would take it? There's only us." One hand clutched her mouth and the other went to her chest. "Please God, not Jessica..." Lizzie's step on the hard flags of the kitchen suddenly registered in Maureen's consciousness and she whirled around. The door to the lobby swung closed.

Lizzie had wondered for a fleeting second whether to leave - it seemed a bad moment – but she thought that might cause Maureen more concern. She spoke as gently as she could. "Hello, Mrs Hodges...or may I call you Maureen?"

"Whichever you prefer." Maureen's reply was a bark and she turned to the stove where some onions were frying in a pan.

"Sergeant McBane has asked us to have a conversation with some of the people at Glenstriven to establish whether they saw anything unusual, any small detail that might lead us to George's killer."

Maureen looked around at her. "You think he was murdered then...didn't take his own life."

"We are sure of that Maureen, otherwise the gun would still have been at the place where he died."

"I suppose that's some relief. It was unbearable thinking that my son had killed himself...that he didn't feel able to come and talk to me."

"I can imagine," said Alice softly.

"Were you aware that George had come back to Glenstriven?"

"No. Had I known, we would have scoured the whole Estate looking for him. It's been several months now since he left."

"Do you know why he left or why he came back?"

Maureen Hodges removed the pan from the hot plate of the range and closed the insulating lid. With a heavy sigh, she sat at the large pine table in the centre of the room. "George became a troubled boy. When he was a child, he was happy and loving. He would spend hours in the woods with his dog as if he belonged there. He obviously felt he did. But he disliked school…it was not surprising really. He struggled with the books, was late to learn to read and some of the other kids were horrible to him because he was a bit slow. That only got worse as he became older. When he turned thirteen, he had grown physically and he was not prepared to tolerate it any more. He was always in fights with other kids and arguments with the teachers. They could not seem to understand that it was his way of crying out for help." Maureen looked up, her eyes appealing.

"That must have been very difficult for you," said Alice.

"It was. I'm afraid his Father tried to deal with it by threats and punishment but that just made things worse. And then there was Jessica of course."

"She did say she felt guilty because she had all the support from the Blairbuies. But she would have been too young to do anything about that."

"Yes. It wasn't her fault but all George saw was her being favoured by the Laird. She was sent to a good school, encouraged to go to university and she was bright, very bright."

"So why did he leave, Maureen?" Lizzie was keen to keep her on track; that was what they needed to know.

"I'm still wondering. I know he wanted more out of life than living here. It's in the middle of nowhere let's face it. But he just took off one day, never said a word, not even …"

She covered her face with her hands and sobbed quietly until Alice went to her and rubbed her shoulder gently. "Now, now, Maureen. You've shed too many tears about his leaving I'm sure."

When she was ready to resume, Lizzie asked, "We heard that George did not get on with Ewan McCrae."

"No. George was supposed to become the gamekeeper, work under Ewan until he knew what to do. But he was difficult, argued all the time, answered back. Ewan is a lovely man but he's not cut out for dealing with a difficult boy."

"And what about your husband? You said he tried to deal with George's behaviour by threats and punishments. That must have caused some friction."

"It did, yes. The rows were awful, both of them getting angrier and angrier and me in the middle trying to calm them down."

"Did your husband tell him to leave?"

"He did, several times... but he didn't mean it." She looked at Lizzie in alarm. "Do you think that's what drove him away?"

"I gather there was some difficulty with Isla or rather her father."

"Isla? Hamish? Not as far as I know. He had little to do with Hamish, nor Isla I think."

Lizzie and Alice exchanged a glance. "Can you think of anyone else who would want to harm George?"

"As I've said, several people were cross with him but I can't believe anyone would want to kill him. They must have realised that he was...not as bright as others. You don't think it was an outsider then, an enemy agent or someone like that? What about the two boys who were poaching? They may have shot him by accident."

"Having talked to them, we don't think they can have been responsible but they'll be arrested by the Police and taken for further questioning."

Alice glanced up at the large clock ticking above the range. We should probably let you get on Maureen or the lunch won't be ready."

Following her prompt, Maureen looked at the clock and, placing both hands on the table, hoisted herself upright. "The World doesn't stop turning though, at the moment, I wish it would."

"You still have Jessica. You must be very proud of her...doing an important job at the Ministry in London," Lizzie offered soothingly.

"Yes, but you can never forget the loss of a child, someone you carried inside you. One day, you'll probably understand that."

◆ ◆ ◆

"So definitely not the two boys then," Robbie McBane murmured, more to himself than to the others present. "It's unlikely that they went into the house, found the pistol and then returned it later. It has to be someone staying at Glenstriven. That narrows it down."

"What shall we do with this fella?" Sergeant MacGregor indicated Gordon McClaughlin.

"You can charge him with theft to start with but you'll want to know who he's selling the carcasses to. You could unearth a whole black market ring."

"Who's your contact in Glasgow, Gordon?" Sergeant MacGregor folded his arms as if he would wait for eternity for an answer.

"I can't say."

"You mean you won't say."

"They're criminal types, dangerous. I had no choice."

"Of course you had a choice. You could have reported it to us."

"You don't know who you're dealing with. They're quite capable of coming for you...or your family."

MacGregor tried to look undeterred but his eyes revealed fear. PC McDonald spoke in a kindly fashion to McClaughlin. "Gordon, you'll do yerself no favours by holding back information. Give us a name. We can do the rest. You don't have to come into it. We can arrange to pick them up as if you've said nothing. You know the kind of thing."

McClaughlin stared at his hands for several seconds. At last he said, "Jimmy Campbell from Glasgow."

Sergeant MacGregor's eyes betrayed increased fear. "He's a big fish but, as PC McDonald said, we can arrange something. I'll contact the Inspector in Glasgow. I'll make sure I mention you're to be kept out of it because you co-operated."

Gordon McCalughlin nodded with relief. Robbie McBane needed to pursue things a little further. "What I don't understand is why you'd risk poaching at Glenstriven when they have a gamekeeper."

McClaughlin shrugged. "Not much risk. Ewan is old and he's been treated badly."

Robbie's eyes narrowed. "Are you saying that McCrae knew about the poaching?"

McClaughlin smiled. "Everyone has his price. If all you have to do is turn the other way, it's easy."

"Lord Blairbuie will be interested to hear that. Now what I really need to know is to whom you are supplying information." Robbie McBane jabbed his finger at McClaughlin.

"I don't know what you mean."

Robbie exploded. "Don't give me that McClaughlin. You can't lie your way out of this. Espionage is a serious crime. You told those boys you would pay them for information about what was happening on the Loch. You're obviously supplying someone else with that information. Who is it?"

Gordon McClaughlin looked up at Robbie. "I've given you a name. It's the same person."

"So Jimmy Campbell is a quisling! He must have a contact with the Germans. I wonder who that is?"

"Keep pulling the wool, Sergeant, and you'll get to the end." Robbie McBane then added quietly, "I think this is much bigger than you or I can deal with. Your inspector needs to take it up. I just hope he remembers where the initial lead came from."

"I'll see to it he does."

"I need to get back to Glenstriven, Sergeant, and you'll need to come over to pick up the two boys. I've interviewed one person about George Hodges' murder who looks like being a strong suspect. I need to talk with all the others."

◆◆◆

"It's an outrage, that's what it is, an outrage!" Dennis Thorney slammed his folder of notes onto the table.

"I'm no fan of Sergeant McBane, Mr Thorney, but he does have to do his job."

"Do his job, Boggen, yes but he as good as accused me of selling secrets to the enemy. I'm hardly going to give years of my life working to produce weapons and then sell them for fifty quid to the enemy. Who does he think I am? I'm making an official complaint to you. You're a senior officer and should be able to court martial him or whatever it is you do in the RAF."

"I will certainly be having a word with his senior officer when I get back to my office but, for now, we must let him pursue his investigation." Paul Boggen was rather pleased at the effect this had on Thorney whom he regarded as an irritating little man, hiding in an office when better men were giving their lives for the cause. Thorney went even paler with rage than he had been before and started spluttering. "Take it easy, old man. You don't want to have a heart attack."

Dennis Thorney turned away and walked to the bay window, hands on his hips, breathing heavily. Boggen watched him, the smile on his face broadening. He was tempted to enrage him further by saying something derogatory about Highball but he chose instead to open discussion on the tests.

"What is your assessment of the test this morning, Thorney?"

Thorney wheeled around. "Highball performed very well. We have a weapon that will devastate enemy shipping such as Tirpitz. We've just got to get your pilots to deliver it properly."

The smile disappeared from Boggen's face. "And what does that mean?"

"It means, Group Captain, that your pilots need to fly at exactly the speed that has been designated."

"What evidence do you have that they were not flying at the

right speed?" Boggen's voice was cold, clipped.

"Well either the bombs dropped short or some crashed into the hull again. We've got the distance right, so it must be the speed or the height."

"You know as well as I do that the height is judged by lights being shone on the water from the nose and tail of the aircraft. When the circle of light from each overlap, the aircraft is at the right height. It works even on a day like today though not so well in bright sunshine. We'll be doing night tests in due course where that system will work very well. I can't see why there would be any difficulty with that."

"So how do you get the speed right?"

"The Mosquitos have an air speed indicator and the navigator adjusts for the wind to arrive at the speed over the ground or, in this case, water. Again, not a difficult thing to do and so I see no reason why there should be any errors." Boggen stood up so that he was talking down to Thorney. "So I conclude that it must be something wrong with your weapon."

All the rage that Thorney had brought into the room after his discussion with McBane now exploded. "There is nothing wrong with our weapon. A few tweaks may be necessary but those would not make a big difference. We need to devise a more accurate way of assessing the speed of the aircraft."

"Please be my guest. That's a job for the boffins...like you." Paul Boggen had had enough. He switched off the radio set and packed it away neatly in a corner of the room letting Thorney sound off without listening to him. The man might be a good scientist and engineer but he was, in other respects, an ass.

CHAPTER 29

"Did you hear her remark when I first went in, Alice?"

"Not fully but she seemed very upset by something."

"She was talking to someone who was in the lobby, her husband perhaps, I couldn't see. She mentioned a letter that had gone. It must have been important or she wouldn't have been so upset."

Lizzie and Alice were climbing the second stairs to their attic bedroom to kill ten minutes or so before going down for lunch. There was a rapid clatter of feet in the corridor above them and, the next minute, Hamish Ferguson came at speed down the stairs. He said nothing, pushing past them and almost knocking Alice over.

"Are you alright, Alice? What an oaf!"

"I'm fine. I wonder what the hurry was about. Perhaps he should be somewhere else and the boys took too long to go to the lavatory." They both giggled. But when they reached the top of the stairs, they could hear sobbing coming from the room opposite theirs, the one where the two boys were detained. Lizzie frowned and they both listened at the door. It was unmistakably Billy.

Lizzie could feel herself softening. Tenderness was not the emotion that usually first filled her breast but something about Billy's vulnerability had touched her...and perhaps she was amused, even flattered by his clear interest in her. The enforced captivity must be preying on Billy's mind. He had now been away from home since Friday evening and was clearly someone who liked his creature comforts.

She unlocked the door and opened it. Rory was slumped on one bed ignoring Billy who was curled up on the other bed, his hands over his head. "Billy, what's wrong?"

"He's a bloody child, that's what's wrong." Rory did not turn his head and spat the words with utter contempt.

"Billy, come with us." Lizzie pulled one arm to remove the hand from his face and continued to pull him firmly until he had to sit up on the bed. "Come on. You can tell us what the problem is."

Billy slowly stood up. He had stopped sobbing when Lizzie and Alice had entered but his eyes were red. He allowed himself to be led from the room. Alice closed and bolted the door behind them. Lizzie, still holding his arm, opened the door to their own room where she sat Billy on her bed. She nestled beside him and noticed the blush that spread over his cheeks.

"What is it Billy? Are you missing home?"

"I am but it's not that." He sniffed and then took a deep breath. "That man...he was trying to make me...you know...say that Rory and I killed that young chap."

"The dead young man's name was George, Billy," Alice said in her soft, calm voice. "Which other man are you talking about?"

"He just left."

"You mean Hamish Ferguson, the Estate Manager?"

"I don't know his name. Big, dark hair, crooked nose."

"That's Hamish. What did he do to you? Tell us everything that happened."

"He took Rory to the toilet and then brought him back. He did the same for me but when he brought me back, he didn't let me go in the room. He grabbed me by the neck and pushed me up against the wall just outside the door. His face was right in mine and I could feel his breath on me when he spoke. It was no more than a whisper."

"What was he saying?" Lizzie asked.

"He kept saying that we had shot that man...George...and that, if I didn't admit it, he would make sure I paid. I could feel his fingers on my neck and he was squeezing. I couldn't move." Billy sobbed and Lizzie slipped her arm around him to stop him crying. She could feel his body relax a little. "And did you or Rory shoot George?"

"No...we only saw him from a distance and then we saw his body. Rory would not do that and I certainly couldn't do it...my eyes."

Lizzie looked at Billy, his glasses grubby and perched at a slight angle on his nose. "If you are not guilty, Billy, you have nothing to fear. I am sure you'll be taken home this afternoon. You will be in court for poaching but that won't be a serious sentence. Perhaps best not to do it again though."

"Don't worry, Miss. I'll never do this again."

◆ ◆ ◆

Robbie McBane pulled the car to a halt at the rear of Glenstriven House, skidding slightly on the gravel. He was out of the Humber and into the house in seconds and strode along the corridor behind the kitchen to the drawing room. As he expected, Paul Boggen was inside, reclining on a sofa with a glass of whisky in his hand.

"Sir."

"McBane. How did you get on?"

"Gordon McClaughlin has been arrested. His contact for disposing of the carcasses and passing on information about activity on the Loch is one Jimmy Campbell from Glasgow. Sergeant MacGregor will be liaising with his superior officers in Glasgow to have him arrested. He's a nasty piece of work, apparently. Fingers in all sorts of pies and all illegal. I almost felt sorry for McClaughlin. He clearly had little choice but to go along with it. I will need to speak with Lord Blairbuie and let him know about something else."

"Well done, McBane. You've obviously made up for the cock-up last night. By the way, you seem to have upset our friend Mr Thorney."

"Upsetting people is part and parcel of my job, Group Captain. I have to ask uncomfortable questions and in Mr Thorney's case there are more to ask."

Paul Boggen raised his eyebrows. "Do tell."

"I don't think that's wise at this stage, Sir. The most important point arising from my visit to Dunoon was a telephone call to Sergeant MacGregor from the science bods in Glasgow Police. The bullet that killed George Hodges was definitely fired from your gun, Sir."

Boggen stared at McBane as if not comprehending his words. He put his glass down carefully on the occasional table next to him and stood up slowly. "What are you saying, McBane?"

"I'm saying your gun was used to kill George Hodges...Sir."

"Now look here, McBane, I've had enough of your insubordination. You stand there and as good as tell me that I murdered that boy. I did not do so. I didn't know him, had never met him and had absolutely no reason to murder him. Is that clear?"

"It is clear, Sir, and I am not accusing you of murder. It is very important though that I know exactly where your gun was left and at what time. Someone picked it up and took it out to murder George and I need to establish who might have had the opportunity to do so. Now, I saw you take it out of your holster to show us all on Saturday evening in Lord Blairbuie's study. Did you put it back in the holster?"

"I don't know, McBane. As I said, I was sure I had put it back in the holster and therefore had taken it out of the Library with me but perhaps I didn't. Perhaps, after a few drinks and a very good dinner, I neglected to do so. If that was the case, anyone in the house could have taken it."

"Yes, Sir, which is why it is so important that you try to remember." Robbie McBane glanced at his watch. "You will need to excuse me, Sir. I must visit the bathroom before lunch." Robbie did not wait for an answer but left Boggen standing open mouthed. As he left the room, Jessica passed him in the doorway on her way in. She smiled weakly and without warmth, her mind clearly elsewhere.

"Ah Jessica. You look very tired, my dear. This must be a terrible strain for you and your parents."

"Yes, it is." Jessica began to walk towards the piano and then stopped and turned. "I trust you were happy with the test this morning, Group Captain."

"It's still not right but we'll get there." He moved towards her. "I wish I could do something to relieve your sorrow, Jessica." He stood close beside her and his arm slid around her waist. She could feel the gentle pressure pulling her towards him. She stumbled a little which brought her body against his and she felt his lips on her forehead. "I do have a very broad shoulder, Jessica, if you want to talk about things." He bent his head and kissed her on the cheek, then lower and then his lips were on her mouth.

She pulled away and faced him. "That is not appropriate Group Captain and will certainly do nothing to relieve my sorrow."

He held his hands up face outwards. "I'm sorry my dear, I couldn't help myself. Even in your sorrow, perhaps especially in your sorrow, you are a very attractive young woman."

"Yes 'young' and not interested in a lecherous old man." She turned abruptly and left the room at speed, leaving Boggen once more open-mouthed.

◆ ◆ ◆

As on the previous day, lunch was delayed until thirteen thirty hours to allow the second test to proceed as planned. Lady Blairbuie clearly did not see any need to forego any of the formality of the household. It was a tense affair. Everyone seemed to be watching others, perhaps trying to guess what their motive might be for killing George. Lizzie was itching to ask Robbie what had happened at Dunoon and even more keen to tell him what they had discovered. She had to content herself with watching Dennis Thorney holding court about anything and everything that was vacuous whilst, occasionally, glaring at Robbie with open hostility. It was not easy for Robbie being the target of such anger.

At last, lunch was finished and, as they left the Dining Room, Lizzie hissed urgently in Robbie's ear that she needed to fill him in on what they had discovered. She and Alice took him up to their own room and he sat self-consciously on Lizzie's bed where Billy had sat while Alice sat opposite him on her own bed and Lizzie stood restlessly by the window.

"Tell us first what happened at Dunoon, Robbie."

"McClaughlin was arrested and eventually admitted the whole thing. He was being pressurised into both the poaching and the information gathering by a dangerous character from Glasgow's underworld. MacGregor's Inspector will pick that up. But he did imply that Ewan McCrae has been taking back-handers to turn a blind eye to the poaching on the estate."

"Ewan McCrae? I wonder if George was on to him…perhaps threatened to tell Lord Blairbuie."

"It's a possibility, Lizzie, but that adds another suspect to the list. The main thing that's new is that the bullet in George's temple was fired from Boggen's gun."

"So he's a suspect too?"

"I think we shouldn't jump to that conclusion, Lizzie." Alice smiled indulgently at her.

"Naturally Boggen denied it and I can't see any reason why he would want to kill George. The infuriating thing is that he can't remember whether he returned his pistol to its holster after taking it out to show us on Saturday night."

"Uh! I'm not surprised," said Lizzie. "If his pistol is a euphemism for something else, I expect he puts it in so many places, he can't remember."

"Lizzie! You are shocking."

"Well come on Alice. Just think about that car journey from RAF Turnberry. He couldn't keep his hands to himself until I made it clear that I didn't want them anywhere near me!"

"I was not using it as a euphemism, Lizzie. Where that pistol was and who had access to it are crucial."

"Sorry, Robbie, but Boggen really makes me cross."

"I'd never have guessed. Anyway, that puts the two boys in the clear. MacGregor will be over at some point today to pick them up and charge them with poaching."

"We've had a busy morning too, Robbie. We spoke with Isla first while you were with Thorney. She said her father, Hamish, had threatened George because he had found him with Isla... doing...you know. Isla thinks that's why George left and that her father may have killed George when he returned. George was going to help Isla get away from Glenstriven and join her Mother in Glasgow. We have just comforted Billy because...listen to this...Hamish used physical violence against him, squeezing his neck, to try to get him to admit to killing George. That has to be a sign of covering up."

Robbie looked suitably shocked.

Alice broke in. "We then spoke with Maureen Hodges. She has no idea really why George left. He did have rows with his Father because David could not deal with him. David often told George to go but did not mean it. Father son rows are quite normal aren't they?"

"But before we started talking to her, I overheard her saying to someone that the letter had gone. No idea what letter and it may be nothing to do with George but worth mentioning."

Robbie stood up and took two paces towards the window. Lizzie moved aside to let him look out. He stood thinking for several seconds. "Let's summarise our progress then. We can discount McClaughlin and the boys, that's a separate issue. Dennis Thorney may have killed George if he had been threatened with disclosure about his willingness to give away secrets to the enemy. Hamish Ferguson may have killed him to carry out his threat regarding George returning. He is very.... how shall I put it?... protective of Isla isn't he? Ewan McCrae may have killed him to stop him revealing his part in the poaching and David Hodges may have killed him in a fit of paternal anger."

"There could be others too, Robbie. Those are just the ones we know about!"

CHAPTER 30

Some minutes after Robbie had left the room, there was a tap on the door. It was Jessica. "I've come up here to... but..."

"What's wrong Jess?"

Jessica's face screwed up but she could not stop a single tear running down her cheek. "That man...he tried to kiss me." She shuddered at the memory.

Lizzie and Alice were on their feet and standing either side of her in a second. "What man?" Lizzie asked, her anger already rising.

"Boggen."

"I knew it. He's a monster. He thinks every woman is there for his pleasure. Probably thinks you should be flattered by the attention."

"It's extraordinary when he knows you are grieving for your brother." Alice stroked Jess's arm.

"He used that as a pretext. You know the sort of thing...'There, there my dear, let me comfort you'. I don't know why I'm so upset by it really. I've dealt with plenty of situations like that before but there's something about him...it felt unnatural somehow."

"I'm afraid it's what I expect from that man."

"I'll be fine in a minute or two...just need to regain my composure then I'll look at the test. It's all so overwhelming." Jessican flopped onto Alice's bed but, within seconds, sat upright. "This will never do. There's a War on." She stood up. "Thanks girls. It's so good to have you two around. I'll see you later." And with that she left the room.

"That Boggen. I'm going to have to say something to him you know. He makes me so angry."

"I hope, Lizzie, you are thinking about why you get so angry. Perhaps there's something you have not dealt with fully."

Lizzie looked at Alice sharply and then looked away. "There is, Alice. You're right, but in good time and besides, we should not accept that behaviour from men. We're not their playthings." She took a couple of steps to the window and looked down on the courtyard. A police car pulled up next to where Robbie had parked the Humber. Sergeant MacGregor stepped out and walked over to the back door. Lizzie wanted to have a word with MacGregor if she could.

A few minutes later, she heard a heavy tread on the stairs and she slipped out of the room to wait in the corridor. Sure enough, Sergeant MacGregor, puffing loudly, reached the top of the stairs.

"Afternoon, Miss," he gasped.

"Good afternoon, Sergeant. I assume you have come to collect the two boys."

"That's correct Miss. I was told they are in this room, first on the right." He pointed to the door.

"Yes, that's the one. But before you go in, could I just have a word. The younger one, Billy, was very upset not long ago because he had been threatened by Hamish Ferguson who was trying to force him to admit he or Rory had killed George Hodges. The bullet that killed George rather disproves that, however, as it came from a pistol not the rifle that they were carrying. I hope you will go easy on Billy. He is not a hard boy like Rory."

"Aye that's very true. I've known them both for years. I was very surprised to hear that Billy was involved in this little adventure. Not surprised about Rory mind. But thank you for the suggestion, Miss. I'll get them back to the station, charge them and send them home."

"Thank you, Sergeant."

MacGregor unlocked the door and led the two boys out. "Don't try anything silly. I know where you live and you'll not avoid a charge."

Rory walked first, his head held high and a sneering smile on his face as if this arrest confirmed him as a proper criminal. Billy shuffled after him but stopped when he saw Lizzie.

He blushed again. "Just wanted to thank you Miss for...you know, earlier."

"It was my pleasure, Billy. Just think carefully before agreeing to anything in the future."

"I will Miss, I certainly will." He managed a smile which, when reciprocated, brought a fresh blush to his cheek.

Lizzie watched them disappear down the stairs and turned to find Alice standing in the open doorway of their room, a broad smile on her face. "I think you have a soft spot for young Billy."

"I think he's a nice boy who has been led astray."

"And the fact that he has an almighty crush on you has nothing to do with it."

Lizzie poked her tongue out. "Of course not."

◆ ◆ ◆

Thorney would have refused to talk to Robbie McBane had it not been for Boggen telling him in no uncertain terms that it was his duty to assist the investigation. In truth, Group Captain Boggen seemed relieved to escape another post-test discussion with Thorney, a man whom, as far as Robbie could see, he clearly did not like and did not respect.

The clock on the mantlepiece in Lord Blairbuie's library ticked in the silence after Robbie's question. He waited several seconds that seemed more like a minute before repeating it. "Did you see George Hodges whilst out for your morning walk first thing on Sunday?"

"I did."

"Did you speak to him?"

"Yes, briefly."

Robbie sighed. "Mr Thorney, this would be over much more quickly if you would simply tell me what happened when you met him."

Thorney stared at Robbie his piggish eyes enlarged through his spectacles. He appeared to make a decision. "Alright, McBane.

I'll tell you exactly what happened. I went out on Sunday morning with a folder of notes about the test to familiarise myself with the scene, the layout of the land and so on as well as to get some air. I was walking along the Loch shore. I didn't see him until he suddenly stood in front of me just a few yards away. He was pointing a rifle at me. I froze. 'Mr Thorney?' he said. 'Yes' I replied. 'I've been sent to offer you a deal.' I asked him what kind of deal he was talking about. As you can imagine, I feared for my life and was really trying to buy time to assess the situation."

Robbie nodded. "I can imagine." Thorney seemed now relieved to be talking.

"He didn't answer for a bit but he lowered the rifle. Then he said he had money for me and there would be plenty more if I were willing to give away the details of the weapon being tested. I asked him what he wanted specifically. He looked confused and said he didn't want anything today but, if I agreed to it, someone would approach me when I was back home. I was worried that if I didn't go along with it, he would shoot me and take the folder anyway. I asked him a few more questions and he didn't seem to know the answers so I became a bit more confident. I said I was not willing to betray my country for a few quid."

"How did he react to that?"

"He started getting agitated…it wasn't really anger but…I don't know, he seemed to be thrown by that as if he didn't know what to do. He obviously expected me to accept the offer. He was dithering about for a bit looking increasingly wild to be honest. So I said I had to go and turned away. My heart was in my mouth. It meant I couldn't see what he was doing and would not be able to avoid a bullet if he fired the rifle. Then he shouted at me to stop. I turned around expecting to be facing the barrel of the gun again but he held it loosely by his side and, in his left hand, he was holding an envelope."

"And what then?"

"I still can't believe it. He threw the envelope on the ground at my feet and walked off. I didn't see him again."

"So you picked the envelope up and brought it back here. Why didn't you report it to me, hand it over?"

"I intended to discuss it with the Head of Security at Brooklands and hand it in then. You'll have to accept, McBane, that I don't know you. Why should I trust you?"

"I think it would have been better to mention it. I have only your account after all and it would have been more convincing had you offered that information at the outset. You have drawn suspicion on yourself, Mr Thorney, and, frankly, I cannot rule you out as a suspect for George's murder. How do I know that you didn't take Boggen's pistol and shoot George to get the money from him? Or perhaps he threatened to report you for taking the money and you needed to silence him."

"I have given you my account and I give you my word, as a gentleman, that my account is the absolute truth."

"Your word as a gentleman? This is not some story for boys – tales of honour and chivalry. I base my judgements on evidence and, at the moment, the evidence suggests you may be the killer. At least I don't have to tell you not to go anywhere. We will almost certainly need to speak again."

Robbie McBane left the room, the horrified eyes of Dennis Thorney following him.

◆ ◆ ◆

Lizzie wanted to talk to David Hodges. She was sure he had been the person Maureen was addressing about the missing letter. She did not know why it was important, indeed she had to admit that it may have nothing to do with George's death, but she was tenacious and would leave no stone unturned to discover what had happened out there by the Loch. Alice had agreed to accompany Lizzie to 'keep an eye on her' she said. David Hodges, Lizzie had discovered, always wound the clock on the stable block at fifteen hundred hours on a Monday. They would go to the hay loft as if they were exploring and come across him as if by chance.

The stable block was now used as a garage as the Blairbuie's had long since sold the horses. At the side of the building was a door that they had been told was the entrance to the hay loft. It was, naturally, unlocked. Lizzie opened it slowly but fortunately it did not creak. She would prefer to give Hodges no warning of their arrival. Inside, a set of wooden stairs led upwards; they were old and grubby but seemed very firm. Lizzie and Alice walked lightly on tip-toe to make as little sound as possible.

A grimy window gave some light onto the small landing at the top of the stairs and a flimsy door presumably gave entrance to the loft itself. The smell of old hay, dusty, almost enough to cause one to cough, filled their nostrils. Lizzie and Alice stopped. There were voices inside.

"Has he talked to you?" The accent was Scottish, but not the broad dialect of Ewan McCrae. It sounded like Hamish Ferguson.

"No. You?"

"No, but he will. We need to be singing from the same hymn sheet."

A creaking sound, a spring being wound perhaps, reached their ears during the brief pause in the conversation.

"I don't feel like singing. My son has been murdered and I'm wondering..."

"Don't go imagining things, Hodges. Let's just discuss what we say. It's best to say as little as possible."

"Sounds like you've been in this position before."

"No I haven't. We don't know what he's already found out but perhaps he knows nothing about that incident."

"Maybe Isla has said something."

"As far as I know, he's not talked to her either. I don't think she would say anything anyway...too embarrassed."

"But if she does?"

"I'll just say that I told George to leave Isla alone...which is what I did tell him."

"There was more to it than that as you very well know."

"Aye there was, but no one except you and I know that."

Again there was a pause in the conversation and the spring

creaked.

"I should never have agreed to it but you forced my hand. You gave me no real choice. If I didn't send him away, you'd have reported him to the Police. He would have ended up in prison. He'd never have coped with that. But what we've never discussed is what else you said to him. Did you threaten to kill him if he came back?"

"Of course not."

"You see, I think you did and that's why I'm thinking you put that bullet in his brain."

"I could never do that, David, whatever he had done."

"It's David now is it? You're the type to do it sure enough. You've a temper haven't you and you don't like being crossed at all. You want everything your way, you want to be in charge, in control. That's why your wife left, that's why Isla wants to leave."

"Don't you bring her into it. And you've got a temper. You rowed with George plenty of times. I know because Isla told me how you treated him. What happened? Did he make you angry? Did you grab a gun? Did you put it against his temple and pull the trigger?" The voice was goading, a vicious snarl.

"Don't try to pin it on me," Hodges yelled. "I would not harm my own son. It was you wasn't it? That's why you've come around here now trying to get me to cover it all up."

"Put that down Hodges, don't be a fool. Think about Maureen."

Lizzie thrust the door open and walked in. The heavy winding handle was held high in the hand of David Hodges. "Good afternoon, gentlemen. We're just having a look around."

CHAPTER 31

The cottage nestled into the edge of the woodland as if trying to hide. There was a sort of garden in front but not much, a patch of grass and some neglected shrubs. Robbie McBane knocked on the door and waited. At last, a heavy tread inside preceded the door being yanked open, screeching in protest.

Ewan McCrae stood in the open doorway, staring at Robbie with no attempt to disguise his suspicion. "Yes. What is it?"

"I didn't know whether I would find you here. Thought you may be out in the woods at this time."

"I've just come back for a cup of tea." There was defiance in his manner, as if daring Robbie to accuse him of neglecting his work.

Robbie smiled, trying to keep his voice pleasant though he was finding it difficult, knowing what he did now know about McCrae. "I need to ask you a few questions, Ewan, as, this morning, I said I would." McCrae stood in silence holding the door. For a moment Robbie thought he was going to refuse. "Perhaps I could come in?"

Ewan McCrae turned on his heel and stomped down the hall to the kitchen at the back of the cottage leaving Robbie to close the door behind him and follow. The kitchen was untidy, dark, the trees outside blocking much of the daylight and the dirty window adding another filter. Unwashed dishes were piled beside the sink but the fire in the range was lit, its warmth filling the room. It was the home of a bachelor and one who was not houseproud. Ewan sat heavily on a chair at one end of the small table that was pushed against the end wall and Robbie turned one of the other chairs to sit facing him.

"I gather that you did not get on with George."

"That's right. He was fine as a kid but he became

argumentative and offensive in his teens...wouldn't do what I told him to do, always answering back. He was a bad piece of work."

"Why did George leave Glenstriven?"

"No idea, other than the obvious. He argued with everyone, obviously hated it here and wanted to get away. Good riddance to him I say. Such a shame for his poor mother. She's a lovely woman."

"I've been told that Hamish Ferguson may have told him to leave in order to keep him away from Isla. Do you know anything about that?"

"No...but Hamish is a man who likes everyone to do what he wants, when he wants."

"I assume that you don't get on with him either."

"No. It won't be for much longer though. I'll be finishing soon."

"Where will you go?"

"Dunoon I suppose. God knows where. I've no family. Perhaps find a room."

"Perhaps your friend Gordon McClaughlin can help you out."

Ewan McCrae looked up sharply. "Why do you say that?"

"Gordon McClaughlin was, this morning, arrested for arranging poaching on this Estate. He set up those two boys. He admitted everything." Robbie noticed how McCrae looked at the floor and shuffled his feet. "He'll no doubt serve time at His Majesty's pleasure. I hope he paid you a good sum of money for turning a blind eye."

"What do you mean?"

"You know very well what I mean, Ewan. I am obliged to tell Lord Blairbuie about your arrangement."

Ewan McCrae initially looked sheepish then shrugged. "Doesna matter now. I'm finishing soon anyway."

"He may of course ask for you to be charged as well."

"Aye... well he should have had more regard for my long service. If you use people and then throw them out, what can you expect? I had every right to try to protect my future."

"What I'm trying to establish, Ewan, is what George's killer hoped to gain. What was his motive? Let's say that George found out about your arrangement with Gordon McClaughlin and threatened to expose you. You may have wanted to keep him quiet."

Ewan McCrae's eyes blazed with anger. "Oh I see. That's it is it? You've come here to pin the blame on me. Well it won't wash. What evidence do you have of that? Hey? What evidence?"

"None Ewan but I had to put it to you. You must admit, it is a possibility."

"How troubled am I that you're going to tell the Laird? Hardly at all. Would I kill someone to stop him telling Blairbuie? Of course not. I'll take the punishment if there is one. They can't do much more to me than turn me out of my home."

Robbie let Ewan's anger subside before speaking again. "Ewan, you have a rifle, the one I saw yesterday. Do you have any other guns?"

"Aye."

Robbie waited for a second or two but McCrae said nothing more. He could see that this interview was not going to become any easier. "What other guns do you have?"

"Shotgun, twelve bore, two barrels."

"Do you have a pistol, any kind of hand gun?"

"No. I've no need for anything like that."

"Could you please show me where you keep your guns."

Ewan McCrae hoisted himself up from the table, sighing deeply with irritation. He led the way into a small sitting room and pointed to a corner where the rifle and shotgun were propped.

"That's not very secure, Ewan."

"Doesna need to be secure out here."

"Do you lock the door of the cottage when you are out?"

"No."

"We have been told that George had a rifle with him on Sunday morning. Where would he have got that? I assume he didn't bring it with him."

"Well it wasna mine. I can tell if it's been moved and it wasn't. Anyway, if he was murdered sometime on Sunday morning as you think, he would have had the rifle with him. Someone else would have had to bring it back here."

"Yes...you're right. The bullet that killed George came from Group Captain Boggen's pistol. Someone took it, shot George and returned it to Lord Blairbuie's library. Was that you?"

"Are ye daft? If I'd wanted to kill George, I'd have taken my own rifle. Why would I go to the trouble of getting another gun?"

"To place the blame elsewhere."

Ewan McCrae turned to face Robbie; there was malice in his eyes and his voice was low, slow and cold. "I did not kill George and you've no right to come into my house accusing me. It's time for you to leave."

◆ ◆ ◆

"I hope Lord Blairbuie doesn't press charges."

"What if he does? It'll just be a fine or maybe a few weeks in the jail house."

"But what MacGregor said...about having a record. That's bad...might cause us problems in the future."

"You're just a bairn, Billy. Stop worrying about the future. Live for the present, that's my motto. We'll deal with whatever happens if and when it arises."

The two boys had just been released from the Police Station in Dunoon with warnings that they may be charged if Lord Blairbuie wished it. Macgregor had promised all sorts of unpleasant consequences if they were caught doing anything like that again, even if they weren't charged this time. Billy had been remorseful, anxious to say he had learned his lesson, even pointing out that he had helped the investigation by mentioning McClaughlin. Rory had sat in defiant silence, a faint smile on his face as if he found the whole thing amusing.

Billy, huddled inside his coat, was trotting beside Rory who was walking purposefully with large strides. “Where are we going now? I need to get home.”

“There'll be time enough for that soon. We have to see Gordon first, find out what he's told them.”

Billy was not looking forward to the encounter. McClaughlin would know from MacGregor that he had spilled the beans. But he didn't regret doing so. They had been foolish to agree to going to Glenstriven and, as for passing on information about the tests, that was completely ni...ni...whatever the word was that MacGregor had used. And he was right. They should have thought it through more carefully. Who but a German spy would want to know what was happening on the Loch?

MacGregor had said that McClaughlin had been released on bail so that he could continue his duties on the ferry. They had been warned by the Sergeant not to say anything about the whole thing to anyone but he assumed that McClaughlin was not included in that as he knew all about it. Rory stopped on the pier, staring out over the water. The ferry was making its way back to the Dunoon side, wisps of black smoke from the exhaust torn away in the wind. The rain had stopped but a dark shroud of grey clouds rolled remorselessly across the water which danced restlessly in the breeze.

It seemed to Billy to take an age for the ferry to pull alongside the jetty, the three passengers to disembark and Gordon to kill the engine. He took his time making the boat fast to the jetty and, at last, moved towards them with a heavy tread. “Now then lads.”

“I wanted you to know, Gordon, that it wasna me that told the Poliss anything.”

“So if not you, Rory, who was it?” Gordon McClaughlin's eyes swivelled to Billy and fixed him with a stare that was accusation, judgement and execution in one.

“I had to tell them, Gordon. They were going to accuse us of murder. I'm not going down for that.”

“Aye, that lad, George Hodges. Had to take his body across the other side yesterday.”

"In future, Gordon, I'll go on me own. Billy here is not up to that kind of thing. He's scared of his own shadow, blabs at the slightest thing. He fancied one of them young women. She was bonnie enough, I'll gie him that, but he was like butter in her fingers. He'd have told her anything. Hoping for a kiss were you not, Billy?"

Billy blushed despite his efforts to prevent it. "Don't be daft. She's miles older than me."

"Didn't stop you dreaming about her though." Billy kicked at a wooden crate on the jetty but said nothing. "Anyway, we saw some things on the Loch if you're happy to pay like you said."

"Thanks to young Billy here, the deal's off. I had to tell McGregor and that RAF man who was behind it. I just hope they do what they promised and pick him up before he gets to me."

"Who was behind it?"

"It's best you don't know, Rory. He's a very dangerous man. I only agreed to the whole scheme because he gave me no choice."

"No choice?" Billy was suddenly assertive. "We all have a choice, Gordon."

"You think so do you?" Gordon McClaughlin took a step closer to Billy so that he was right in front of him. He leaned forward and glared into Billy's eyes. Billy shrank back a little but did not move. "You have a choice alright. You can choose to go along with it or you can choose to have your fingernails pulled out one by one, your ear cut off and sent to your Mammy or they might just get it over with quickly and blow your head off wi' a shotgun. You call that a choice, Billy. I don't!"

"You could have told the Poliss."

McClaughlin shook his head slowly. "It's nice that you have so much confidence in MacGregor and McDonald but the man I'm talking about would have done something to you before those idiots would have dressed in the morning."

They fell silent and Billy looked out across the water. Where the sky thinned, a patch of lurid, orange light moved ominously towards them. The sky looked angry and Billy could feel unaccustomed anger growing inside him. Images flashed into Billy's mind from the newsreel he had seen at the cinema a couple of years ago. It was in black and white of course but he could imagine the colours: London burning in the Blitz and, another time, piles of rubble in Glasgow after a German raid. How could he ever have agreed to give information to an unknown person who was probably selling it to the Germans?

Rory broke the silence. "When it's all died down, we can go again…without Billy this time."

"Damn right, without me. I'll no get myself involved in that kind of thing again. There's a better way to live than crime. And giving secrets to the enemy is not something I'm going to let happen. If I get any hint of you doing that again, I'll be straight into that Poliss Station."

Both Rory and Gordon McClaughlin stared at Billy. Never before had they seen such confidence, determination, clarity from him.

"I may wear glasses but, somehow, I'm going to do my bit in this War." He turned and walked away, leaving them gaping on the pier.

CHAPTER 32

Lizzie and Alice saw Robbie McBane trudge back to Glenstriven House, hunched against the rain that had started falling again. He came through the back door, through the lobby and they intercepted him in the corridor.

"Robbie, we've got something for you, something important."

"That's good. I'm getting nowhere."

Lizzie took his hand and led him to the stairs which all three ascended in silence. Once inside Lizzie and Alice's room, Lizzie looked excitedly into Robbie's eyes. "Alice and I went to talk to David Hodges who always winds the clock in the stable block on a Monday afternoon. We walked to the top of the stairs and were about to go into the hayloft when we heard voices. It was Hamish Ferguson and David Hodges and they were getting very angry with each other."

"To cut probably a long story short," Alice broke in, "and putting what we heard together with what we already know, it sounds as though Hamish Ferguson told David Hodges to send his son away or else he would tell the Police that George had abused...perhaps stronger than that...Isla. David Hodges became very angry that Ferguson had effectively given him no choice."

"And then he pretty well accused Ferguson of murdering his son when George came back to Glenstriven." Lizzie took over the narrative again. "It sounded as though Hodges was going to attack Ferguson so we went in, all innocent, saying we were just looking round. David Hodges had the heavy iron clock-winding handle in his hand raised above his head and clearly about to bash Ferguson on the head with it. There was a very tense moment and then Ferguson left very abruptly."

Robbie McBane looked from Lizzie to Alice. "So this is more

evidence that Ferguson might have been responsible for the murder but it is speculation, not hard evidence."

"It is, yes. But the incident this afternoon also suggests that David Hodges might have killed his own son in a fit of temper. He was well and truly roused and would have hit Ferguson with that handle. It would probably have killed him."

"It adds another suspect to the list, Alice, but everything in human nature would prevent a man from killing his own son."

"Not necessarily, Robbie. There's been plenty of murders committed by close family members in hot blood."

"How did you get on with Ewan McCrae, Robbie?" Lizzie asked.

"As you know, he's another one with motive though I'm not convinced his motive would have been powerful enough to lead him to murder George. He was very defensive, had no regret about cheating Lord Blairbuie and no fear of whatever consequences might follow. It seemed a case of, now he was losing his home, he had nothing else of value to lose…not even his freedom. It's sad when a working life ends like that. I do wonder that Lord Blairbuie made that decision."

"But wasn't it Hamish Ferguson who wanted him off the Estate so he didn't get in the way?"

"Yes it was , Alice."

"Hamish Ferguson again."

Robbie slumped onto the bed with a sigh. "McCrae did say that Ferguson wanted everything done his own way and expected everyone else to comply."

Although not heavy, the rain was sufficient to make some sound against the windows and leave spots of water which occasionally dribbled down the panes of glass, gathering other drops as they did so.

"We mustn't forget Thorney. He's not in the clear."

"No he isn't, Lizzie. I just can't think how we can prove or disprove his account of the meeting with George yesterday morning."

"If it was Thorney, perhaps what happened is George grabbed one of his papers and Thorney grabbed it back, leaving that corner of paper in George's hand. If that's what happened, one of the papers in Thorney's briefcase will have a corner missing."

"If I ask Thorney to show me his papers, he'll either claim they are top secret and I don't have clearance or he will remove the torn paper before showing me."

"So let's not tell him we're checking them."

"How do you mean, Lizzie?"

"She means that she will go into Thorney's room, get into his briefcase and check the papers without Thorney's permission or knowledge."

Lizzie smiled. "You know me too well, Alice."

You can't do that, Lizzie. If he is the killer and he catches you..."

Lizzie smiled again. "Just a thought."

◆ ◆ ◆

Alice stood nervously at the bottom of the stairs that led to the attic rooms. They had made sure that Thorney was not in his room but they did not know where he had gone. Alice had tried to dissuade Lizzie from going into his room again but she knew she could not stop her and therefore the next best thing to do was to keep watch. If Thorney appeared, she would have to keep him talking somehow and find some way of warning Lizzie. Achieving the first would be hard enough but she had no idea how she could achieve the second. If she had possessed a whistle, she could have blown it but how she would explain that to Thorney she had no idea. Anyway, it was academic as she did not have a whistle.

Her position allowed her to see the length of the corridor on the first floor from which the main guest rooms were accessed. It was considerably more impressive and comfortable than their own, attic corridor with a richly-patterned strip of carpet stretching its length and pictures of former Blairbuies adorning the walls. Some five yards along it, was the top of the stairs which led to the ground floor. If Thorney returned, he would emerge from those stairs, turn towards her and head for the stairs to the attic rooms. She would have those few, short yards to delay him.

What would other women do? She smiled to herself at the thought of slowly sliding her hand up her thigh, lifting the hem of her skirt. She knew she could never do that, it simply was not her and the thought of the short, tubby, balding Thorney would make it very difficult to try even the most innocent of flirtations. Lizzie had suggested she ask him about some of the things he had been boring everyone with. He could talk for hours on any of them and the occasional remark feeding his sense of his own worth would be sure to keep him occupied.

Alice was not as confident as Lizzie that she could do that but she would try. If she failed and Thorney found Lizzie in his room, she could not conceive how Lizzie would deal with it. She would just have to accept the tirade of angry abuse he would direct at her. But, as Lizzie had said, what could he actually do? Report her to Commander Trueman, their boss? She would get a dressing down but she was far too good a pilot to lose from the ATA. Lizzie was very confident, perhaps over confident, about her ability to deal with situations. The conversation had concluded by her saying that she was certain Alice would be able to stall Thorney for long enough. The pressure was on her then.

Every minute that passed made Alice easier. Surely Lizzie would not take more than a few minutes. The longer no one came up those stairs, the less likely it would be that Lizzie would be caught.

She waited.

Then she heard steps, muffled by the carpet, on the stairs from the ground floor. She tensed, ready to give a bright smile and a hearty greeting to Thorney. She would ask him about piano playing, might even ask him to go with her to the drawing room to play something. Despite this idea, her heart was pounding and she hoped that the smile she gave would not be an ugly grimace.

When she judged the figure was about to arrive at the top of the stairs and come into view, she forced a smile onto her face and took one step forward. But…it was not Thorney who appeared; it was Group Captain Boggen. Her smile disappeared with the surprise but she quickly brought it back to her face.

"Group Captain Boggen. How nice to see you."

Boggen looked at her in surprise and then his eyes lit up in response to her smile. "And it's lovely to see you my dear. Where are you off to?"

"Oh…I thought…I might…actually I don't know. I'm at a bit of a loose end."

He smiled indulgently and came towards her. "So am I as it happens. There's not much to do out here is there?"

"No, not when it's raining."

"You know I've been wanting to have a chat with you. I am really fascinated by your role in the Air Transport Auxiliary. Young Miss Barnes is quite frosty but I know you and I could have a very good conversation. Why don't you come along to my room and we can chat while we look at the view of the Loch. Even on a day like today, it is spectacular."

"Oh no…I can't…you see I've just remembered I'm waiting for Lizzie."

He chuckled to himself and slipped his left arm around her waist pulling her to him. He lifted his right hand and stroked her face gently with the back of his fingers, looking into her eyes. Then his lips were on hers, hard, pushing, passionate. His right hand moved down to her breast and she tried to pull away but he was too strong. With his lips still on hers, he began to move her slowly along the corridor towards his own room, her hands pushing ineffectually against his chest.

◆ ◆ ◆

"I'll come straight to the point, Mr Ferguson, did you threaten George Hodges with violence if he didn't leave or if he tried to return to Glenstriven?"

"No."

The face was sullen, defiant and Robbie knew he was unlikely to achieve anything from the interview but he was determined to persist if only to make clear that he would not be deterred from carrying out a thorough investigation.

"Tell me about the incident between George and your daughter, Isla."

"That's none of your business."

"George is dead, Mr Ferguson. I know there was some issue about what he might have done to your daughter and it is very relevant to this investigation."

"If you know about it, why are you asking?"

"Because I don't know every detail. What did George do?"

Ferguson stared back fixedly and Robbie thought he would say nothing but, after a few seconds of hostile silence, his words came in an angry torrent. "I found him with my daughter. She was only sixteen, just, and he had her pinned on the sofa, lying on top of her, with his hand up her jumper and kissing her. He was an animal. How dare he touch my daughter like that? If I hadna come in at that moment, I know what he would have done next. He would have raped her."

Robbie let Ferguson subside a little, though anger had not left him by any means. "Are you sure George Hodges was acting without Isla's consent?"

"Consent? What do you mean? He was taking liberties, that much was obvious."

"Did you discuss it with Isla afterwards?"

"There was nothing to discuss."

"I think there was, Mr Ferguson, I think there was. I believe Isla and George had a relationship – girlfriend and boyfriend – and Isla was not a victim of sexual abuse but a willing participant in a romantic encounter, the sort that boys and girls do have."

"I suppose you think you know my daughter better than I do?"

"Know her? I don't claim that but perhaps I understand her

better. You see, your argument with Isla in the kitchen was overheard and it was clear that she was not at all happy with the way you had dealt with that incident." Robbie could see Ferguson's anger building but he needed to press the point home. "I don't think you are capable of listening to Isla. You don't understand that she is a young woman needing to find her way in life. You are too keen on imposing your will on her...and everyone else apparently. You have a temper which is visible now. Your conversation with David Hodges earlier was overheard and it is clear that you threatened to report George to the Police unless his father told him to leave Glenstriven. You have access to this house. You had the opportunity to take Boggen's pistol from where he had left it and go in search of George. You had a clear motive to murder George Hodges. Did you do so?"

Ferguson was on his feet and shouting. "I'm not going to sit here and listen to these groundless accusations. How dare you? How dare you? I did not like George...he was a poor specimen of a boy and I did not want him near my daughter but I did not kill him."

He turned towards the door.

"You're going to lose your daughter, Mr Ferguson, unless you listen to her, respect her needs and wishes."

Ferguson turned back and, with the ferocity of a lion, growled, "I'll not lose my daughter. She's mine, understand, mine and no one is going to take her from me."

The door of the library slammed behind him.

CHAPTER 33

It was the briefcase Lizzie knew she had to find. Thorney had made no attempt to hide it; it was in plain sight sitting beside the bedside cabinet. She lifted it onto the bed and knelt in front of it. It had two catches set close to the ends with buttons that slid to the side to release them. She pressed one holding her other hand over it to dampen any sound it might make when it flicked open. The button did not move and the catch did not release. She tried the other one but the same thing happened.

"Blast," she whispered. Each catch had a three digit combination lock; Thorney had probably used the same combination for each side but what could it be? Three digits. What would one use as a combination? She thought of the chain and combination lock she had used as a child on her bicycle. It had to be something easily remembered but something a stranger would not know. She had used her date of birth, the day and the month: ten and three for 10th March 1920. That was the place to start. How could she discover Thorney's date of birth?

The bedside cabinet may contain something of his. She opened the drawer but there was nothing in it. The cupboard underneath it was similarly empty. Dennis Thorney certainly travelled light. She felt under the mattress, running her hand carefully along each side and the bottom. She checked under the pillow and managed to get her hand under the headboard to check the top end of the mattress. Nothing. Looking around the room, she realised that there was only one other place she might find something...the wardrobe.

The door needed a little tug to open it and she grimaced at the sound made when it gave. Inside was a jacket hanging on a hanger and a few clothes on the shelves. Thorney's suitcase was at the bottom of the hanging space; it was not locked but when she opened it, she found it empty. The jacket then. She checked the outside pockets: a handkerchief and a packet of cough sweets in one, a comb in the other. The inside pocket was more fruitful and with a smile of satisfaction, she withdrew a wallet.

Flicking it open, she saw a photograph of Thorney in a very smart suit with a buttonhole and beside him his bride. Her eyes suggested a shyness, unused to being in the limelight, but there was certainly also pleasure, even a hint of pride. Thorney was beaming straight at the camera, shoulders back, head held high. The round stomach had not yet formed but his sense of his own importance was very evident. Were they a happy couple, Lizzie wondered? People had such different expectations of a relationship and it was, of course, the way of things back then – perhaps still in the present time - that the man would assume a dominant role. The photograph was evidence of Thorney's personal life; he had a wife and perhaps children. A dim sense of guilt infected Lizzie. Perhaps she had been too quick to condemn him.

She dragged herself quickly back to the task in hand, flicking through the items in the wallet but ignoring the money. With a small surge of excitement, she found in a pocket of the wallet a Brooklands identity card, which gave his name and section in the organisation, and, on it, was his date of birth. Lizzie carried it speedily to the briefcase on the bed and used the day and month of birth in numbers as she had done with her bicycle lock: four, zero, five. Again she tried to push the latch buttons aside but the locks did not release. The urgency she now felt made her nervous, desperate. What about month and year? She rolled the numbers around to five, nine, nine on one lock and tried it. With a soft click and to her relief, the latch flew up. The other latch responded to the same numbers.

Inside were two folders. Opening the first, she took out the wad of papers inside and turned them over, examining the corners of each. Nothing missing. She repeated the exercise with the other folder but again no corners were missing. Perhaps Thorney was in the clear.

Suddenly a door slammed somewhere in the house and she jumped with a start. Swiftly, she put the folders back in the briefcase and closed the latches. She could hear other noises below, scuffling, voices. Returning her attention to the locks, she realised she had not memorised the numbers that had been set when she first took hold of the briefcase. She would have to turn the dials randomly and hope that Thorney did not notice.

She had just replaced the briefcase when she heard a shout. The voice…it was Alice's. Thorney must have returned and Alice was struggling with him to prevent him discovering the intruder in his bedroom. Lizzie leapt to her feet and rushed to the door but with a jolt realised she had left the identity card and wallet on the bed. Almost whimpering with frustration, she grabbed the card, pushed it back into the right section of the wallet and returned it to Thorney's jacket. She was out of the door and running down the corridor in a second.

◆ ◆ ◆

Robbie McBane was feeling something of a failure. Thorney had stormed out of his first interview with him and now Ferguson had done the same. Both incidents suggested guilt but they couldn't both be responsible for George's murder…or could they? He sighed. This case was as impenetrable as the two murders he had dealt with at RAF Silverstone in February and RAF Cranwell in March. He now needed to find Lord and Lady Blairbuie to establish their movements and ask whether they had seen anything unusual. He also needed to break the news to Lord Blairbuie that his gamekeeper had been taking back-handers. James Blairbuie was an honourable man, a gentle soul, who would never suspect anyone else of foul play. The knowledge of Ewan McCrae's disloyalty would be hard on him.

There was no sign of James Blairbuie in the drawing room so Robbie McBane decided to try his 'den' as the Laird called it. Robbie had been wondering what was in the room. He tapped on the door and after a few seconds it was opened enough for Blairbuie's head and shoulders to be visible though his body prevented Robbie from seeing into the room.

"Ah it's you McBane." He opened the door wider and nodded for Robbie to enter. "Forgive the caution but this is my private space and I guard it jealously."

Most of the room was taken up with a huge model railway arranged in a large U shape and set at table height. On the opposite wall, was a workbench with tools and various parts of rolling stock, scenery and materials laid out. Being at the front of the house, the window gave a view of the lawns falling gently to the Loch, the boathouse sat half in and half out of the water.

"My private obsession...model railways."

"It's very impressive, m'Lord."

"James please, Sergeant."

"Thank you, Sir. Did you construct it yourself?"

"Yes, every piece of it and I built most of the engines and rolling stock too. I buy the parts of course, the clockwork motors and so forth. There's an excellent shop in Glasgow. That's my guilty treat to go there occasionally. It's strange really that I should have this interest and yet love this place for its serenity. But it's a great diversion when the weather is poor."

"I can imagine, Si...James." Robbie was intrigued and would have loved to be given a demonstration of the railway in operation but he knew he must press on with the matter in hand. "I must, firstly, let you know about something that has emerged as a result of my investigations. Ewan McCrae... I'm afraid he has been taking back-handers from that man we apprehended last night, Gordon McClaughlin, to turn a blind eye to poaching on the estate. I think that's why he wasn't keen to investigate the camp too thoroughly."

James Blairbuie looked shocked and then saddened. He sat in a chair and looked out of the window. "I should have handled him differently. It was Hamish's advice to remove him. I understood the logic of it and yet it seemed a harsh way to treat a man who has worked on the estate for so long." He looked back to Robbie.

"I assume that was why he did it."

"Yes, he said as much. I have to keep in mind the possibility that George discovered what he was up to and threatened to tell you. Perhaps McCrae decided to silence him."

"Good God! Surely not? I can't believe Ewan would go that far, even though he didn't like George."

"In his defence, he did point out that he was not troubled when I said I would be telling you. His response was that, as he was losing his home, he had little else to lose."

A look of pain settled on James Blairbuie's face. "Losing his cottage has hit him harder than I would have imagined."

"McClaughlin has been charged with conspiracy to commit theft; I think Sergeant MacGregor would like a steer from you as to whether to charge the two boys and McCrae."

James Blairbuie again gazed out of the window. It was a good minute before he spoke. "Those two boys were young, easily led. I think a warning may be sufficient. Perhaps one of them could be an assistant gamekeeper. There's no one more committed, you know, than a former poacher. But that's for the future. As for Ewan, I would be grateful if Sergeant MacGregor would leave him up to me. I need to have a conversation with him. I should not have treated him as I did."

"I'll let MacGregor know your thoughts, Sir, but if you change your mind…"

"I'll not change my mind, Robbie."

"I also have to ask you your movements late Saturday evening and early Sunday morning. Did you leave the house?"

"No I didn't. Virginia takes the dogs for a walk in the morning and again late afternoon though of course they spend a fair bit of time running around the estate too."

"Did you see anything unusual?"

Lord Blairbuie shook his head slowly. "No…apart from that craft in the Loch."

"Do you know by any chance why George left Glenstriven or why he returned?"

"No to both questions. I've always assumed that he left

because he was fed up with being nagged by everyone. He didn't get on with anyone here I don't think."

I haven't caught up with Langford as yet. He gives nothing away does he? Always hovering in the background."

Janes Blairbuie smiled. "Yes, the perfect butler. He was my Father's batman in the second Boer War and after it, my Father employed him as butler. He's been with the family since. He is utterly loyal, completely discreet and gentle, though," Blairbuie chuckled, "my Father said he could be ruthless in battle. He's certainly not your killer, Robbie.

"Thank you, Sir. I now need to find Lady Blairbuie."

"She'll be in her room at the other end of the house, what we call the morning room."

◆ ◆ ◆

Lizzie bounded down the stairs from the attic, unconcerned about who might hear. She rushed along the first floor corridor, hearing voices raised, Alice and...Boggen, it must be. When she reached the door of the Green Room, she flung it open and strode in, stopping just inside. Alice was struggling with Boggen whose back was to Lizzie and who was gripping Alice tightly, trying to keep one hand over her mouth to stifle her protests.

Lizzie took a deep breath and shouted as loudly as she could. "Let her go, you animal, let her go."

Boggen had been so pre-occupied, he had not noticed Lizzie's entrance. He let Alice go and whirled round. "Don't you ever knock?"

"Not when my friend is being attacked. How dare you? Is Virginia Blairbuie not enough for you? Is that it? You have to try it on with everything in a skirt. Good God!"

Alice ducked away from Boggen and stood beside Lizzie. She was trying to look calm but Lizzie could see she was trembling.

Boggen's face distorted into an ugly, contemptuous sneer. "Why are you being so precious about it? Jealous are you? You want some attention too perhaps?"

"You disgust me. You're a senior officer. You should be setting an example. We should not have to fear for ourselves around you. What happened to decency and chivalry?"

"You may not have noticed, Dear, but there's a War on. Not much decency and chivalry in war."

Lizzie exploded again. "But that's what we are fighting for, you imbecile, to preserve decency, fairness...

Alice tugged at Lizzie's sleeve. "Let's just go, Lizzie."

"How dare you?" Boggen stepped up to Lizzie, threat in his snarling face and in his body, arched towards her. "Who do you think you are? You are addressing a senior officer in His Majesty's Royal Air Force and I can get you booted out of that tinpot organisation you are in. Just remember that in future." Boggen jabbed his index finger at Lizzie, pushing it into her chest between her breasts.

"And when I report you to your senior officers, where will you be?"

Boggen stepped back and laughed. "Report me? Who's going to take your word over mine?"

Lizzie was furious but said nothing for a few moments. "Was it you? Did George challenge you about your antics? Perhaps he found you attacking Jessica and you killed him to silence him." With that, Lizzie took Alice's hand and left the room slamming the door behind them.

CHAPTER 34

Robbie tapped on the door of the morning room. There was no instruction to enter so he opened the door and stepped inside. "Lady Blairbuie...I hope I'm not interrupting you."

"Sergeant, come in. No you're not, I'm just reading. Apart from walking the dogs, there's precious little to do around here except read. I have to stock up with books when we go to Glasgow, which is not very often. Anyway, what can I do for you?" She had been reclining on a sofa but now swung her legs onto the floor and sat up. She patted the seat beside her. "Come and sit down. Any diversion is welcome."

Robbie sat beside her though ensuring he was as far away from her as the arm of the sofa allowed. He turned towards her. "I just need to catch up with you Lady Blairbuie, as I said I would do, to find out your movements late on Saturday and early Sunday morning and to ask if you had noticed anything unusual."

"Well, let me think. I took the dogs out on Saturday afternoon, probably at about three o'clock. I had not long returned to the house when all you people arrived. On Sunday morning, I took the dogs out again as I usually do before breakfast."

"That's your usual routine is it? I thought you tended to rise late in the mornings."

"Occasionally I do but, most mornings, I take the dogs out before breakfast. James likes to believe that I'm lying in bed." She smiled and shifted a little closer to Robbie.

"Erm...and did you see anything unusual on your walks? Did you see George for example."

"No...no, I didn't. But then I walked the other way along the Loch, going South. George was found to the North of the house I believe."

"Yes he was. I think you heard gunshots on Friday night?"

"That's correct. I assumed we had a poacher on the Estate. We do have them sometimes."

"May I ask you what you thought about George when he was living on the Estate?"

Virginia Blairbuie shrugged. "I don't know what to say really. Obviously, I had nothing to do with him really. You know you don't really notice the children of the servants."

"But you did notice Jessica."

Lady Blairbuie became brisk, the smile fading from her eyes and her face becoming hard. "Jessica is different. As you have probably discovered yourself, she is rather special. She was as a child. It was clear that she was very intelligent and her talents would have been wasted had we not provided a good education for her."

"I have the impression that George resented that."

"Perhaps he did. I don't know but George struggled with learning. Spending a lot of money on his education would have been pointless." She smiled again. "So, Sergeant, have you made any progress in your investigation?"

"I can't really discuss that with you, Lady Blairbuie, but we have made some."

"No prime suspects as yet then?"

"No. It is proving complex."

Lady Blairbuie leaned closer. "Tell me...Robbie – it is Robbie isn't it?"

"That's right."

"Tell me...what gave you such a fine...physique?"

Robbie shuffled uncomfortably but he could not move further away unless he stood. "Fine physique? Well thank you, Lady Blairbuie. I suppose it was playing rugby and all the training."

"Ah yes. I can see the muscle in your legs." She placed the tip of her finger on Robbie's knee and drew it slowly up his thigh. She leaned even closer towards him until he could feel her breath on his cheek. "Do you find me attractive, Robbie?"

Robbie was on his feet. "Well thank you, Lady Blairbuie, I

really must get on."

Virginia Blairbuie seemed amused by Robbie's confusion. She stood and moved close to him, pressing her left breast against his body. "You can call me Virginia, Robbie. Why don't we meet later...in my room?"

"I must go," he said, hurriedly stepping away from her and leaving the room.

◆ ◆ ◆

Lizzie took Alice up the stairs to their own room and sat her on her bed. She lowered herself to be close beside her and put an arm around her. At last Alice was able to speak.

"Thank you, Lizzie. I don't know what I would have done if...."

"You would have found the strength to kick him where it really hurts and you would have got away."

"I wish I was like you, Lizzie."

"Don't wish that, Alice. I'm a mess. I can't believe that man. What right does he have to treat us like that? I'm afraid you've had the worst of it Alice."

"Probably thought I wouldn't resist."

"I'm not sure he even thinks about it. He lets his animal instincts take over and yet he tries to present himself as civilised and sophisticated." Lizzie stole a glance at Alice's face. Naturally, she looked shaken. "Are you going to be alright, Alice?"

"Oh yes. I just need a few minutes to calm myself." Alice's breathing was now slower and steady. "You certainly gave him a sting with your tongue, Lizzie, but what did you mean about Virginia Blairbuie?"

"The first night we were here, I couldn't sleep so I went for a little walk. I went into the room opposite and looked out over the Loch and then, when I came out, I went down the stairs. At the bottom, I thought I heard voices and I walked along. They were coming from the Green Room – Boggen's room that is. It was Virginia Blairbuie and Boggen. I think they must have known each other a long time ago and they were being…amorous."

Alice said nothing for a minute and Lizzie did not push her to talk. She would do so in her own time. At last, Alice said, "Lizzie, you have said before that something bad happened to you… something to do with a man or men. Is that why you are so angry about men who try to take liberties?"

Lizzie felt the lump in her throat that always came when she thought of the past. "I have had a couple of bad experiences when a man tried to take liberties as you put it. And yes, it does make me very angry. But the problem started when I was a child. I was abused by a so-called friend of my parents. If I'm honest, I've never really come to terms with it."

Alice looked up into Lizzie's eyes but she turned away, feeling the smart of a tear. "You know, Lizzie, it is good to talk about these things. You can't let it rule you for the rest of your life. Robbie McBane is a good man. He's not like Boggen and he loves you, I know he does. You should hold onto him, Lizzie. Don't let a good man slip away."

"I know I should but…"

"But what?"

"It's so hard because I think, what if I can't…you know… if the memories come flooding back and stop me from…giving myself?"

"The memories won't come back, Lizzie, because you are in love. It's not the same."

Lizzie stood up. "I hope you're right, Alice."

"I am, Lizzie, I know I am. I know you are in love with him though you don't seem to have realised that yet. You should go and find him. Tell him how you feel."

"But I don't know how I feel."

Despite her recent ordeal, Alice smiled. "Something will happen to reveal your feelings."

"I must go and find Robbie anyway to tell him about what Boggen did. Is that alright for me to do, Alice?"

"Yes, it is but I don't expect him to do anything about it. Now leave me to recover please."

"We can report him when we get back to White Waltham. Trueman will support us. When I've gone, Alice, pull the bolt across the door. I'll see you later." Lizzie bent and kissed Alice on the cheek.

She moved down the attic stairs to the first floor half hoping she would see Boggen again so she could give him another salvo but also half hoping she would not see him. He would be prepared this time and ready for her. She needed to find Robbie and let him know about her search of Thorney's room. She would also vent her anger at Boggen and hope Robbie would be prepared to make a complaint through his senior officer as well as the complaint that she and Alice would lodge with their own boss.

She met him in the corridor by the drawing room, walking towards her from the end of the house...Virginia Blairbuie's morning room. His face looked somehow grey, his eyes troubled. "Robbie, I need to up-date you on two things. I went..."

"Not here, Lizzie. Let's go into Lord B's library."

She followed him in silence, stifling the urge to rant about Boggen. She would deal with Thorney first. Robbie entered the library, knocking as a precaution and putting his head around the door to check it was empty. She followed him and closed the door. "So, firstly, Robbie, I found nothing in Boggen's room that suggested he had ripped one of his papers from George's hand. Everything was intact. I managed to get into his briefcase by finding his wallet in his jacket and using his date of birth."

Robbie smiled weakly. "You'd make a good spy, Lizzie."

"It doesn't mean we can discount Thorney as a suspect of course but it looks less likely that he was responsible." Robbie nodded. "But the other thing, continued Lizzie, "is that Boggen, monster that he is, attacked Alice...pulled her into his room and tried to put his hand...you know. Alice and I will make a formal complaint about him when we get back to White Waltham but I think you should too...or do something to him."

"What can I do, Lizzie?"

"You're in the RAF Police. Surely there's something you can

do? I mean RAF people can't behave like that however senior they are."

"I'll see what I can do, Lizzie."

"Do you know what he said when I told him we would make a complaint? He said 'It's your word against mine and no one will believe you.' He's insufferable!"

"Right now, Lizzie, I need to concentrate on trying to solve this murder. We have suspects but nothing conclusive.

"But Robbie, aren't you even going to say something to Boggen, let him know that you know and that you'll make a complaint. Next time, he may succeed in achieving his evil desires."

"No, Lizzie. I need to concentrate on George's murder."

"You know, Robbie, sometimes I think you would achieve nothing if I didn't nag you."

Robbie suddenly turned to face her and his face was angry. "And sometimes, Lizzie, you interfere too much. I've given you my answer now leave me to think things through." He turned away.

Lizzie felt stung as if she had been slapped on the face. She opened her mouth but no words came. She turned away so he would not see that her eyes were beginning to water and left the room, closing the door quietly behind her.

She needed to go somewhere she could recover. Not her room because Alice would probably be in there and Alice would know however much she tried to hide it. Soft piano music was drifting along the corridor from the drawing room. It did not sound like the rather pompous music that Thorney would play. She opened the door quietly and peered in. Jessica was sitting at the piano, a book spread on the music stand, her hands lifting and falling gently on the keyboard, rich and tragic chords constantly shifting and changing. She did not notice Lizzie until she had finished the piece and Lizzie coughed.

"Lizzie!"

"That was beautiful, Jessica. What was it?"

"A very short piece by Chopin. I love it for its sombre tones, especially now. This is my way of trying to recover from George's death. It's what I most like to do at Glenstriven anyway."

Lizzie could feel Jessica's eyes on her. "I wish I could play like that," she said, turning away to look through the window at the clouds scudding over the Loch towards the House.

"There's something wrong, Lizzie."

The sympathy, the understanding in Jessica's quiet voice undid Lizzie. She squeezed her eyes closed tightly but could not stop a tear rolling down her cheek. She felt Jessica's arms around her. "It's nothing," she sniffed, "just had a disagreement with someone."

Jessica turned her round so they were facing and she put one finger under Lizzie's chin to raise her head. "Let me guess...with Robbie."

Lizzie looked surprised. "How did you know?"

Jessica smiled, leaned forward and kissed Lizzie on the cheek. "Because I've seen the look in your eyes and the look in his. You love him don't you?" Lizzie could feel tears start again and could only nod. "The fact that you are so upset proves it. If you didn't care for him, you would be cross not upset."

"He called me interfering. That doesn't sound as though he likes me."

"He's just under pressure, Lizzie, and, when under pressure, we all take it out on the people we know won't desert us. And you must not give up on him now because you've had a little tiff. By the way, have you told him you love him?"

Lizzie shook her head. "To be honest, I didn't know I did until just now."

Jessica looked almost pityingly at Lizzie. "Don't let him slip away, Lizzie. You will regret it for the rest of your life."

CHAPTER 35

"Thank you Mr Langford for making time to meet me."

Langford sat stiffly in the chair, clearly uncomfortable being seated in his master's library. From his starched collar to his highly polished shoes, he was the classic image of a butler. He wore pin-striped trousers and a morning coat with a grey waistcoat. A chain, presumably gold, made a graceful arc from the buttonhole on his waistcoat to the side pocket. "My time is always at the disposal of others, Sir."

Robbie almost smiled at the formality of the response, the subservience so habitual that he suspected Langford could never depart from it. He was a creature that lived by the wishes and whims of others and Robbie imagined him consulting the fob watch frequently to ensure that everything ran on time. He wanted to put him at ease. "I gather you have been with the family for many years."

"Yes, Sir. I was the former Lord Blairbuie's batman – that's the present Laird's father – during the second Boer War and he very kindly gave me employment after it. I have worked for the family since 1902, forty-one years." The accent was slightly cultivated but Langford's London roots just occasionally broke through the polished surface.

"You've seen many changes then."

"Yes indeed, though some things, the essential things, do not change."

"What sort of things are you thinking of?"

"The basic qualities of service, duty and loyalty."

"You have certainly shown those qualities in abundance to this family."

"I like to think so, Sir."

"Do you have a family?"

"No, Sir. I never married...I suppose because I went straight into service after the War – the Boer war I mean - and the opportunity for courtship did not arise."

"But you have siblings, brothers and sisters?"

"No, Sir, and my parents are long dead. My family is this household whether they be in London or here."

Robbie nodded slowly. Langford was the archetypal, inscrutable servant, giving away nothing, not because he was secretive but because his role demanded that his own personal concerns should never be revealed. What a tragedy that someone should deny themselves a life to serve others. But perhaps not. Fulfilment was the most important thing to achieve and Langford had obviously found that in his role as butler to the Blairbuies. For a moment, Robbie's mind flashed to the recent encounter with Lizzie and he felt a pang of guilt, fear, a sickness in his stomach. Had he destroyed a promising relationship? Would he end his days like Langford? But then Lizzie had always said that she would not entertain a relationship until the war ended and her task in the ATA was done. Duty before personal happiness. It was a noble sentiment.

Robbie pulled himself back to the present. "I need to ask you about your movements late on Saturday and early Sunday morning. Did you leave the house at all?"

"My duties are confined to the house, Sir."

"Did you see anything unusual, perhaps George somewhere."

"No, Sir, nothing unusual...except Group Captain Boggen's pistol in this room."

"Yes, it was careless of him to leave it."

"It's not my place to comment on the actions of the guests, Sir."

"No, quite. How did you get on with George when he was here?"

"I had no dealings with him, Sir. He spent his time on the estate when he was older and, as I said, my duties are confined to the house."

Robbie looked out of the window. Even if Langford knew

something, he would say nothing. He remembered Lord Blairbuie's description of Langford. It was glowing, warm and Robbie could see it fitted the man who sat placidly in front of him. But one of Blairbuie's comments...'he could be ruthless in battle' echoed in Robbie's mind. He could not see this mild-mannered man as a ruthless warrior. Perhaps age and servitude had dampened any fire he may once have had. Blairbuie was almost certainly right: Langford was not George's killer.

Langford took his watch from his waistcoat pocket and glanced at the time. "You will need to excuse me, Sir, I need to set up the dining room for dinner."

◆ ◆ ◆

The bell on the stable clock chimed six times and Alice decided she would go downstairs. She checked her face in the slightly distorting old mirror on the dressing table in their room and smiled at her reflection, not because she was pleased with her appearance but because you had to 'prepare a face to meet the faces that you meet'. The line from T S Eliot's poem had stuck in her mind since schooldays. When Boggen had first attacked her, she had been shocked, then upset but now...now she was angry. How dare he? She would confront him before dinner, even if that meant doing so in front of others. In fact, perhaps it would be best to do so with others at least nearby in case he tried again. Discretion was, after all, the better part of valour.

She set her face in the mirror to determination. That's what she felt now. She was determined not to be intimidated. Speaking in a whisper, she told herself that she was a professional woman doing a difficult and necessary job and no one...no one had the right to treat her like a...a woman of the night.

Holding her head high, she made her way downstairs, intending to go to the drawing room and wait for Boggen to arrive. However, when she reached the corridor on the first floor, she saw Boggen heading towards her. She could easily make the stairs to the ground floor well before he reached her. As she descended the next staircase, however, she decided that her new resolve to assert herself should not allow her to scurry away. At the bottom of the stairs, she took a few paces along the corridor and waited.

Moments later, Boggen appeared at the bottom of the stairs. For a moment, he looked startled but then a sickly smile spread over his face. "Miss Frobisher...what a shame..."

"You can be thankful, Group Captain, that I have met you here and not in the drawing room where others would hear what I have to say to you. What you did to me earlier was utterly unacceptable. How dare you think you have the right to satisfy your own desires without seeking the agreement of a woman? Do you suppose that your seniority in the RAF allows you to use those more junior for your own pleasure? Let me tell you plainly that it does not and I will be making a complaint to Commander Trueman who is head of the ATA about your conduct."

"Now steady on, Alice,...it was just a bit of fun."

"Fun? Fun! For you perhaps but it was not fun for me. You grabbed me, you forced me against my will into your room, you put your hand on my breast, you tried to lift my skirt. How is that 'fun' for me?"

Boggen suddenly looked boyish, his head slightly lowered, his lips twisting to one side as if ashamed. "Thing is, Alice, you are a very attractive young woman and I'm a red-blooded male. I can't help it if your beauty prompts me to..."

"What kind of defence is that? You are blaming me and my appearance for your scandalous behaviour. That's like a thief saying it was the fault of a beautiful painting that he stole it. It's no one else's fault, Group Captain, except yours." Alice made her voice steely, something she had never done before. "And if you come near me again, I will kick you very hard where it will hurt you most."

Boggen's face turned ashen and he recoiled from Alice. She turned and walked away.

◆ ◆ ◆

"I don't want to interrupt you but may I stay and listen?" Lizzie wanted a few more minutes to think through the contretemps with Robbie.

"Of course, but don't expect too much. This is an intermezzo by Brahms, one of my favourite pieces."

Grand chords started the piece followed by a delicate melody. It was slow, expansive, rich, tragic and suited Lizzie's mood perfectly. Soon she was lost in thought, sitting on a sofa out of Jessica's line of sight. 'Interfering' that was the word that had cut her. She knew she was eager to sort things out, she knew she nagged Robbie because he did not seem to grasp things as quickly. But perhaps it was just that he liked to think things through more fully. She was a bit impetuous, she knew that and she tended to jump to conclusions. That had been demonstrated on the two previous trips when she had worked with Robbie.

But it was not those rational thoughts that troubled her. It was the sense of rejection. She had always protected herself from that by never allowing herself to become attached to anyone, not really attached. But now she had. Like the incoming tide slowly creeping along the shore of the Loch, Robbie McBane had seeped into her very being. She had vowed she would never form an attachment whilst working for the ATA. But how could one resist the motions of the heart?

And now she had ruined everything.

Would she be able to look him in the face? Dinner would be served soon and there would be drinks beforehand in this room. Would she be able to avoid him until they all left the following day? She knew she ought to do something about it. She ought to go to him, apologise, tell him she cared for him, tell him she wanted to help him. But she struggled with that. Pride. She knew that's what it was. She had never, since childhood, let any man see her weak. She had always been resolute in the face of any attempt by a man to intimidate or mis-treat her. But Robbie had not mis-treated her or ever attempted to belittle her.

This feeling was new to her, a feeling that tore at her insides, drained her resolve always to be strong, destroyed her sense of herself. 'Do not let him slip away.' Jessica's words lashed her. She must not allow this disagreement to go without speaking to Robbie and if he rejected her...her heart lurched at the thought... if he rejected her, she must deal with it.

The last chord of the piece died away. Jessica stood and started to sift through music stored in the piano stool. Lizzie forced herself to put thoughts of Robbie aside and stood up. "I'd love to hear you with the piano fully open. May I lift the large lid."

As Lizzie lifted the heavy lid and propped it up, she noticed a piece of paper dropped just inside; it was not touching the strings. She picked it up and stared at it. One corner had been torn off. Quickly, she folded it and slipped it into her pocket. Jessica sat once again at the keyboard.

"Beethoven. This is perfect for my mood...the Moonlight Sonata. I'll play just the first movement. People think it's beautiful and of course it is but, to me, it is laden with tragedy."

Lizzie returned slowly to the sofa out of Jessica's line of sight. As the triplets trickled from Jessica's fingers, she pulled out the piece of paper and began to read. Her mouth opened with shock and a hand clutched her heart. This was what George had tried to hold in his left hand, she was sure of it. She must show it to Robbie without delay.

As if on some silent cue, the door opened and Robbie entered followed by Alice and a few steps behind, Boggen.

CHAPTER 36

Isla was lying on her bed, a book on her lap, but she did not seem to be reading it. She was deep in thought. There was a knock if it could be called that and then the door was thrust open. Her Father stood in the doorway.

"Shouldn't you be away over to the big house to help with the dinner?" Hamish's voice was not the usual angry snarl he adopted when talking to his daughter.

"I'm aware of the time." She did not look at him.

Hamish stopped, uncertain how to proceed. He knew he had to be reasonable but he found that difficult; he was much more used to barking orders, expecting immediate obedience. "Isla, we need to talk."

"What about?"

"This mad notion you have of leaving Glenstriven."

"There's nothing to talk about. I'm going and that's all there is to it."

"Where are you going?"

"That's my business."

"It's my business too, Isla. For God's sake, girl, I'm responsible for you and you're still a bairn."

Isla snapped the book shut and thumped it on the bedside table. "That's your problem isn't it? You can't accept that I've grown up. I'm not a child any more. I'm sixteen."

"The law says you're not an adult until you're twenty-one."

"The law also says that I can get married at sixteen."

Hamish's eyes opened wide. "You're not telling me you're going to get married surely? That would be madness at..."

"No, I'm not getting married. Who the hell would I marry? I don't know any young men any more now that George is dead... and I wasn't planning to marry him."

The two fell silent, Hamish looking at his daughter's rigid form now sitting upright on the bed and Isla's head turned to gaze through the window. Both were angry. After almost a minute of mute hostility, Isla stood and, looking directly at her Father, spoke in a measured but determined voice. "I will be leaving soon so you need to get used to the idea. I will be going to Glasgow to find my Mother."

"Your Mother is no gud..."

Isla suddenly shouted. "How dare you judge my Mother! That's all you've ever done isn't it? Judge people as if you're always right, as if you're some kind of God. You drove her away and deprived me of the one thing a child needs...a mother's love. You will not be able to stop me...unless of course you kill me like you killed George."

It was Hamish's turn to shout. "I did not kill George. How dare you shout at me and make such a ridiculous allegation?"

"Ridiculous? You told him when he left that if he ever came back, you would kill him. I know you did because he told me. You think you were protecting me from him. You weren't. I liked George...he was the only friend I had here and we were not having sex when you interrupted us but, frankly, I would have slept with him eventually just to get some kind of joy in my life."

"Isla, Isla. You are completely wrong. He was taking advantage of you because he knew you had no other friends here. He was using you but you were too young to see it." Isla said nothing. She suddenly grabbed an apron from the chair and pushed past him. "Where are you going now?"

"I'm going to the kitchen, not because I want to do that boring job and not because you came to remind me. I'm going because I want to help Maureen. She's just lost her son, remember, but still has to work."

Isla left him standing speechless, anger fighting with an awful pain in his chest. He knew he had lost his daughter.

◆ ◆ ◆

Billy sat on the bench overlooking the harbour. The rain had stopped some time ago but clouds were still racing over the water towards him. At least now there were some breaks, some occasional flashes of blue amongst the grey and the wind seemed to be slackening. What was over the water? He had never been even to Glasgow. There was a whole World out there waiting to be discovered and, with a thrill of excitement in his stomach, he knew he was going to explore it.

But how could that be achieved with his poor eyesight? What sort of job could he do to help the war effort? And would he have a criminal record because of the antics at the weekend?

He sat for a long time contemplating these questions until he became aware of a figure walking along the harbour wall towards him. It was PC McDonald.

"Now then, young Billy? What're you up to? Not waiting for a boat to take you poaching again I hope." PC McDonald sat heavily on the bench beside him.

"No, Constable, I'll never do that again. It's not right."

"That's true…it's not right."

"I'm just wondering whether Lord Blairbuie will press charges. Sergeant MacGregor said he might."

"Aye he might. We'll just have to wait and see. I think it won't go hard on ye though. I mean Gordon should have known better than to use you two lads and Rory was the one who led you astray was he not?"

"Yes, but I should have known better. I should have told him I wasna interested. It's just that there's never any excitement round here. I thought it would be an adventure."

"I understand the need a young fella has for adventure. We've all felt that in our youth. There'll come a time when you'll be happy to avoid adventures but I suppose that comes after you've had a few of them."

"I was also wondering what I could do…you know for a job. I mean with my eyesight, they'll no let me into the Army or the Navy or the Air Force. I won't even get into the Poliss will I?"

"What d'you mean 'even'? You make it sound like it's the last resort."

Billy looked embarrassed. "No, I didn't mean it like that. I just meant that I want to do something for the War effort and, if I canna get into any of the services, I won't be able to."

"What do you know about the Civil Defence Service?"

"Is that the same as the ARP Wardens?"

"The wardens are part of it and it used to be called the ARP - Air Raid Precautions - but now that's part of The Civil Defence. They oversee the fire services, ambulance crews, first response after a bomb, messages from the ground to the command. They do vital work. Many are volunteers but they do have paid jobs. You could try that."

"But there's only wardens in Dunoon telling people to turn out lights."

"Aye, that's right, but Glasgow has a big need. You know Glasgow was badly bombed back in 1941...May it was...trying to hit ships and the docks on the Clyde."

"I know. I've seen newsreel films about it and London too in the cinema."

"They even bombed Gourock just the other side of the water here."

"I know. Would they let me in to the Civil Defence you know with my eyesight?"

"Don't see why not. You'll have to go to Glasgow and ask. Actually, come into the Station tomorrow. I think we might have some leaflets and we can make a telephone call for you perhaps."

"Would you do that for me? Even though I might have a criminal record?"

"Everyone makes mistakes when they're young, Billy, and some keep making them. But you obviously have realised the error of your ways and now you want to do some good in the World. That is to be encouraged." PC McDonald stood up, pleased to have given guidance to a young person. "I must be getting along. Probably time for you to go home, Billy. I'll see you tomorrow perhaps."

"Definitely. Thanks PC McDonald. I might be of use after all."

The officer smiled. "Oh, you'll be of use right enough, Billy. Take care now."

◆ ◆ ◆

Lizzie walked over to Robbie and Alice before they had taken more than two steps into the room. She forced herself to look at Robbie's face and saw there a haunted expression, a sadness. What had she done to the poor man?

"Robbie, I need to speak with you."

"Lizzie, I'm so s..."

"Not here, Robbie. We need to go somewhere else."

She walked past him, trying to smile at Alice and glowered at Boggen. Robbie fell in behind her and, when in the corridor, they walked in silence. Lizzie climbed quickly up the first set of stairs and then up the second, her heart thumping not with exertion but with trepidation. But she had to face it whatever was his reaction. It could not go unspoken.

Inside her own room, she turned to face him. He closed the door quietly and looked at her. Perhaps he saw on her face the same tightness, anxiety she had seen on his. She was sure it must be evident, her feelings were so strong. They both spoke at the same time.

"Robbie, I..."

"Lizzie, please..."

"Let me go first please, Robbie. There is something important I have to show you...about the murder, but first there are some things I need to say. I know I am a pain in the neck sometimes. I don't mean to be but I know I nag you and jump to conclusions and I always condemn men whom I find unpleasant and I am sorry, Robbie, I am so sorry." She fought hard to stop herself crying.

"No Lizzie, it's me who should apologise. I snapped at you because I am under pressure. There seem to be no certain leads in this case, nothing except speculation. I'm sorry, Lizzie. I cannot forgive myself for treating you in that way. You don't deserve it."

"I do, Robbie, I know I do and I know I need to be put in my place sometimes. It's hard for me to admit it, but it's true. But the thing is...the thing is..." Lizzie felt the sting of tears in her eyes. Could she bring herself to tell him what she wanted to say?

"The thing is, Lizzie, I care for you very much."

Lizzie looked up and saw the tenderness in his eyes, almost a look of being lost. Her mouth seemed to go rigid and she could say nothing. She took a step forward, longing to fling her arms around him but held back by years of suspicion, anger, fear. His arms slipped around her waist and only then did her arms slide around his neck. He held her tight and kissed her on her cheek. She felt the warmth of his body against her, the comfort of his arms around her, the joy of laying her head on his shoulder. They stood motionless for several minutes until Lizzie felt able to speak.

"I care for you too, Robbie. It has taken me so long to realise it and to admit it to myself but, Robbie, I need to tell you something about me...before you commit yourself in any way. I am damaged goods and if you want to walk away, I will not blame you...much." She managed a smile.

"I can't believe there is anything so bad that I would walk away."

"Let's sit down." They sat side by side on Lizzie's bed and she drew in a deep breath. "I'm not going to give you the story in detail, Robbie, but, when I was a child, I was abused by a friend of my family. On my tenth birthday – he and his wife were staying with us – he came to my room and ...and "

"Raped you?"

Lizzie nodded and again fought the tears threatening to ooze from her eyes. She felt Robbie's arm tightening around her, pulling her in closer. "Oh Lizzie. You poor thing. And you've carried that around with you ever since. Have you ever spoken with anyone about it?"

"Just once. At Silverstone, you may remember there was a young nurse called Patricia. We were locked up overnight and, in the darkness before dawn, I told her everything. I am so ashamed of it."

"Ashamed? Lizzie you have no reason for shame. The shame is on the animal who did that to you."

"I know that on one level, but at the same time, I can't feel anything other than shame."

"And this is why you have been unable to commit to a relationship with a man. Not surprising at all. But, Lizzie, I will never harm you, please believe me."

"I know that, Robbie. I know that." Lizzie turned her face towards him. She needed to be certain. "And now you know my dark past, can you still… love me?"

"Even more than before. I never thought anyone could replace my first love, my fiancée, my poor dead Catriona," he stifled the catch in his throat, "but here you are and you have. I know that she would be pleased that I have found someone so admirable, intelligent, vivacious…"

"Stop there or I'll become very big-headed."

Robbie looked at her and smiled. "What you mean even more so than you already are?"

She hit him playfully on the arm and kissed him on the lips. She could never have imagined that such a simple act could be so wonderful, transformative, exhilarating.

Suddenly she remembered the letter in her skirt pocket. "Robbie, you need to read this. I think this will solve the murder."

Robbie took the letter and read. When he had finished, he looked at Lizzie. "Where did you get this?"

"It was under the large piano lid, presumably put there by the killer."

"We need to think carefully how we handle this. Say nothing until after dinner."

CHAPTER 37

Dinner was almost unbearable, participating in trivial conversation whilst the letter nestled in her skirt pocket. Lizzie had slid close to Jessica in the drawing room and whispered that she wanted to speak with her in private immediately after dinner. It would be easier as Lady Blairbuie had asked Jessica to dine with them, it being her last night at Glenstriven. Robbie had spoken with Lord Blairbuie and asked that everyone proceed to the drawing room after dinner as he needed to speak with them. He had asked that Jessica, Maureen and David Hodges, Isla and Hamish Ferguson, Langford and Ewan McCrae be asked to attend. James Blairbuie looked surprised but gave Langford instructions.

When Lady Blairbuie topped up her wine glass and rose at the end of dinner, Robbie, according to the plan they had hatched, would tell her quietly that he wished to speak with her. Depending on her answers, he would then speak with her husband privately before informing the assembled group. Lizzie felt dread in her heart at the part she now had to perform in the drama. With Alice at her side, she moved close to Jessica as the other diners began to leave the dining room and, when the last had disappeared through the doorway, asked her to sit down again.

"This may be a great shock to you Jessica…unless you already know. I found this letter which I think you should read. If you wish afterwards that I had not shown it to you, I am sorry, very sorry, but I feel I must let you read it."

She handed the letter to Jessica who took it and began to read. Lizzie watched her face as the implications of the letter hit her, the horror, the anger and the devastation. All she could do was put her arm around Jessica and hold her tight while the other sobbed. After several minutes, she gently took the letter back.

"We have to go into the drawing room, Jess. Will you be able to manage that?"

"I wish I could run away...but yes, I will manage it. I can't vouch for my conduct in there but, hopefully, people will understand if I lose control."

There was surprise and consternation on the faces of many in the drawing room, surprise that they had been summoned again so soon after the meeting that morning and concern lest something would perhaps be revealed that each would prefer to remain hidden. Lizzie herself was surprised to see Virginia Blairbuie seated majestically and unflustered in her usual armchair. She passed close to Robbie and raised her eyebrows.

"She insisted she had nothing to hide," he whispered. "She obviously does not realise the letter has been found. Perhaps I should have told her but..."

Lizzie and Alice, with Jessica between them, sat close together on a sofa; Ewan McCrae, Hamish Ferguson, Isla and the Hodges hovered at the edges of the room, the same reserve evident that they had shown in the morning. Langford was distributing coffee, though only to the Blairbuie's and the guests. Alan Thorney was trying to talk with Group Captain Boggen about the tests but Boggen showed little interest.

Robbie waited until Langford, pushing the coffee trolley ahead of him, had left the room. "Ahem. Ladies and gentlemen, thank you for coming here again so soon after the briefing this morning. I want to let you know about the events of today and something that has been discovered which might lead us to George's killer. Gordon McClaughlin, the ferryman, was arrested today and charged. The two boys may be charged depending on whether Lord Blairbuie wishes to press charges" Robbie turned to him. "Have you any thoughts on that matter, Sir?"

"I see no point in charging the boys, provided MacGregor gives them a strong warning."

"Thank you, Sir. I'll communicate that to the Sergeant when I see him. Group Captain Boggen, could you please update us on the tests.

Boggen slowly stood and surveyed the room. "As you all know, the tests on the Loch have finished for now but no doubt will resume when some adjustments have been made. Mr Thorney will let us know when they are ready for more and I'm afraid we'll be back." Boggen allowed no questions and eased himself back into the armchair.

Robbie resumed. "As you know, I or Miss Barnes have talked with all of you now and have become aware of tensions especially in relation to George. However, we have no strong evidence that points to any one individual...until now that is. I'm afraid Ladies and Gentlemen what you are about to hear will be shocking to you. I apologise for that especially to those most closely concerned. This afternoon, Miss Barnes found a letter hidden under the lid of the piano in this room. It appears to have been written and signed by you, Lady Blairbuie."

Lizzie saw the narrowing of Lady Blairbuie's eyes; there was cunning there, an attempt to hide fear and there was anger. She also heard the involuntary gasp from Maureen Hodges. Jessica kept her eyes on the carpet.

"I wonder, my Lord, if you would be good enough to look at the signature on the bottom of the letter and see if you recognise it."

Lizzie took the letter to Lord Blairbuie, folding it so he could see only the signature at the bottom.

"That's Virginia's signature without a doubt."

"Let me see it." Virginia Blairbuie advanced on Lizzie and reached out to grab the letter but Lizzie turned away, keeping it out of her reach.

"It's quite alright, Lady Blairbuie," said Robbie. "The contents of the letter will now be read by Miss Barnes."

Lizzie stood up and cleared her throat.

"Dear Mr and Mrs Hodges, I thank you so much for helping me in my difficulty. Your agreement to our arrangement has lifted a weight from my mind and I will always be grateful to you. This letter is to confirm the main details of the arrangement we have made. As soon as the baby is born, you will take it as your own and raise it. In return, I will ensure that you both have employment in the Blairbuie household, whether that be in London, Scotland or elsewhere, as long as you desire it. Furthermore, I will ensure that my husband and I cover the costs of education and other expenses you will incur until the child is eighteen or has passed through university. As a gesture of my sincerity in this, I have arranged for the sum of ten thousand pounds to be paid into your bank account. You will undertake never to tell anyone, especially not the child, that I am the mother and you will raise it as your own. I look forward to seeing it grow and flourish and will have the satisfaction of knowing its future and safety are guaranteed. Lastly, if the child is a boy, please call him James after my husband but, if a girl, please name her Jessica for a young friend of mine. Yours sincerely, Lady Virginia Blairbuie."

Lizzie looked up and saw the shock on the silent faces around the room. Lady Blairbuie was ashen, her mouth open and her eyes wide with fear.

Robbie spoke. "The letter that Miss Barnes holds has one corner missing. When George's body was discovered, his left hand was holding a corner from a piece of paper. It is this scrap of paper here." Robbie reached into his pocket and produced the piece of paper taken from George's hand. He walked across to Lizzie who held up the letter. Robbie offered the corner to it and the tear matched completely. "As you can see, the corner was torn from this letter. It is reasonable to conclude that George had the letter in his grasp and it was snatched away by whoever then killed him."

"Before we get to that, Robbie, I want to hear what my wife has to say. Virginia, what on earth is this about?"

Lizzie felt sorry for Virginia Blairbuie. The arrogance, the supercilious expression on her face, the haughty assumption that she was better than everyone else had all gone and in its place was naked fear. "I'm sorry, James, I'm sorry to everyone but I was young and didn't know what to do. Please forgive me James. I did what I thought was best and Maureen and David were so kind as to help out and it suited them too. They had tried to have a child for some time but without success and I thought this would solve their problem also."

James Blairbuie stood and his voice was uncharacteristically hard. "Just tell me what happened, Woman."

"It was just before the Great War had ended and you were still away with your regiment. There was a party and I suppose I had a bit too much to drink. I had a...a liaison with a young man and a few months later, I realised I was with child. I couldn't admit that I had conceived out of marriage – it would have been terrible for you as well as for me. Maureen and David saw how distressed I was and offered to bring up the child. We came up to Scotland so that people would not discover my condition and you see what a lovely and clever young woman Jessica has become."

James Blairbuie sat down on his chair again, his shoulders slumped and a tone of utter weariness in his voice. "But, Virginia, I would have raised Jessica as my own. I would have been glad to have a child. You know I cannot give you children. Why didn't you tell me?"

"And admit that I had been unfaithful, foolish, be shunned by all the people I knew. Better to keep the arrangement secret and watch Jessica grow."

Maureen Hodges burst into loud tears. "Oh Jessica, Jessica, please forgive us. We did what we thought best for you. We never intended to lie to you and we have loved you and will always love you as our own."

Jessica was trembling but holding herself together. "I know you love me, Mum. I've never doubted that. And, as far as I am concerned, you are still my parents and I love you both as such. I think I probably had the best of both Worlds." She turned to James Blairbuie. "You have often said I am the daughter you never had. You have loved me, provided for me as a second father and I love you for that." She turned to Virginia Blairbuie and her eyes blazed. "But you! How could you? All these years you have watched me grow and never once admitted you are my birth mother. What kind of heart could do that, deny her own child and yet see her daily? You may have given birth to me but you are not my mother." Jessica stood and walked across to David and Maureen, standing between them and putting an arm around the waist of each. "These are my parents; you are nothing to me."

Lizzie looked at Alice whose own mother was cold to her; her eyes were brimming with sympathy for Jessica. Isla's hand was clutching her mouth. This must have echoes for her and the way her mother left her. Lizzie wanted to go and comfort her but that would have to wait.

"What I want to know is who was the bounder who took you to bed?" James Blairbuie was angry again.

"Yes, who is my natural father? You have a duty to tell me that at least."

Lady Blairbuie hesitated, her eyes flicking around the room as if registering that her humiliation was complete. Then she looked directly at Paul Boggen. "Do you remember that party Paul? It was at the Mitford's house I think and you took me home. I thought it very gallant of you. You were so hungry and so was I. We hardly made it to my bedroom."

Paul Boggen looked stunned. "Are you saying that I…do you mean that Jessica's father is…"

"Yes, Paul. You are Jessica's father."

"My father!" Jessica's face was a dreadful mask of horror.

"If I were a younger man, I would meet you outside with pistols. Do you have no morals, man, no sense of right and wrong?" James Blairbuie was no longer the gentle man Lizzie had seen so far. He was on his feet, breathing heavily, fists clenched.

"I'm sorry…I had no idea. I was young, probably drunk too much also and Virginia was willing so…"

"She can have been only eighteen. You took advantage of that. You will leave my house tomorrow morning and you will never return."

Jessica stood, trembling. It was anger. She advanced on Boggen who stood up in alarm. "And you tried it on with me! A father wanting to have sex with his daughter. You're a filthy, perverted animal." Her hand suddenly whipped across his face. He managed to avoid the worst of it but the slap was strong enough to make him stumble.

Lizzie and Alice turned to confront him. "He attacked me earlier today as well."

"And tried it on with me in the car on the way up."

"But it's just a bit of..." Boggen stopped, faced with the hostile glares of three young women and one older man.

CHAPTER 38

There was a terrible silence again in the room. At last, Robbie McBane said, "We need now to return to George's murder and what this letter suggests about the identity of that person. We believe that the killer is the person who had most to lose by the letter being discovered. What did George want, Lady Blairbuie? Was it money to buy his silence? Did you find Boggen's pistol and meet George?"

Virginia Blairbuie sat like a shattered statue. At last she said in a frail whisper, "He wanted money to keep silent. He must have found the letter at home and thought he could use it to blackmail me. He said he wanted as much money as had been spent on Jessica."

"When was this?"

"I met him on Saturday afternoon when walking the dogs. He had a rifle with him. I agreed to meet him early Sunday morning with some money, just what I had, as a first payment."

"But you realised you had to silence him for good. You shot him."

"Me? No, no! I did not kill George. How could you think I would do such a thing?" Virginia Blairbuie turned to Maureen and David Hodges. "Maureen, David, I did not kill George. I could never do that when you have been so good, so faithful to me. You must believe me."

"Who else had a motive to kill him as strong as yours?"

"I do not know how to fire a gun, Sergeant. How could I have shot him? How could I have obtained Paul's pistol?"

Lizzie remembered the murmuring voices in the Green Room on their first night at Glenstriven. "Quite easily, Lady Blairbuie. On Saturday night, I couldn't sleep and I went into one of the front attic rooms to look at the view of the Loch. I don't know what it was that took me down the stairs to the first floor but, when I did so, I heard voices coming from the Green Room. The voices were yours and Group Captain Boggen's."

James Blairbuie's anger burst like a dam, gushing out in a torrent of words. "You absolute scoundrel! You cuckold me under my own roof, you try to have your wicked way with three lovely young women – you disgust me! As soon as we are finished here, you will pack your bags and I will have you driven to Dunoon. You are not going to spend another moment in this house."

When James Blairbuie had resumed his seat, Robbie McBane continued quietly as if it were an everyday matter being discussed. "I think it is clear how you obtained the pistol, lady Blairbuie. You took it from Group Captain Boggen's holster when he was...distracted, or perhaps asleep. You then put your husband's spectacle case into the holster so the pistol would not be noticed."

Lady Blairbuie rose, trying to preserve some dignity. She looked directly at Robbie. "Sergeant McBane, I did not kill George Hodges or anyone else though I admit I did take Paul's pistol in order to protect myself. George had a rifle. I didn't know whether I could ever use the gun but it was the thought of a desperate moment."

Lizzie looked at the disgraced woman. An image flashed across her mind of George lying on the ground, the bullet hole in his right temple stained with darkening blood. Another image lay in the recesses of her brain, a gong held in the right hand and hit with a beater held in the left. She picked up Virginia Blairbuie's glass of wine from the table and held it out towards her.

The older woman took it in her right hand and gulped it greedily. "Thank you, Lizzie, thank you."

"I don't believe you did shoot George, Lady Blairbuie, but I think you know who did," Lizzie said.

Lady Blairbuie looked directly at Lizzie. The knowledge of what had happened to George was in her eyes.

Suddenly, there was an explosion nearby, from another part of the house. "That was a gunshot I think." James Blairbuie was on his feet. "With me McBane."

"Please wait here all of you," Robbie shouted as he strode after James Blairbuie.

The two men rushed from the room followed by Lizzie and Alice. They headed down the corridor, past the kitchen, to where the sound appeared to have come. Robbie opened the kitchen door and looked in – nothing. He did likewise with the pantry door. James Blairbuie pointed to a door at the end of the corridor.

"Langford's quarters." Slowly he approached the door and turned the knob. When the door was pushed open, the sight that greeted them was horrific. Langford was sitting in a windsor chair, the end of a rifle barrel in his mouth, his head partly blown away. Blood spattered the walls behind. He was still.

Lizzie and Alice pushed past Blairbuie and Robbie and rushed to him, Alice feeling his wrist for a pulse. "Nothing," she said, "he must have died instantly."

Robbie McBane surveyed the room and his eye was drawn to an envelope on the table. He picked it up. "It's addressed to you, Sir."

Lord Blairbuie opened it, unfolded the sheets inside and read aloud.

Dear Lord Blairbuie,

I am sorry, very sorry, that my time in your employment should end this way but I have failed in my duty and must pay the price. I wish I could undo what I have done and I ask you to give my most sincere apologies to George's family.

Late on Saturday evening, Lady Blairbuie summoned me and explained to me in confidence what had passed between herself and George that afternoon. I knew of course of the arrangement she had made with Maureen and David Hodges over the upbringing of Jessica. I apologise again for not telling you about this but Lady Blairbuie was most insistent that I didn't. There is always a difficulty when duty to one employer

conflicts with loyalty to another. I hope you will forgive me for my silence but I felt it would not serve your marriage well for you to know.

Lady Blairbuie asked me to meet George by the Loch on Sunday morning at seven o'clock. She said she would meet me at the back door at six-thirty to give me something. She gave me fifty pounds and said I was to give it to George in exchange for the letter. She also gave me a pistol, saying I should take it for my protection as George had been armed.

I met George as arranged and he had the letter with him. He also had your rifle – I recognised the stock – which he must have taken during the night. I gave him the fifty pounds and asked for the letter. He refused to hand it over and began to taunt me, saying I was Lady Blairbuie's lackey, why didn't I stand up for myself - that sort of thing. I hope you have found me to be a very self-controlled man; I believe myself to be that but I'm afraid his jibes made me see red. His willingness to exploit the situation was reprehensible. I became angry and demanded the letter. He still refused and, before I knew it, I had shot him.

I pulled the letter from his grasp, rummaged in his pocket to retrieve the fifty pounds and took the rifle which he had dropped as he fell. I returned the rifle to your cupboard and gave the letter and money to her Ladyship. She was in the drawing room at the time. The pistol I put in your Library as I had seen Group Captain Boggen show it to you the previous evening.

Needless to say, I am ashamed of myself. I would do again what I did in helping Lady Blairbuie. You and your family have always had my complete loyalty but to allow myself to lose control as I did was unpardonable. I am sincerely sorry for the trouble my action will bring you. I cannot, at my age, face the disgrace of being taken to court and thence to prison. It may be regarded as cowardice but, in my book,it is honourable to end matters this way.

I have taken your rifle again to perform this last act. I hope you will forgive this and I apologise unreservedly for the trouble this will bring to your household. I must end it now. I have served you as faithfully as my poor talents have allowed and want you to know that it has been the honour of my life to serve you and your Father before you.

With my sincere apologies,

Robert Langford

James Blairbuie laid the letter carefully on the table and slumped in a chair, his hands covering his face. After some seconds, he looked up and his eyes were wet. "That poor man. He never shirked his duty even when it brought him to this."

"I don't think there is any mystery about his death, Sir, but we must inform the Police and have his body removed. I will go back to the drawing room and tell everyone what has transpired. We'll need to keep his quarters locked until this can be cleaned up…not a pleasant task for anyone."

Robbie McBane led Lizzie and Alice back to the Drawing Room, leaving Lord Blairbuie to say his farewell to his faithful servant. The room was silent but Boggen was absent. As soon as they walked in, Thorney sat up. "What's happened McBane?"

I regret to inform everyone that Robert Langford has shot himself. He left a letter addressed to Lord Blairbuie explaining what happened. He went to meet George on behalf of Lady Blairbuie but George would not hand over the letter in exchange for money. Instead he taunted Langford until the man could stand it no longer. He had been given Boggen's pistol by Lady Blairbuie and, before he could stop himself, he had shot George."

"Oh my God! I didn't intend him to do that. The pistol was to protect himself so George would not try anything."

"Langford explained that in his letter. What puzzles me, Lady Blairbie, is why you left the letter under the piano lid."

"Because, when Langford gave me the letter, I heard someone coming so needed to hide it quickly. I then did not get a chance to retrieve it because people were in the room."

"You accused me of George's murder, McBane. You accused me of being a German informant, a Quisling. I shall make sure your superiors know about it."

"I did what I had to do, Mr Thorney, and, had you told the truth at the beginning, I would not have needed to be so forceful. The same applies to others of you. Should you ever be in such an unfortunate situation again, I strongly recommend you tell the truth, the whole truth, from the beginning. And now we must make some arrangements. Mr Ferguson, I know this has been a very difficult time for you as it has for everyone but would you be willing to drive Group Captain Boggen to Dunoon and fetch Sergeant MacGregor? Please explain that Robert Langford has taken his own life and he will need to remove the body."

Shock and sadness were still etched on Hamish Ferguson's face. When he spoke Lizzie detected weariness and, almost, an uncharacteristic self-doubt. "Aye, that will be no problem but I need to have a word with Isla first. Will ye come with me my dear?"

Isla looked at her Father, surprised at the gentleness of his tone. She followed him silently out of the room.

"Thank you, all of you, for your patience. Ewan, I think Lord Blairbuie would like a word with you about your future but that would best be done tomorrow. He is very upset at Langford's death."

"Aye, he would be. The man worked for the Blairbuie's a long time. I know what that is like but sadly..."

"Don't make assumptions, Ewan. I do not know what his Lordship will say to you but it may be to your advantage. Now, ladies and gentlemen, you are free to leave."

CHAPTER 39

Lady Blairbuie did not show her face at breakfast but all the guests, except Boggen, were there. Isla was serving and Lizzie noticed a significant change in her. Her movements were sprightly and her face was bright, smiling. She moved around the table pouring tea.

"You look happy this morning, Isla."

Isla smiled broadly at Lizzie. "Yes, Miss, I am."

"Is there a particular reason?"

"Yes Miss. My Dad and I had a talk after that meeting last night...before he went to Dunoon. I think what happened yesterday made him realise how important a mother is to a daughter. It's the first time I've been able to talk – really talk – with my dad for years. Anyway, he said he would take me to Glasgow soon and we'd find my Mum. He's agreed I can stay with her if she'll have me as long as I come and visit sometimes."

"I am pleased for you Isla. I'm sure you'll enjoy being in a bigger place but...you won't forget the deal will you? You must come and see your Dad. He does love you."

"I know, it just didn't often feel like it."

"Love is so difficult isn't it? The need to protect and, yes perhaps, to possess. I think some people find it very difficult to express love...it can feel like a weakness."

"It can indeed for some people, Lizzie." Alice's eyes lit with a gentle smile and Lizzie blushed.

Isla looked keenly from Lizzie to Alice. "Yes...I think I know what you mean. Perhaps you...?"

But Dennis Thorney impatiently rattled his cup and Isla moved on.

After breakfast, Robbie took Lizzie aside. "Well done Lizzie. You cracked the case again. What made you so sure that Lady

Blairbuie had not killed George?"

"When I handed her the glass of wine, she took it with her right hand...a natural thing for a right-handed person to do. But, unless George's killer was behind him, he must have been shot by a left-handed person. I remembered Langford ringing the gong for dinner using his left hand to operate the beater. A right-handed person would have held the gong in the left hand and the beater in the right. Knowing how obedient, or perhaps I should say loyal, Langford was to Lady Blairbuie, I thought he had probably killed George on Virginia's behalf. I may have been wrong of course but as it happens..."

"You were right again." Robbie smiled. "Lizzie, I have a request to make of you. I had arranged to have some leave for a couple of days so I could visit my Mother in Glasgow. I wondered if...but perhaps you would not..."

Lizzie looked at the uncertainty, anguish on Robbie's face. "I'd love to Robbie."

"But I haven't asked you yet."

"No, so do get on with it."

"Would you be able to come with me and meet my Mother. She'd love to see you and you would be able to stay...that is if you can delay your return."

"What about Thorney and Alice? We'd have to get permission from Commander Trueman."

"You could telephone from Dunoon; I'm sure MacGregor wouldn't mind, given that you solved the murder for him. Alice would be very welcome too, if she didn't mind but I'm afraid I draw the line at Thorney."

"Let's find out. I'll ask Alice, you speak with Thorney."

Five minutes later, it was arranged. Dennis Thorney wanted to stay at Glenstriven for another two days to check distances and measurements. Perhaps, Lizzie thought, he just wanted a short holiday in a very attractive place. Alice was happy but only after seeking numerous assurances that she would not be in the way. "Ok, I'll be your chaperone provided you agree to behave. No more murders please."

By ten o'clock, they were loaded with Jessica into the shooting brake. Lord Blairbuie, Hamish Ferguson, Isla, Maureen Hodges and Ewan McCrae were there to see them off. Robbie had a brief word with Ewan who told him that Lord Blairbuie had rescinded the instruction to leave his house. He would be seeing out his last days at Glenstriven and helping to train whoever was appointed to replace him.

Jessica flung her arms around her Mother and held her for several seconds before turning to her Father and doing the same, even though he would be driving everyone to Dunoon. "I'll be back," she said through tears, "for the funeral. It won't be long and I'll make sure that I see you more often now that...now that I'm the only one."

"You're a wonderful daughter, Jessica, and we've never for a minute regretted the arrangement we made. We should perhaps have told you long ago but we had agreed to say nothing to anyone." David Hodges wiped his cheek. "Now don't forget, Lord Blairbuie," he added quietly.

James Blairbuie looked forlorn, standing a little apart from the assembled group as perhaps he felt his status as Laird demanded and, no doubt, embarrassed by his wife's infidelity. Jessica went to him and looked him in the eye. "Thank you, James, for everything you have done..."

She did not complete the sentence. James Blairbuie held up his hand signalling she should go no further. "Your parents have always been so kind allowing us to be part of your life and I will always treasure that, Jessica. I love you as if you are my own daughter...I hope you know that."

Jessica's wet eyes sparkled with a smile. "I've never had any reason to doubt that, James, and I love you as a second father which is what you have been to me. You've never demanded anything in return, just given me so much. I'm so sorry about Lady Blairbuie...I'm afraid I cannot call her Mother."

"No...that is perfectly understandable, my dear." James Blairbuie reached out his arms and Jessica stepped into them. The hug lasted as long as it had with her parents, both clearly reluctant to let the moment go. At last they drew apart and Jessica walked quickly to the car.

◆ ◆ ◆

They were in the Humber as there were only the four of them and enough room in the generous boot for their luggage. Robbie sat next to David Hodges in the front whilst the three young women were in the back; the width of the car meant it was not squashed but pleasantly intimate.

"I'm not sure I should ask this, Jessica," said Lizzie cautiously, "but what are your feelings towards Group Captain Boggen?"

"My view of him has not changed. He's a monster who thinks women exist to provide for his sexual desires. I refuse to acknowledge him as my natural father. But...he wrote me a letter...quite extraordinary."

"A letter?"

"Yes, slipped under the front door of our house last night, presumably as he was leaving Glenstriven."

"And what did it say?"

"He said he was sorry, firstly for attempting to...you know... do things to me and, even more sorry, that he did not know he was my father. He said, had he known, he would have been a part of my life. He said he would like to do that now if I would let him."

"He sounds just like an honourable man doesn't he? But I fear it's not a position he would sustain."

"I agree, Alice." said Lizzie.

"Yes I think I agree too." Jessica looked out of the window at the spray rising in wonderful displays from the rocks as the car cruised close to the coast.

"Will you reply to the letter?"

"Maybe in time I will but, at the moment, I can't deal with it. It's a strange feeling suddenly discovering you're not who thought you were."

"I can imagine. But Lady Blairbuie…your natural mother… what a thing to do!"

"That woman is never going to be my mother. How could she do that? How could you deny the existence of your own daughter when you are seeing her everyday as she did when I was growing up. Just so she could go to parties. I was an inconvenience."

The three young women sat for a long while in silence until Alice said quietly, "I often think my Mother would rather I had not been born. She has never shown any interest in me."

Lizzie, sitting between Alice and Jessica put an arm around the shoulders of each. "I'm so sorry that you have both had to deal with these situations. But try to use them to make yourselves stronger. There are so many people…men mainly… trying to put us down and we women have to be resolute to counter it. As long as we stick together and fight for each other, we can be strong."

"Amen to that," said Jessica.

◆ ◆ ◆

The Humber drew up at the harbour. Gordon McClaughlin was sitting on the quay by the ferry; he scowled at them as they stepped out of the car.

"I need to go up to the Police Station to have a last word with Sergeant MacGregor," Robbie announced.

"We'll come with you, won't we Alice?"

"There's really no need, Lizzie, I won't be long."

"There is a need. Come along Alice."

Robbie did not protest – he had learnt that, when Lizzie was determined, nothing would stop her. But as they walked away from the harbour she said, "We need to give Jessica and her father a little time to themselves to say goodbye. Besides which, we need to try to telephone Trueman to ask for permission for leave."

"A good thought, Lizzie." Robbie smiled at her.

In the Police Station, they found Sergeant MacGregor and PC McDonald concluding a lecture to Billy and Rory. Billy was nodding, his eyes earnest and relief exuding from him. Rory's face was unflinching, hearing without really listening. He was a hard one and unlikely to be deterred from further crime by the dressing down.

"About our conversation yesterday, Billy," said PC McDonald laying a paternal hand on his shoulder, "would you like me to telephone someone in Glasgow about Civil Defence?"

"Yes please, Constable." Billy turned to Lizzie and added sheepishly, "I'm going to try to do something for the war effort. Civil Defence maybe."

"I'm so pleased Billy. I'm sure you'll do a great job."

Rory snorted and walked out of the Police Station.

"Don't mind him, Billy. I think he's a lost cause."

"I suspect you're right, Miss." Sergeant MacGregor pointed a finger at the doorway through which Rory had just passed. "I'll be keeping a close eye on that one."

"Lord Blairbuie is not going to press charges, Miss, so I won't have a criminal record."

"That's wonderful, Billy. I'm sure you'll make the most of the opportunity you've been given."

The necessary telephone calls were made with the desired outcomes, while Billy and PC McDonald waited for their turn. After taking their leave, Robbie, Alice and Lizzie walked towards the door. Before Lizzie had reached it, Billy stepped close to her. "Miss, I just wanted to say...thank you for helping me to see what I needed to do. I think you are a very lovely lady and..." He stopped, his face red and the blush spreading down his neck.

"Well thank you, Billy. You have shown real courage in standing up for what you believe in." Billy held out his hand which she took but then, on an impulse, she leaned towards him and kissed him on the cheek. She left immediately, surprised and slightly embarrassed at what she had done. She realised in herself a change, a different kind of confidence. It was not necessary always to be guarded and hostile; being secure in one's ability allowed one to deal with the trials that life put in one's way.

As soon as she had left the office, she could hear Sergeant MacGregor and PC McDonald begin to rib Billy. "You'll be alright there, Billy. Quite a catch."

Billy responded and Lizzie could imagine him doing so with a new confidence. "Don't be daft, she'd not be interested in me. But she is a lovely lady."

"Aye, she is that."

Lizzie had to bite her lower lip as she felt a little tear in the corner of her eye.

Wednesday 12th May 1943

CHAPTER 40

"You do realise what this visit means I hope."

"Whatever do you mean Alice? It's just a visit."

Alice smiled pityingly. "Lizzie, when a man asks you to meet his mother, it's a form of vetting. Provided she approves, a proposal will follow."

"Nonsense! Robbie knows that I am not ready to marry whilst this War is on and I have a useful job to do."

"The war won't last for ever, Lizzie, and a proposal can be made well before the marriage occurs."

"Anyway," Lizzie said, "what about you? We need to find a nice man for you, Alice. Now here's a thought, you could marry Hamish Ferguson."

"Don't change the subject, Lizzie. You know as well as I do that Robbie loves you and you are making sure you make the right impression which is why you are taking so much time getting ready to go down to dinner."

Lizzie was sitting at the small dressing table tying her hair at the back. She did not have the patience to tie it in a bun the way Alice did and, besides, that look suited Alice but not her. "I'm just making sure I look presentable."

"Of course...that's exactly what I'm saying." Alice raised herself from the bed on which she had been sitting and stood behind Lizzie. Her arms slid over Lizzie's shoulders and joined together at the base of her neck. "You look lovely as always, Lizzie, and you deserve happiness. Make sure you grab the opportunity for that because we are all so vulnerable. We could be killed tomorrow."

Lizzie's hands rested on Alice's arms. "Thank you, Alice. You are a true friend and I want you to be happy too. There is possibly an obstacle to my happiness with Robbie. I'm not sure if you know but he was due to be married to a girl, Catriona, who was staying with her aunt here in Glasgow when the City was bombed. She died. Robbie carries her photograph in a frame wherever he goes. I'm not sure he can let her go, Alice, and I certainly don't want to force him to. I think he still loves her."

"Perhaps he does, Lizzie, but he wouldn't have asked you to come here if he didn't also love you. Besides, you can love more than one person and it's not as if he would be seeing her."

"It's just that…I don't know…would her ghost always be there between us?"

"If that happens, you must love her too, for his sake. Don't fight it and he will love you the more because you treasure someone he holds dear."

◆◆◆

Both Lizzie and Alice admired Mrs McBane. She was tall for a woman and, naturally, had put on weight from her youth but she had a lovely face and her eyes exuded kindness. More than that, she had a stoicism that had enabled her to endure the loss of her husband. That was a quality so necessary in wartime. After breakfast, while Alice went to brush her teeth, Robbie led Lizzie into the small front room, the room that was only used on special occasions.

With a degree of panic, Lizzie wondered if this was it. Would he be dropping on one knee? What would she say? Her rational mind told her to accept but all those ghosts from her childhood told her to get away.

"Lizzie, this morning I want to do something that I have wanted to do for a while. I want to visit the place where Catriona died and then go to her grave."

"Of course, Robbie. Alice and I can walk into the City and have a look around."

"No…I want…I was hoping you would come with me."

"Are you sure about that, Robbie. Won't I be in the way?"

"No you won't. I would really like you to come with me."

"Of course I will if you're sure."

Alice declined the opportunity to join them "I'm not going to play gooseberry," she said to Lizzie. And with a teasing smile, "I'll want to hear all about it when you get back. I'll go shopping with Mrs McB."

A little later, Robbie and Lizzie walked through the morning streets of Glasgow. Robbie was carrying a paper bag with something in it. Signs of the bombing raids were still very evident though some attempts had been made to repair the houses that had suffered only minor damage. At last, Robbie turned into a cul-de-sac, a row of terraced houses lining each side. As they walked down the road, Lizzie could see a gap in the buildings on one side of the road, like a tooth missing. Robbie stopped in front of it. Rubble was piled in the gap, wooden beams projecting at crazy angles from the dusty pile of masonry.

"It was here," Robbie said quietly.

Lizzie took in the scene. A saucepan, dented and covered in dust, lay amongst the bricks nearest the road. Caught further up the pile was a piece of rag, perhaps once a woman's skirt. Lizzie gently pulled her arm from Robbie's and slipped it around his waist.

"It's terrible." She looked up at him and felt a sudden explosion of love within her. One tear was sliding down his cheek. "Robbie, you don't have to look at this."

"I do, Lizzie, I do. This is part of it."

They stood for a long time in silence, Lizzie not wanting to disturb the memories and emotions that Robbie must be experiencing. At last, Robbie turned. "There's somewhere else I want to go now."

They walked in silence back through streets that spoke of normality, a sense that jarred with what they had just seen. A church spire seemingly untouched by the bombs rose above the rooftops and, when they reached it, they turned in to the graveyard beside it. Robbie knew where he was going and they walked, arm in arm, through the graves until he stopped in front of one. A simple headstone gave Catriona's name and her dates.

"Her parents said she may as well be buried in the City where she died. I suppose it was easier than taking the body back to Edinburgh."

Lizzie nodded, not wishing to say anything that might disturb his mood. And, after all, what could one say? Robbie slipped his arm from Lizzie's and took the paper bag in his hand. He opened it and pulled out a framed photograph.

"This was Catriona."

Lizzie took the photograph and studied it. "She is lovely, Robbie. You can see the intelligence in her eyes. I think she was a kind person."

"She was. She didn't deserve to die, Lizzie."

"No, she didn't. Few people do."

Robbie stepped forward and, bending over, propped the photograph against the hard headstone. He stood again and returned to Lizzie's side. "I have to let her go, Lizzie. It's time to do that."

Lizzie could feel tears in her own eyes. "But you can keep her memory alive, Robbie. Always hold onto her in your heart."

"Can I do that? I need to make space for another." He turned to her and she saw the uncertainty, the agony on his face.

"Of course you can, Robbie. Love is not a finite thing. The more you love, the more you are capable of love."

He looked at her keenly. "Do you really believe that, Lizzie?"

"Yes I do...and I would never resent you treasuring Catriona's memory."

"I must be the luckiest man alive. To have loved and lost such a beautiful woman and to find another."

"Who's that then?"

Robbie laughed. "You are such a joy, Lizzie. This afternoon, we need to go into the City to buy a ring."

"A ring? What kind of ring?"

"An engagement ring of course."

"But you haven't asked me to marry you yet!"

HISTORICAL NOTE

Everyone knows about the Barnes Wallis designed bouncing bomb used to destroy German dams in the Ruhr Valley. It was code-named Upkeep and the mission was called Operation Chastise although it is now more commonly known as the Dambusters' Raid after the book and subsequent film. Highball was a smaller bouncing bomb developed to be used against enemy ships and particularly the Tirpitz which hid in a Norwegian fjord and was heavily protected. Whereas Upkeep was cylindrical, Highball was shaped like a very large golf ball but the two operated in a similar way.

Testing of Highball began in November 1942 at Chesil Beach and Reculver but was moved to Loch Striven on the West coast of Scotland in May 1943. Modified Mosquitos flying from RAF Turnberry were used to drop the bombs. Glenstriven House was indeed used by observers and one account states that all residents in the house had to stay in the rear rooms during the tests. There were some issues with Highball and the tests revealed the need for modifications. Testing continued in various locations until well into 1944 but Highball was never used in action.

At the same time, Loch Striven was being used to develop another secret weapon: the X Craft, the base for which was Port Bannatyne on the Isle of Bute. The Navy also commandeered Ardtaraig House at the head of Loch Striven as a training base where Lizzie, Robbie and Alice are taken. The X Craft was a small submarine some fifty feet in length. The intention was to tow it with a larger submarine to the operational area and then put an operational crew on board to carry out the mission. X Craft were used in September 1943 in Operation Source, an attack on German battleships including Tirpitz which was damaged in the attack. She was repaired but later destroyed by an air attack.

Highball's older sister, Upkeep, was of course successfully used in the Ruhr later in May 1943.

ALSO BY KEVIN O'REGAN

The Lizzie's war Series

New Swan Stone February 1943: Can Lizzie's powers of observation help find the murderer of a young civilian girl at RAF Silverstone despite the ghosts of her own past?

Meteor March 1943: RAF Cranwell in Lincolnshire. Someone is relaying information to the Germans and a young airman is murdered. Lizzie must untangle a web of deceit.

Eager for the Air A prequel to the main stories. May 1940 and Lizzie is one of 8 new recruits to the ATA at White Waltham near Maidenhead. One of them is murdered and there are several suspects. Can Lizzie establish the real culprit and free her friend from prison?

The Dresden Tango
It is 1889 and a ship, The City of Dresden, carrying nearly 1800 poor Irish migrants, arrives in Buenos Aires after a nightmarish journey with inadequate provisions. Rose is coerced into prostitution whilst Patrick, a young priest, accompanies some 300 migrants to an area 400 miles South of Buenos Aires to found a farming community. Both suffer unbearable hardships and meet again in Buenos Aires. Can they restore each other's self-worth?

All available now on Amazon as e-books or paperbacks.

ALSO BY KEVIN O'BRIEN

ACKNOWLEDGEMENTS

I first came across the important role that the Air Transport Auxiliary (ATA) and especially its female pilots played in World War II when reading 'Spitfire Women of World War II' a non-fiction book by Giles Whittell. I am very grateful to the Air Transport Auxiliary Museum for providing such a wealth of information on their web-site (www.atamuseum.org) and at the museum itself, which, though small, is well worth visiting.

I am indebted to those who have once again read an early draft of the novel and provided such valuable feedback: Patrick Sanders, Mark Kenny and Paul Boggeln. I am also grateful to Paul for allowing his name, albeit in an altered form, to be used for a rather unpleasant character. I would like to thank my publishers for their continued belief in the value of the Lizzie's War series and for bringing another book to public attention. Finally, thanks to my wife, Carrie, for her patience, encouragement and support.

www.ingramcontent.com/pod-product-compliance
Lightning Source LLC
Chambersburg PA
CBHW070658180626
46817CB00006B/2421

* 9 7 8 1 7 3 9 2 2 0 6 5 5 *